THE SWORDS OF GOD

AN IAN QUAYLE SPY NOVEL

CALIBER
BOOKS

Also from ALAN CAILLOU

CABOT CAIN Series
Assault on Kolchak
Assault on Loveless
Assault on Ming
Assault on Agathon
Assault on Fellawi
Assault on Aimata

TOBIN'S WAR Series
Dead Sea Submarine
Terror in Rio
Congo War Cry
Afghan Assault
Swamp War
Death Charge
The Garonsky Missile

MIKE BENASQUE Series
The Plotters
Marseilles
Who'll Buy My Evil
Diamonds Wild

IAN QUAYLE Series
A League of Hawks
The Swords of God

DEKKER'S DEMONS Series
Suicide Run
Blood Run

The Charge of the Light Brigade
A Journey to Orassia

Rogue's Gambit
Cairo Cabal
Bichu the Jaguar
The Walls of Jolo
The Hot Sun of Africa
The Cheetahs
Joshua's People
Mindanao Pearl
Khartoum
South from Khartoum
Rampage
The World is 6 Feet Square
The Prophetess
House on Curzon Street

IAN QUAYLE: THE SWORDS OF GOD
Book Two

For further information visit the Caliber Comics website:
www.calibercomics.com

CHAPTER 1

Ian Quayle's explosive little Mini-Cooper "S"—the one with the twin Strombergs that could take it to an easy 125 mph on its ridiculous little four-cylinder engine—had never been in better shape as he hurtled it along the narrow, hedge-bordered Surrey lanes to his Fifteenth-Century cottage, an historical masterpiece with the finest thatched roof in the whole of southern England.

And why shouldn't it have been? It had just spent three weeks in the loving care of old man Perkins, tuned up to hell and gone, and given a thick and shiny new lacquer job that made it sparkle like the jewel it was.

"Someone else's been fooling around with her bodywork," the old man had said accusingly. "What d'you think we found when we stripped 'er down? Bullet-'oles is what we found. And they'd been plugged with chewing gum, that's no way to treat 'igh-class machinery."

"Er, Rome," Ian Quayle had said apologetically, as though that explained it all. "Even tourists aren't safe from terrorists these days. Terrible, isn't it?"

But now she was right as rain again, the late afternoon was yellow-bright with slanting sunlight filtering its way through the green foliage of the chestnut trees that lined the road near the cottage, and the girl beside him was gorgeous, splendid as the weather and far more predictable.

Her name was Melanie something or other, a student from Eddie Forbes' fashionable modeling studio in Shepherd Market, just off Curzon Street, London. She liked to call herself 'Melancholy Melanie,' because she worried about the fact that no one, but no one, was interested in the intellectual capacity she fancied she had; just in her spectacular body.

And she was right; no one was.

At the age of thirty-one, she looked like a teenager, slim and athletic; and she moved with the easy articulation of a jaguar on the prowl.

She was tall and willowy, with sensibly shaped breasts over an almost non-existent waist, nicely-rounded haunches, and long, long legs with perfection in every inch of them. Her hair was always left to just hang there, silky-shiny and down to her waist. It wasn't just ordinary hair, but a strange ultra-blonde color like the patina of the ivory keys on a very old concert grand piano. Her eyes were cornflower blue and enormous, with constant surprise in them, and her complexion, almost entirely devoid of make-up, was what the English liked to call 'peaches and cream.'

All in all, Melanie was quite a dish, and for Ian Quayle, this promised to be one hell of a weekend.

Arm in arm they strolled through the lovely garden of the white-washed cottage, and as the sun began to set over the lush green hill, Melanie said, a trifle plaintively, "But am I just supposed to smell flowers? Is that what you brought me all this way for?"

"More exciting things to come," Quayle said easily, "take my word for it."

"Well, I hope so. And meanwhile, could I have a drink? I'm gasping, really I am."

"Of course. But first, you have to meet Horace."

"Horace? Who the hell is Horace? I thought there'd just be the two of us."

"Horace is my ferret."

Melanie stared. "A *ferret*? Isn't that some kind of a rat?"

"No. They kill rats. That's why I have one."

They were moving to a steel mesh hutch, and Ian Quayle opened it up and took out the yellow-furred creature there, a bundle of restrained energy that reflected his own. He held it up to his cheek, practically kissing it.

"Would you like to hold him?" he asked. "He has great taste in women."

Poor Melanie was in shock. "That'll be the day," she said, "keep it away from me for God's sake! And where's that fabulous dinner you promised me? I'm hungry."

"You can't be hungry at twilight," Ian said, "it's not civilized. In the country, we dine at eight-thirty."

He looked at his Omega. "But perhaps it's time to start things moving. All right, come and help me cook."

He put Horace gently back into his cage, whispering, "Okay, Baby, I'll bring you some nice fresh lettuce before you go hunting tonight..."

"Something to drink," Melanie said plaintively, and he sighed. "Follow me, luv." The darkness was falling now.

The ceiling beams in the low, low kitchen were black with age against the rough white plaster, only inches over their heads. Quayle reached up and touched one of them with a kind of affection, and he murmured, "You know about the Black Prince?"

Melanie nodded, suddenly very angry. "Sure I do," she said. "Ascot, last June. Eddie put fifty quid on him for me. Came in five lengths ahead and the bloody jockey got disqualified for foul riding; lost me a bundle."

"Not that one," Ian said patiently. "The Thirteen

Hundreds, son of Kind Edward the Third, he fought the French at Bordeaux..."

He broke off, knowing it didn't matter very much, and said glumly, "Anyway, these beams were taken from French ships the Black Prince destroyed. Swords into ploughshares, that sort of thing."

"Well, how nice."

"So let's get dinner started. You know how to make Lyonnaise potatoes?"

"Isn't that sort of fried?"

He was at the frig, taking out the shish kebab, lamb, onions, peppers and tomatoes on elegant brass headed Turkish skewers. "Boil them in their skins," he said wearily, "then brown them in lashings of butter with a touch of onion."

But she was staring at the kebabs, and she said, horrified, "But Ian darling, I can't possibly eat that! That's meat!"

He said, "Well what did you expect?" The light dawned, and he said, aghast, "You're not...not *vegetarian*, are you?"

He made it sound like an affront to his sensibilities, and she answered, "Well, of course I am, I thought you knew. I was hoping for something like nut cutlets."

"Oh Jesus Christ." In despair, he said, "I do have hazelnuts fresh off the trees..."

"Carrots?"

"In the ground."

"Herbs?"

"The best herb garden in south of England."

"Oh goody-goody, everything fresh. I'll do all the cooking then, and you'll have the best dinner you ever tasted."

She was showing off the famous smile now, "And you have yeast fiber?"

"No. So tell me what you'd like to drink?"

"Brandy and Coke, please. A large one."

There was only a moment of silence, and then: "No Coke.

Settle for Brandy and Soda? That's what Gordon used to drink."

"Gordon who?"

The sigh again. "*General* Gordon, killed in Khartoum, January 26, 1885."

"Oh. Well never mind, I'll settle for soda. But it's better with Coke, really it is. It's the only drink Eddie ever gives us at the studio, he says it helps to slim the thighs."

Only a merciful moment later, they heard the soft *pht-pht-pht* of an old Bentley coming up the driveway, and then the beep-beep of the horn, and Ian Quayle said happily, "I do believe that's Eddie Forbes in his ancient four and a quarter, what joy."

"Oh God, no...!"

Melanie was in shock. "But what's he doing here? Looking for me? I honestly hope not! And how did he find out where I am, I honestly didn't tell a soul."

"Eddie's a very bright man," Ian Quayle said, "and he probably knows where every one of his models is every hour of the day or night."

He leaned forward and took her hand in what he thought of as nice, conciliatory gesture.

"Worry not," he said earnestly, "tonight you belong to me. The hell with your boss."

Quayle went to the door and flung it open, and there was his old friend Eddie Forbes, slim and tanned and muscular in a startling red jumpsuit and a scarf of electric blue silk at his throat, looking like a million dollars. He liked to pump iron when he wasn't either making a fortune with his studio or tinkering with his beloved Bentley $4^1/_4$ Park Ward convertible, more than a half million miles on the clock and still purring like a sewing machine.

Eddie threw out his arms and shouted a boisterous, "Surprise, surprise...!"

There was a great deal of back-slapping, and Eddie held out a bottle. "Glenlivet," he said, "best Scotch in the world, I thought it might mitigate the awful pain of separation."

"Of *what*?"

Pushing into the room and closing the door, Eddie went on: "Got to take her away from you, old boy. You're going to hate me for it, but I need Melanie tonight."

"Eddie," Quayle said evenly, "I need her tonight too."

"Ah, but you don't pay her. At least, I hope you don't. And I'm the man who guides her career, her Svengali. Carson Productions wants her on the steps of St. Paul's at the witching hour of midnight, with no less than the great Neville Mariner himself providing the music. Just time for a quick drink, and we'll be on our way. Business, Ian, and very high-class business, the break she's been waiting for."

"You rotten bastard."

Melanie was staring, wide-eyed. "Carson Productions?" she whispered in absolute awe. "They've always turned me down before..."

Eddie nodded. "And they finally wised up. This is a big one, you get to play two roles, Odette and Odile, tutus, chiffon, that kind of stuff."

"Who's Odette? Who's Odile?"

"Swan Lake," Ian Quayle said, and got in a low blow just for the joy of it. "But you told me yourself, Eddie...Melanie dances like the Camel Corps of the French Foreign Legion, for Christ's sake!"

Eddie had the grace to bluster. "I never said any such thing, and you know it! You want to crack this bottle?"

"Why not?"

As Quayle poured, Melanie said, excited, "What's the product, Eddie?" and Forbes nodded his appreciation. "That's my girl, always the first question you have to ask, isn't it, what's the product? I mean, we have to be careful, don't we, what with all these disgusting suppositories being hawked on the bloody tube like so many hot cakes... It's perfume, *Parfum LaRouche*.

We've already shot the master with the whole Corps de Ballet, the pros, and you do the close-ups. You get to say: 'I wear nothing under my costume except *Parfum LaRouche*, that's why I smell so sweetly as I dance.' Isn't it great? You get a teleprompter so's you won't blow it."

"You're a shit, Eddie," Melanie said coldly, "I never blew a line in my life."

"Ha!"

Eddie figured he'd made his point, and as soon as he had gulped down his thirty-quid-a-bottle Scotch he shepherded Melanie out into the silent garden. Ian Quayle took time out to admire once again the fabulous lines of the old Bentley, listened appreciatively to the whisper of the engine...and Melanie whispered soulfully, "Business is business, Ian."

He grunted. "I'll never forgive either of you, you know that, don't you?"

Eddie grinned. "I'll have her back for you tomorrow night," he said "Nothing beats the expectation of pleasures."

"No you won't," Quayle said. "I'm off to Paris tomorrow to visit my family. Tonight was to have been a sort of farewell to the cottage for a while, two weeks' leave."

"Oh, that's tough."

Eddie brightened suddenly. "Send me a wire when you're on your way back, I'll have her in your bed, waiting with baited breath."

"A shit," Melanie said again. "That's what you really are, Eddie." And she whispered to Ian, "I'll make it up to you, truly I will..."

And then they were gone, the 18-inch tires spitting out dirt under the wheels as Eddie put his foot to the floor. There was just time to hear Melancholie Melanie shouting: "See you, Ian! I love you..." and then they were gone.

In sad silence, Quayle went to the gate and closed it, and then found his way to the patch where the romaine lettuce was growing. He troweled two of them and held them under the garden faucet for a while because Horace was fussy about dirt on his food, and turned and walked slowly to the little ferret's hutch, round the corner of the old stable where he kept his Mini Cooper.

And there, he pulled up in sudden surprise...

"Well, I'll be damned," he said, "Where in hell did you spring from?"

The woman there turned in the semi-darkness, hugging Horace to her small tight, up pointing breasts, as she hand-fed him lettuce. Her face was lined by the moonlight, a profile to chase away all the miseries of an unsatisfactory world. Her figure was the kind that drives men to distraction, and her dark dress molded every smooth curve of it.

Ian Quayle felt an unexpected lump rise in his throat, and what could have caused it? Only a week had passed since last he'd seen her, since last he'd run the tip of his searching fingers over her long, smooth body, receptive to his caresses.

Only a week?

He said tightly, "Eddie Forbes, the friendly pimp, bringing me a replacement for the ever-lasting love of my life. So that's how he knew where to find Melanie! And how the hell did you know she'd be here? Or is that a stupid question?"

"Yes it is. And you're a sonofabitch, Ian Quayle."

Wendy Hayworth, age 30, Case Officer Grade III, working out of the most secret of all of London's secret offices, a place that went by the innocuous name of The Continental Liaison Board, one of MI6's many cover names. She was soft as the finest Genoese silk velvet, and as hard as a barrel of shrapnel when she had to be; as sensitive as a fallow deer, and as jungle-tough as a hungry tiger.

She was nice, and no one to tangle with at all. Sometimes you'd think that butter wouldn't melt in her mouth, and then—to your sorrow—the fangs would suddenly appear, headed straight for your jugular.

"A sonofabitch," she said again. "I'm not a replacement for anyone, certainly not for that moronic nympho Melanie whatever-her-name-is. This is a business call, and am I in time for dinner?"

He took Horace from her and said gently to the writhing, agile bundle of yellow fur, "Time to go hunting, Baby..."

He set her down for an instant disappearance into the shrubbery, and took Wendy's arm. In the kitchen he look at her and saw yet again how lovely she was, that Renaissance face with the calm—sometimes—blue-green eyes and the high, intelligent forehead, the aristocratic nose and full, sensual lips that told so much about her.

He laid his hands lightly on her breasts, and he said quietly, "Business? I'm on holiday, two weeks, off to Paris tomorrow. You must know that."

"You *were* on vacation," Wendy said. "It has to be postponed, Ian."

"Bloody hell..."

"I know. But it's important, and very, very urgent. Did you hear about the bomb in Dover's Five Ports Hotel?"

Ian Quayle nodded. "On the way down here, the car radio. Why the hell should anyone want to blow up the Five Ports? It's just a small family hotel, isn't it?"

"Sort of. But not this afternoon."

She was frowning darkly as she went on, "I suppose you could call it a minor summit. Our people and the Deputy Heads of three others of the Secret Services were meeting with their French, Italian, and West German counterparts, top secret like you won't believe. And Dover's just a country town well away from the beaten track, enough foreign tourists to account for the European contingent, and an unlikely place for this kind of meeting. It was a good choice. But the bomb was in the very suite where the first of the meetings was being held."

Ian Quayle had taken out the shish kebabs again, and was

staring at them as though all the secrets of the universe were skewered on the blades. "A damn good. marinade," he said. "Olive oil, cider vinegar, tomatoes and lots of rosemary."

Not changing his tone in the slightest, he went on: "The radio said two people killed, seven wounded, three of them critically. But it's still a matter for Scotland Yard in cooperation with MI5, it's not for us."

"They've both asked for our help," Wendy said at once. "Specifically—for *your* help. They know that what's needed now, in a hurry, is someone who knows what research really is, know where to dig deep and quickly and some up with at least some of the answers."

There was a certain look on her face, and as Ian put the potatoes on to boil, he said quietly, "The dead, the wounded. Anyone we know?"

"Five people were killed not just two. Three of them were from the French contingent, one from the Swedish—and the other was Gavin O'Brien, who was the number three man at MI5. One of the critically hurt was our own Robin Harris."

Quayle stared. "How badly?"

"He lost two fingers on his left hand, and Robin's not the kind of man to worry too much about a trifle like that... But he also too a hunk of concrete in his stomach..."

"Oh my God..."

"And the surgeon's got a great sense of humor, says it was so big they needed a fork-lift to remove it."

Quayle's face was white, "Where is he?"

"St. Mary's Hospital in Dover."

"Less than a couple of hours from here in the Mini. We'll go there *now*."

"No."

Wendy was very firm. "They won't let us see him till tomorrow afternoon at the earliest. We just have to sit it out, Ian."

"Doesn't take much to put me in a pretty damn foul humor," Quayle muttered, and Wendy said, "There's more to come. We need your cassette player."

They went to the living room, and Wendy took a cassette from her purse and held it up. "A man called Abu Jildi," she said. "He called the Daily Telegraph, claiming responsibility."

"Abu Jildi?"

There was a tiny bell tinkling at the back of Ian's head, the little flash of memory that all born researchers soon develop. A good researcher didn't have to know very much, actually, he just had to be damned sure he knew where to look it up, even if it meant finding a 1750 Atlas, an obscure reference book published in China a hundred years go, or a Hungarian report on the Soviet invasion of 1956. But that sudden flash was confusing, a smidgen of recall that was gone almost immediately.

He said nothing, and Wendy went on, noticing the look on his face but knowing that questions wouldn't help now. "Three other groups called various papers to make the claim too, but we figured this is the only one that mattered."

"Why?"

"Because," Wendy said, "it's the only one that shows any inside knowledge. The others are just the usual crap, unfounded claims for the sake of media publicity. The Telegraph taped it, a matter of routine."

"And is this the only copy we have?"

"Of course not, this one's for you. Several others floating around, everyone in sight working on voice prints, independently. Us, MI5, Scotland Yard."

"Let me have ours the moment it comes through."

"Sure."

Wendy slipped the tape into the little Marantz and sat down, as Ian went to the dresser and gestured with a bottle. "Campari Soda?"

She nodded and touched the button, and the heavily-accented voice came through loud and clear:

> *'I am Abu Jildi, first leader of Swords of God, and this is my message for capitalist imperialist pigs of British, French and Germany Governments. Is warning to all of you, there will be no more meeting by Intelligence people, which they call Summit for deciding war against freedom-fighters everywhere. We know where all meetings are held, who is speaking, who is listening, what is object of all this foolish talk. Is destruction of Freedom guerrillas everywhere, we know where they are always, they be killed at time I decide, I am Abu Jildi, a servant of God, who is strong, the only one. Next meeting is Hotel Esplanade, not so? Maybe bomb there too, you search, I tell you this so that you understand I do not speak foolishly, I know. Remember Swords of God. Remember Abu Jildi. I speak to you again, very soon.'*

There was an audible click, and the tape continued on in silence for a moment or two before Wendy pushed the stop and ran it through twice more.

"At a guess," Ian Quayle said at last, "I'd say he's an Arab, an accent you hear all over London these days. What about the Hotel Esplanade?"

"They went through it with a fine tooth comb, a hundred and forty-two guests evacuated for more than five hours. And they found nothing. I suppose that was to be expected."

"And that's truly where the next meeting was to be held?"

Wendy nodded. "He knows too goddam much, doesn't he?"

"So who set-up the schedule?"

"Whitehall, high level Foreign Office. The Minister himself, so top secret you won't believe it."

"And who was informed?"

"'Eyes Only' to the top brass at Scotland..."

As she spoke, there was the distant and muffled sound of a shot and the breaking of glass. Ian Quayle fell to the floor and yelped, reaching for his shoulder and finding a rip in the cloth of his jacket, just a sticky touch of blood there; there was almost, no pain at all.

White as an aspirin, Wendy almost threw herself at the light-switch and clicked it, but Quayle was getting to his feet and saying instantly, "No, leave them on."

When she did not respond immediately, he said furiously, "Dammit, leave them on! I know what it was."

He strode to the door, lived with rage, flung it open and shouted, flaring-tempered and at the top of his voice, "What the bloody hell do you think you're doing, you fucking bastard...?"

There was only silence out there in the darkness as the lights came on, and Wendy was beside him, fingering the tear in his coat. "You're wounded," she said, and he answered her abruptly, "Well, that's a bright observation, isn't it?"

He relented at once. "Don't worry, it's just a scratch, as they say. But I'll have that bastard's guts for a necktie if I catch him."

Wendy was aghast. "Ian, someone tried to kill you!"

"Oh balls!" he said. "It was a poacher, it's happened before. Got a stray shot through my greenhouse only a few months ago. And last year, someone put a bullet hole through Charlie's kennel."

"Charlie?" She was already stripping off his jacket, unbuttoning his shirt.

"Albert's dog," he said patiently.

She found a rag and soaked it in his expensive cognac, and patted at the wound with it. "Does it hurt much?" she asked.

"It does now. That bloody stuff burns like hell."

"Best disinfectant there is. If we get it nicely cleaned up, you'll probably live. Yes, it's just a scratch. Who's Albert?"

"Albert's the farmer who lives just down the road, the man who looks after this place when I'm in town, feeds Horace and the hens and so forth. You met him once."

"Ah yes. But...but, poaching with a *rifle*? At nighttime?"

Quayle nodded. "They strap a bloody great flashlight to the gun's barrel centered on the target bulls-eye. It's illegal, and it's a lousy way to hunt anyway. But the woods here are full of deer, a cheap and miserable way to get a year's supply of venison."

"Ian, you can't be sure it wasn't something far more deadly.

But Quayle ignored her and picked up the phone and dialed.

"In a moment," he said: "Albert? You hear that shot? We've got a poacher out there again... Yes, I know, I didn't hear his truck either, it means he's left it way down the road... Right, if he's got himself a deer, maybe we can nab him before he can pick it up. Why don't you join me... Okay."

He slammed down the phone and looked at Wendy. "Going hunting myself," he said tightly. "You want to come with me?"

"Sure..."

Wendy was still uncertain, but they went out together to the Mini, and drove slowly and without lights down the long and winding lane, north first for a couple of miles before deciding they'd chosen the wrong direction and doubling back.

And all the time, Ian Quayle was wondering, beset with second thoughts...

'*Someone tried to kill you,*' Wendy had said, and Wendy was the kind of gal who cut through the tinsel and the polish and the gorm and got down to basic possibilities very quickly indeed.

'*For Christ's sake,*' he kept telling himself, '*all I do is research, who the hell would want to kill me*?'

Okay. Once, a while back, he'd made like a Field Officer

for a spell, putting his life on the line like they all did, and had come within an inch of being carted home in a plain pine box.

But that was in Rome, and this was in Surrey, England; not even London where, admittedly, mayhem was running rife these days. Surrey, a place of ancient cottages, and friendly pubs, and winding, leafy lanes where all was well with the world.

But when his common sensibility returned to him in a while, he knew that the frantic excitements of the recent past had left a mark on him, a mark that was clearly labeled: *paranoia*.

He grunted, not even aware that he was voicing fears he was ashamed of. "Let's hope we really do find someone loading up a dead deer..."

Wendy looked at him and read his thoughts, and she said nothing.

Saying nothing was something at which she was very expert.

And in less than twenty minutes, they found what they were looking for—a late-model Ford pick-up carefully concealed in the shrubbery at the side of the road.

"That's it," Wendy said quietly. "Do you have a gun?"

"I do not need a bloody gun," Ian said, "to take care of a poacher. If we find him, which I doubt, he'll tip his cap to me respectfully and call me Sir, and all he'll want is to get the hell out of here before Sergeant Tim Berry turns up on his bicycle. And if we're lucky enough to find that he has a deer carcass thrown across his shoulders... Well, we'll take it from him, and tomorrow I'll run it into Guildford. There's a butcher there who carves venison up for you and packs it away in his freezer, we'll have enough meat for a year."

Wendy knew when not to argue, and she just sat there, tightlipped.

But she delved into her purse nonetheless, to assure herself that the Parker fountain-pen she habitually carried and very seldom used—was still comfortingly there.

19

It was one of the old-fashioned Parkers, a work of art in itself, with a barrel that was as thick as a strong man's index finger and would hold almost a year's supply of equally old-fashioned ink.

But Ops. E. in the office had done some work on it for her, and now, that man-sized barrel contained 85 grains of compressed cyanide gas. Point it in the right direction and push the clip, and that beloved old fountain-pen sent out a stream of lethal gas for almost twelve feet.

Killing dose...five grains.

CHAPTER 2

Twice they-drove past the concealed pick-up, looking for any sign of life, but there was none, just an owl hooting its annoyance at them from a nearby branch. They were in deeply wooded country here, and the silence was eerie.

They went back and stopped at last for a closer look, and they sat in the Mini, waiting and watching, till Quayle said at last, irritably, "What the hell are we waiting for? Let's take a look."

The pick-up was almost brand new, but mud had been slapped all over its bumpers and the other brightwork, not to catch the occasional light of the filtered moon that streamed through the clouds and the trees.

And there was nothing at all in the back except a large blue tarpaulin and several coils of rope. And as they rooted around, Albert came along in his beat-up old Bedford van.

Charlie the mongrel dog leaped out of the window and clambered all over them with his muddy paws, slobbering to show how much he loved them, and then Albert Ray got down, a large and grizzled old man with a moustache of the kind that could easily be seen from behind, and a gray beard almost down to his navel. He was lugging out a shotgun, breaking it and slipping two shells in.

"London license plates," Ian Quayle said, and the old

farmer nodded. "A good supply of venison in Lunnon Town tomorrow, Mr. Quayle. Unless we catch the bugger."

He looked at the tarp and the ropes in the back, and he said, "Yep, that's a poacher alright. They bundle the carcass up to hide it, because, can you believe it, the coppers can't untie it without a search warrant. So they let the buggers go; it's not worth their time."

So, it was indeed just a poacher after all, and Ian Quayle breathed a sigh of relief. He remembered the formalities. "Wendy, you met Albert, I think? Albert Ray, Wendy Hayworth."

The old man touched his forelock, "Miss Hayworth," and Ian said, staring out into the darkness: "Yes, a poacher, and he might just be sitting out there and listening to us, waiting for us to move on. Draped in venison over his shoulders."

But Albert shook his head. "No," he said with assurance. "He's not within three or four hundred yards of us, or Charlie here would be raising blue murder."

He scratched at his beard. "Six hundred quid," he said, "that's what a good deer fetches in Lunnon these days. But he won't show himself till we've gone, will he?"

"So let's make it not so easy for him," Ian said. "What do you say?"

One by one, he unscrewed the valve covers of the tires, extracted the cores, and threw them away, watching in great satisfaction as the nice new tires collapsed.

"When I get back to the house," he said, "I'll give the Sergeant a call, that pick-ups not going to get very far tonight."

"Why don't *I* do that?" Albert asked, "I owe Tim Berry a favor. Half of them day-old-chicks I sold him last month died on him, he thinks it's my fault. But you can't trust a copper to look after day-olds the way they're supposed to be looked after, now can you?"

"No, I suppose not. Okay, just give him the license

number, let him take it from there. It'll give him something to do."

He helped Wendy squeeze back into the Mini, and clapped Albert on the shoulder. "You take care of Charlie now. Take care of yourself too."

Albert touched his forelock respectfully for Wendy. "Been a real pleasure, Miss Hayworth. And if you're staying down here for a while...perhaps you'd like a basket of peaches fresh off the trees to take back to Lunnon with you?"

"You're very kind, Mr. Ray," Wendy said. "Yes, I'll be staying overnight, I got a lift here, left my car in town."

The young people these days, the old man was thinking, *they're not brought up the way we was...* But he reflected that scarcely a weekend passed without some young lady or other coming down from the City for Mr. Quayle's pleasure. None of his business, of course, and they made such a nice couple together...

"Good-night, Mr. Quayle."

"Good-night, Albeit."

Ten minutes later they were back in the cottage, and Ian Quayle said, "Now, after that pleasant interlude, where were we?"

"You were asking me," Wendy said promptly, "who was informed about the schedule of those meetings."

"Ah yes."

"It was 'Eyes Only' to the top brass at Scotland Yard, at MI5, and us. No one else."

"And now, what about the rest of them?"

"They'll go on, of course. But they'll be held in London now, for tighter security. I don't quite know where. So what do you know about the Swords of God?"

"I can answer that in one word," Quayle said: "Not a bloody thing."

"Ian...! You must know *something* about them!"

"Well, I don't. But the name Abu Jildi rings a bell. There was a report in one of the French papers a week or two ago, *Le Monde* I think it was, yes, I'm sure of it. About a man named Abu Jildi who claimed responsibility for a bomb in the basement of the Saudi-Arabian Embassy in Cairo, a janitor and his daughter killed and a lot of damage done. The paper said the Egyptian police had no suspects. It figures."

Wendy frowned. "What, no suspects? When a man claims responsibility...?"

"It seems that Abu Jildi is just a nickname. It means 'Father of Leather', might be applied to anyone. And all we know about him at the moment is that he's probably an Arab, we can't even be sure of that."

Wendy was deeply concerned. "I hope that doesn't mean you're thinking of the Middle East as a place to start looking? I won't allow it, Ian. And if I can't stop you—then I'll see to it that Robin Harris will, I don't care how sick he is."

"Two things," Ian Quayle said tartly, "First of all, just because this Abu Jildi seems to operate in London and Cairo, it doesn't mean that I have to traipse off to bloody Egypt and ask every Tom, Dick and Harry on the street: '*Has anyone seen Abu Jildi lately?*' And secondly, I am not a Field Officer, I'm not trained as a Field Officer; and I'd hate to become a Field Officer, it scares the death out of me. The first and last time I tried that caper on for size I damn nearly got myself killed, not once, but three times, for God's sake! Or was it four? Quite apart from the almost irreparable damage they did to my Mini..."

"You're being stubborn again..."

"Besides which," Quayle went on, "the logical place to start is not in Egypt, but in the British Museum, where they have every foreign language newspaper and magazine under the sun, with lots of bright young birds to translate for me in languages I don't really know. And if you'll excuse me, I have to make a phone call."

Wendy sighed and wandered back into the kitchen as Ian spoke at great length to his mother in Paris, and to his young daughter Pia, an illegitimate child whom he discovered only a year ago. Studying ballet, Pia was working out with her grandmother, the famous Claudine Andrassy, once the greatest of all the legendary Prima Ballerinas.

But that was before that damned Russian defector had dropped her on stage and had ruined her career as a Prima forever. How could she hope to dance after shattering a kneecap?

He loved them both dearly, Ian Quayle, with a devotion that passed all the bounds of reason, and it was hard for him to tell them: "We'll have to postpone it, darlings, just for a little time. I'd say a week or so."

When he'd finished at last, he smelled the ripe scent of well marinated meat sizzling, and found that Wendy had finished frying the *pommes Lyonnaise* and had grilled the shish kebabs, and that all was ready.

As they sat down to eat, Wendy asked, "Tomorrow?"

"We'll run down and cheer Robin up first, then we'll hightail it to London and I'll start work. Shouldn't take me more than a few days to find out all there is to be found out. About Abu Jildi I mean, and his bloody Swords of God. How's the grub?"

"Fantastic," Wendy said. "So I'd better stay here tonight, no? I don't have my car here, do I?

Ian nodded. "Sure," he said, nibbling on a chunk of lamb, "the bed in the spare room's made up."

She threw him one of her glances. "Well, how nice! Are you still mad about Moronic Melanie? I hope not, because that would make you a moron too. You really have to choose your dates more carefully."

"I don't have to," Ian said cheerfully. "The fates always seem to choose them for me. I've always thought that fornication and conversation ought to go hand in hand. With poor Melanie

I'd have had too much of the one and not enough of the other. You, on the other hand, are at least competent in the intelligent exchange of ideas."

"Not a moron," Wendy said caustically, "just a goddamn sonofabitch, first class. I truly, honestly, *hate* you! You know that? You're just a pain in the fucking ass."

The next morning at seven, the spare bed was still made up when Ian Quayle shook the slim body beside him awake, and whispered, "Shower together too?"

Wendy Hayworth nodded, and she groaned. "And then some coffee, for Christ's sake. For God's sake, some *espresso*! Jesus, how much did we drink last night? You don't have to get me drunk, you know, whenever you want to sleep with me."

She shivered half to death in the cold shower that Ian liked to take on his more vigorous mornings, and it was his turn to suffer when she switched over to hot. And then the phone rang downstairs, and he swore.

He slipped into a robe and went down to find it was Sergeant Tim Berry from the local police station.

"Hope I didn't get you out of bed, Mr. Quayle sir," Sergeant Berry said, "but about that pick-up truck. It was still there at six this morning when I went to take a look at it, no one there at all, and no dead deer around either. I didn't like the look of them London number-plates. Most of the poachers around these parts come from Guildford or Dorking, where the big meat markets are. So just on a hunch, you might say, I called a buddy of mine at the Yard and he ran it down for me. He says the truck's registered to an Arab, one of them Syrian Arab Sheiks London's lousy with. Name of, hold on a minute, can't read me own writing... I got it. Sheik Najir Mohammed el Afwan bin Sousa. Why can't they all be called Smith or Jones?"

"Well!" Ian Quayle said, "I find that very, very

interesting, for reasons I won't bother you with. I don't suppose you've got an address for him, have you?"

"No good doing things by halves, Mr. Quayle sir. Yes, he lives at Number 307, Marlborough Towers. That's that fancy new building just off Berkley Square, on Charles Street. Costs a million quid just to look at one of them flats, so he doesn't sound like a poacher to me. But whoever's walking around our woods in the dead of night with a gun in his hand—I want to know who it is."

"And so do I," Quayle said. "And I have friends at the Yard too, so let's both see what we can find out, shall we? We'll keep in touch. And thanks, Sergeant, thanks a lot."

"It's my pleasure, Mr. Quayle."

Ian thought about it deeply, wondering if he could hide the awful worry that was on him when he told Wendy, as he'd have to. He went upstairs slowly, and found her drying herself off, and he took the towel from her automatically and began patting that splendid body down.

He said lightly, trying to make little of it, "Seems we stuck our necks out last night. That was Sergeant Berry down at the local police station."

Her eyes were wide, alarmed already, sensing that something was very wrong, knowing that she could read her lover like a book.

"And...?"

"It wasn't a poacher after all. It was an Arab, a man named Sheikh Najir Mohammed."

"Oh God. Then he was trying to kill you!"

"It's a possibility, at least. But why, can you tell me why?"

"No, I can't. I can only tell you why *not*. I don't believe it can have anything to do with Abu Jildi..."

"Of course not, I haven't even started work on him yet, there hasn't been time...!"

"So, what other possibility is there? Do you have..."

She broke off, not at all sure of herself, and she went on at last, not liking what she had to say: "Don't misunderstand me, Ian, but...well, you are a bit of a philanderer, aren't you? Do you have any Arab girl friends?"

"No, I don't," he answered, and he sounded a bit testy.

"Any of your girlfriends maybe have an Arab husband?"

Exasperated, he said, "God dammit, Wendy, there aren't that many Melanies! Just once in a while, I must admit. Something I'm trying to cure myself of..."

"As long as you don't try and cure yourself of *me*..."

"That, never," he said earnestly.

"Oh shut up!"

He sighed, "Okay, tell me one thing I must know. Who put me onto this Swords of God business? Mrs. Bloody French, I suppose."

"In Robin's absence, yes."

"Who else knows about it?"

"A hell of a lot of people. The P.A. to the Director, for starters, that's Jackie. All the department's heads and their secretaries, at least seven or eight people in Operations A total, I'd say, of twenty or maybe thirty. But even if there is a leak there, as you seem to suspect...they haven't had time, Ian! It doesn't make any sense at all!"

"Unless we postulate," Ian said tightly, "that Abu Jildi not only knows a hell of a lot about what's going on—he also knows it almost before it happens. And in the absence of anything that makes more sense—that's what I'm going to assume for the moment. Who's your best contact at the Yard?"

"The Deputy Chief, Metropolitan Area."

"Good, I've only got a couple of Supers. Let's give him a call."

Wendy shrugged herself into her dress, a nice little piece she'd fashioned for herself out of some Shanghai silk she'd bought on Rupert Street. It was light blue and very fine, and when she moved, the dress moved to, it was very fetching indeed; if she stood with her back to the light, it was murder.

They went downstairs together, and Ian picked up the pad he'd scribbled on. He said, "A man named Sheik Najir Mohammed el Afwan bin Sousa, he lives at 307 Marlborough Towers. Tell him it's a long shot, but there just might be a connection to the Five Ports bombing. Will he ask too many questions?"

"No, nothing I can't handle, he's been working with us for a very long-time."

He listened attentively while she spoke on the phone, and interrupted her only once: "Ask him to find out if the Sheik has any guns registered to him, like a hunting rifle."

Wendy nodded and went on with her talk, and when she put the phone down, Ian Quayle said abruptly: "So let's get going, we have a hospital call to make."

And very soon, they were on the road in the souped-up little bomb of a car, hurtling along the narrow and winding byways of Surrey and Kent.

And at four minutes past mid-day, they were ushered into the private ward in St. Mary's Hospital, Dover, to find Robin Harris, white as the sheets he lay on, white as death itself, flirting mildly with the pretty young nurse who sat beside him.

"Just a short visit," the Matron said sternly, "He's still in great pain."

She turned to the young nurse. "And you. Be about your business."

When the three of them were alone together, Robin Harris managed a grin, and he said weakly, "Great pain my ass, I'm shot so full of analgesics you could jump up and down on my stomach in football boots, and I wouldn't feel a thing. How are you, Ian? Wendy? Good of you to come..."

He eased himself painfully on the bed and said, "Sit

down, both of you. We've a lot to talk about now."

CHAPTER 3

Robin Harris was a gentleman of the old school, a man who saw absolutely nothing wrong in opening doors for ladies or in leaping promptly his feet when one of them entered the room.

He was head of the foolishly named Continental Liaison Board, which was largely concerned with what, in its earlier days, was known as 'Dangers to His Majesty Realm,' but which in these more trying times, boiled down mostly to the threat of terrorism.

He was a born aristocrat, and looked the part—tall and slim, gray-haired and distinguished-looking in his immaculate Savile Row suits, a member of all the proper clubs, and a man of considerable sensitivities; he sometimes wondered what the devil he was doing in MI6, dealing with all those dreadful people.

He was completely unflappable, and highly regarded for his great erudition (the end result of schooling at Harrow, Cambridge, and the Sorbonne,) and for his persuasive skills in what he liked to call 'fitting the pieces together.'

He was charming and witty, and all in all a very pleasant old gentleman.

He was smiling at them now, glad that Wendy was emotionally hanging onto his hand, a very worried look on her face.

"I won't ask you how you feel," Ian said, "I can guess.

The question is, do you feel you can put up with it."

The smile broadened. "Modern medicine," Robin Harris said. "No trace of pain or suffering anywhere. And I have the strictest orders—if I feel the slightest twinge, all I have to do is press a button, and that pretty little thing hurries in with a damn great needle which she thrusts lovingly into my bum. A drug called, I think, Nepenthe."

"So how much do you know," Quayle asked, "about what happened?"

The smile vanished at once. "Five minutes after I came around," Harris said, "I bullied them into giving me a phone, it wasn't easy. But I've been in touch with the office. They told me about Gavin O'Brien. Poor bugger was a member of two of my clubs, nicest old goat you could wish to meet. Knew one of the dead Frenchmen too, Jean-Claude Perot, not a bad sort at all, considering. But that's behind us now, isn't it? Question now is—what the devil are we going to do about these damn Swords of God? Mrs. French tells me she's put you on it. I'm glad. Any idea who they might be?"

Quayle shook his head. "Not yet. But whatever *is* known about them—I should have it under my belt in a very few days. They're new, that much I'm sure of, or I'd have heard of them."

Way back in his student days, Quayle had read history and languages at London University, but the lovely young Italian girl he'd fallen so desperately in love with, the only child of a senior Roman Police Officer, had been studying criminology, so it seemed quite natural that his masterly thesis should be a study of secret and criminal societies in history, from the Sicarii at the time of Christ (Judas was a member) to the Mafia, the Liberators of Corsica, the Society of Friends in South-East Asia, and the equally clandestine terrorist organizations operating worldwide. (It was this famous thesis that had first brought him to the notice of MI6.)

"Not only new," Robin Harris said, "but highly

competent. They seem to have known too damn much about those meetings, I don't like it, don't like it a bit."

He paused, and seemed to search their faces, and he said at last, slowly, "You're both what, Grade Four, aren't you?"

Wendy shook her head, "No, I'm Grade Three..."

"Ah, good..."

"But Ian's only five. You might want to do something about that someday."

"Grade bloody Five," Ian Quayle said, "It means I'm not supposed to know an awful lot that I should know."

"But I'm going to tell you anyway."

He thought about it for a moment, then looked at Ian Quayle and said, "Rome, last year, the matter of the League of Hawks. You came to the conclusion that there was a double agent working out of our office." He sighed heavily. "I'm afraid events have proved you right."

"Good, I was sure of it. You know who it is? Was?"

"No, we have a code name, that's all. '*Bahram*', it's the name of several Persian Kings."

"Quite," Quayle said; tending to pontificate. "Taken originally from the God Vahrana. I wonder if that presupposes a man rather than a woman?"

"Not a conclusion to leap at," Wendy said tartly. "It could have been imposed on him or her, by almost anybody. But if it's Middle Eastern, Persian, it might be one of the spies from Khomeini's Hezbollah."

Quayle grunted. "It's a thought. The last King Bahram, Bahram V, was known for his persecution of the Christians."

He turned to Robin Harris. "Are there any Muslims in the office?"

"There were two," Harris said, "both girls from Lebanon, in the cypher department, which is the obvious place to start looking. But some years ago, when Arab terrorism started up with a vengeance, we practiced a little discrimination. They were both quietly reassigned. And then, one day, one of our men saw a fellow named John Reston on the edge of a crowd of Arab in Hyde Park, listening to one of their hysterical speakers. You know the type, the type that can do nothing but scream obscenities against the country that's given them refuge. Back home, they'd be carted off for execution, but in London..." He grimaced, and went on: "Reston worked in the office Mail Department, innocuous enough, but our man said he seemed to understand what was being said. In Arabic. And Arabic was *not* one of the languages he listed on his application. We found that very strange."

"And so?"

"He was fired. I think the excuse was drunkenness or some such triviality. But that was long before the present leak, which is a very dangerous one."

It seemed that the effort of talking was too much for Robin Harris, and he was whispering now and trying to hide the pain Ian knew he must have felt in spite of his bluffing. "But all that's our concern, not yours. Yours is to find out about these damned Swords of God and their Abu Jildi. And let me for once lay down the law. If you feel that your research should take you to the Middle East—I forbid it absolutely. You will *not* go there, you understand?"

"It stipulates in my contract that I work at home," Quayle said happily. "That means—in my London flat or my weekend place in Surrey. And I always keep to the letter of my contracts."

"I feel guilty still about what happened to you in Italy," Harris went on. "It was Mrs. Bloody French's idea, and I should never have allowed it. With all of your sterling qualities, you're still the world's worst Field Officer, never forget that."

"Nice to know," Wendy said mildly, "that *someone* agrees with me."

But those weary eyes had closed, and Robin Harris had fallen into a sleep or coma.

Wendy touched the button, and when the pretty young nurse came hurrying, Quayle said quietly, "I think it's only sleep, we just wanted to be sure he's alright."

She fussed over him, and said at last, smiling, "Such a nice old man, yes, he's fine."

She was laughing suddenly. "And you know what? Dr. Gerhardt told him about the lump of concrete that had opened up his stomach. Mr. Harris asked me to, find it for him. He wants to use it as a paperweight..."

Quietly, they left their boss to his dreams and headed for London.

London and the British Museum.

As they walked together down the long and silent corridors of the Museum to the Polish Section, Wendy asked, "Are you truly hopeful about this?"

Ian Quayle nodded. "I learned a long time ago," he said, "that the Eastern European papers always know first, and most, about what's happening in the terrorist world. Sometimes they get news of a calamity so fast have to wonder just who's feeding them. Bulgaria especially, Poland too. Yes, I'm very hopeful. And Sonia's a doll, you'll love her."

Wendy sighed. "Another of your conquests?"

"Not quite," Quayle said, grinning. "Though I did get her the job she's been holding down for the last few years. Believe it or not, she was my teacher once, she taught me German and Russian, and used to chat with me in half-a-dozen other languages as well, just to keep me in practice. She speaks more languages, knows them fluently, than you can shake a stick at. She's worth her weight in diamonds, and more."

They found her poring over a copy of the Polish DZIENNIK ZWIAZKOWY, and making quick, incisive notes on a yellow pad. She left her desk as they approached and ran to embrace Ian like a long-lost son.

"Ian!" she almost shrieked in the silence. "It's *years* since I saw you...!"

He held her off at arm's length, and said cheerfully, "And you never looked better. You haven't met Wendy Hayworth, have you? An associate of mine. Wendy, Sonia Walenska."

The two women shook hands, and Sonia asked, "And what is it this time? I always find your requests so very, very exciting."

"And this one is of enormous importance. And urgency. I'm looking for an organization called the Swords of God, and a man named Abu Jildi."

"Tonight's *Evening Standard*," Sonia said promptly. "They're the people who planted that bomb in the Five Ports Hotel. Three people killed, several wounded, all tourists."

"Ah, so it's common knowledge now. Good. I a like you to search back for any mention of them at all in the Bulgarian, Rumanian, Czech and Polish press. Go back about six weeks for a start, if you don't find anything, try another six. After that—we'll have met a dead end, I'm afraid. How long will that take you?"

"Just a day or two, with help. I can put some of the girls on it..."

"And if you do it yourself?"

"Ah, it's like that is it? Very well, mum's the word. Do I have a week?"

"As long as you need. I'll be in touch, but call me the moment you find anything, okay?"

They chatted for a while, Wendy and Sonia good friends already, and as they drove round to Wendy's place on Sydney Mews, a honeysuckle sort of retreat from London's bustle, Ian said, "I think I'll go to Paris tomorrow anyway, I've been thinking about that article in *Le Monde*, it *was Le Monde*, I'm certain. They have damn good investigative reporters, and if I can track down the man who wrote it, I can get his notes, always a good source. The stuff that slips through the presses unseen."

Wendy sighed. "I wish I could come with you, but I can't."

"Mrs. Bloody French?"

"Of course. I haven't even checked into the office today, she'll be furious with me."

"The hell with her."

Wendy said wistfully, "But maybe she'll be too busy, in Robin's absence, manipulating the upper echelons, trying to fulfill a lifelong ambition. To wriggle into his job."

As they pulled up in the delightful Mews, with honeysuckle climbing everywhere over the timbered walls and little pots of geraniums at every window, Wendy asked, "Can I fix you dinner? It's only leftover stew, but it's great."

"Why don't I take you to that little Thai restaurant in Soho instead?"

She shook her head, "I have to call my father at ten. That's six a.m. Washington time, catch him before he goes on his morning jog."

"Ah... Then say hello to the old fart for me, will you?"

"I somehow don't feel," Wendy said coldly, "that that is quite the correct way to refer to His Excellency the British Ambassador. I will, however, frame a suitable greeting. What time are you leaving for Paris?"

"I'm catching the nine o'clock hovercraft from Hastings to Boulogne. Get me to Paris in nice time for lunch with Claudine and Pia."

"God, I wish I could come with you, just to see them both again! Give them my fondest love, won't you?"

"Of course. Goodnight, my sweet."

"Night, darling. Call me as soon as you get back."

"Will do."

They embraced and kissed, long and lovingly, and

Wendy whispered, "You do realize, don't you, that even at the research level, the potential for trouble is quite strong? You're tangling with a group about which we know nothing—except that they're ruthless and very knowledgeable. And don't forget about Bahram, either. Remember that I'm your Case Officer, you deal only with me now, no one else."

"Yes Ma'am, Take care."

He waited till she had unlocked the brightly blue-painted door and was safely inside, and eased his Mini-S into the heavy traffic of Fulham Road, the short cut down Flood Street, almost past his own flat, to the Embankment and over Chelsea Bridge, weaving the little car in and out like a shoulder-fired Stinger missile searching out its prey and seeking the fast route tor Croydon and Leatherhead, then turning south along the winding country roads where he could put his foot to the floor and watch the speed sweep up to the nineties...

And when the distant church clock in the tiny village of Austel-in-the-Woods struck midnight with its sonorous bells, he pulled up at last outside the cottage. He sat in the car and listened to the dying notes, thinking about a man named Abu Jildi, the 'Father of Leather'.

What kind of man could he be?

An Arab sometimes got to be called that if his weathered old face was lined and grizzled, but this didn't sound like an old man, though the possibility couldn't be shunted aside. Sometimes, anyone who fancied he was tough as camel-leather gave himself the name, a sort of Arab *machismo*.

Somehow, it conjured up a country sort of image not at all the kind of nickname that would settle on an urban, educated man, and yet...in the terrorist battle, toughness was all that counted.

He thought of the tape he'd heard; the English was lousy, but enough to presuppose some kind of schooling; chalk that up, not a peasant. It didn't mean much, but a little something at least.

The voice-prints might help, but only if they matched up with the print of some other terrorist already more experienced than a newcomer would be. Every well-known terrorist's print was on file at Scotland Yard, so if it turned out to be Arafat under another name for his new venture, or Abu Nidal, or George Habash, or Bassam Sharif, or Ahmed Jibril, or Naif Hawatmeh, or any one of a hundred others...

Wishful thinking, nothing more...

He left the car at last, went into the lonely house, soaked for a while in a hot bath, set the alarm for five a.m., and lay awake half the night still thinking about an enemy he had not yet met and could not yet even envision.

But when he fell asleep at last, the only thoughts in his mind were of a different kind of excitement—the excitement of meeting once again with his lovely daughter Pia, and with his even more lovely mother Claudine.

Dreaming, he thought: the most wonderful women in history...

CHAPTER 4

Madame Marie-Louise Constant, concierge at the elegant St. Cloud apartment of Claudine Andrassy and her granddaughter Pia, was not like most of her watchdog sisters-in-trade.

Throughout almost the whole of Paris, your typical concierge was always a formidable harridan. Tightlipped and taciturn to all but her charges, and ever complaining about the trials and troubles of her demanding existence.

But not here, in this very upper-class environment.

Madame Constant liked to think of herself as almost a lady too, only the slightest degree lesser in stature than the gentry to whom she was responsible.

"But M'sieur Quayle," she said, apologetically and as though it was all her own fault. "They are not here! They have gone to the seaside."

"Oh bloody hell..."

"Madame Andrassy herself told me, she often chats with me, that she was expecting you, and then *not* expecting you. For a few days, she said. And so...they left this morning, both of them, just for the weekend."

"At the seaside..."

"*Mais oui, M'sieur*. To the villa in St. Tropez."

"*Merde!*"

"But the maid is there, of course, if you wish to stay for a while. A meal, perhaps..."

"Yes, I'll just take a look around."

"Of course. I'll call her to tell her you're coming up."

"*Merci, madame.*"

"*C'est moi...*"

As he took the rickety elevator up to the top floor, she was primping at her gray hair, thinking 'What a nice young man, M'sieur Quayle...'

The maid was standing at the open door to the apartment when he finally arrived, and she ushered him in, fluttering and smiling to show how fond she was of him. "I will cook lunch at once, M'sieur Ian," she said, "if you will tell me what you would like..."

He shook his head. "No, Cecile, thank you. Just some of your excellent coffee and a glass or two of Armagnac."

"*Bien, M'sieur, a votre service.*"

For a while he wandered around the rooms, looking, remembering, even smelling the perfumes on the air. He picked up the famous photo in Claudine's bedroom, an old press photo from the far-off days when he had rescued Claudine from the clutches of the Russians; Budapest, November 1956, as the Hungarian Freedom Fighters were awaiting the second Soviet attack. And he'd been just a child then!

He remembered the streets littered with dead bodies, sprinkled with lime that tuned them into dreadful statuary, remembered the burned-out tanks that casually moved over them. By the end of the second assault, 25,000 civilians had been killed, and the Russian 'Liberators' were in firm control of the once beautiful city. It was a time of great sadness and of terror.

He'd found his mother in the apartment of one Colonel Malakov, who had raped her repeatedly, and he had somehow smuggled her to the border and beyond it, where an alert Austrian photographer had recognized the great Prima Ballerina, bedraggled as she was, a child by her side, not knowing even the basics of their close escape.

He sighed and put the photo down as Cecile brought him his *cafe filtre,* and went to the expansive living room where the phone was.

He thought for a while: What was the name of the Editor-in-Chief at *Le Monde,* the man Claudine had spoken of so highly and so often? Boideleau? No, but something like that.

He summoned the maid again with the bell-pull: "Cecile, do we have a copy of *Le Monde*? It doesn't have to be today's..."

"I will see, M'sieur Ian..."

When she brought it to him, he searched the editorial page and came up with the name *Gerard Savarin Boileau, Chef du Bureau Etranger...*

He called, and sipped his coffee through the interminable waiting, wondering how long it would be before telephonic France caught up with modern technology. But at long last the girl was on the line: "*Bureau de Monsieur Boileau.*"

"My name is Ian Quayle," Ian said, "and I am calling from St. Cloud, the apartment of Claudine, Andrassy, who is my mother. Please ask M'sieur Boileau if he can spare me a few moments of his time."

"*Ne quitez pas M'sieur...*"

And then, there was the *chef* himself, effusive and amiable, saying cheerfully: "Mr. Quayle! What a pleasure to hear from you! *La merveilleuse* Claudine has spoken of you so often that feel I already know you intimately...and I must congratulate you on your choice of mothers, surely the brightest star in the Parisian sky!"

"How kind of you... I won't take up much of your time, which I know must be valuable..."

"For Claudine's son...just tell me how I can help you, it will be for me the greatest pleasure imaginable."

"Ah... You have a reporter named Paul Diderot..."

"One of our best."

"And I wonder if you could arrange for me to meet him? At a more confidential level than I could expect if I were to call him direct. After all, he's never even heard of me, and going in cold..."

"I know what you mean. When is it convenient for you?"

"Any time at all, the sooner the better."

"Tell me when and where, I'll have him there."

"The Mediterranée. For lunch? In about an hour?"

"Oh-ho, the Mediterranée! Journalists do not usually eat so well! He will be delighted! And if there is anything else I can do for you, don't hesitate."

"You are most kind, M'sieur Boileau."

"And is your mother there now? Just to say hello?"

"She's at the seaside with her granddaughter."

"*Ah, quel dommage...*"

"A pity indeed. *Au 'voir*, M'sieur Boileau. And I thank you."

He rang off, and wandered into the huge kitchen to find the maid. "Call the Mediterranée for me, Cecile, would you? Book me a table for two at two o'clock."

She nodded. "*Oui M'sieur*," and he somehow thought that only the women of Paris could say 'Yes sir,' so sweetly.

He penned a note and stuck in. on Claudine's bathroom mirror: "I was here, I will return. I love you both *a la folie*... Ian."

Ian Quayle, for no sensible reason at all, had expected a much younger man.

But Paul Diderot, rising to his feet now at the table for two, was a skeleton of an old man, in his later severities, perhaps, bald-headed but with an imposing white beard almost down to his waist and no moustache at all. His eyes were pale blue and twinkling, and he shot out a hand and said: "How very nice to meet you, M'sieur Quayle. I have never had the honor of meeting the great Claudine Andrassy, but...who does not know her reputation? I've had the great pleasure of seeing her dance on numerous occasions. Before her tragic accident, of course." He sighed. "A tragedy for the whole world of Ballet. So tell me how I can be of service to you?"

"Well, first of all," Ian Quayle said amiably, "you can accept my gratitude for agreeing to meet with me. Then, you can help me decide what we're going to eat. The lobster, I suggest, but—Thermidor or Amboricaine? Staring a live lobster face to face, this is the question a gourmet must always ask himself: *Amioricaine or Thermidor*? It taxes the imagination of even the strongest man, M'sieur Diderot."

The old man was grinning broadly at this sally: "Ah, perhaps the Amoricaine? I was born and bred in a place called St. Brieuc, which is in Brittany..."

"Once called Amorica," Quayle said happily; "and the home waters of the world's best seafood. *Amoricaine* it'll be, then. And the wine. A fairly new Pouilly-Fouisse?"

"An excellent choice indeed."

And excellent it all was.

When their palates began to luxuriate in satisfaction, Ian Quayle said abruptly, "A few weeks ago, a bomb was exploded in the basement of the Saudi Arabian Embassy in Cairo, you remember? You wrote a quite short report on it, which I read at the time and it seemed to me, reading through the lines, that you left a great deal unsaid that might have been said. Was I right?"

The old man nodded. "Yes, you were. Are you a journalist yourself, Mr. Quayle?"

"No, I am a professional researcher, I find out things that other people want to know about. And my employer is very interested in the man named Abu Jildi, who claimed responsibility."

There was a little silence, and then Diderot murmured, "I

will not embarrass you by asking you who your employer might be. I will tell you instead how I chanced upon that story. It's one of those scoops a journalist always dreams about, and seldom succeeds in covering. I just happened to be in Cairo at the time."

"You were?" Quayle was already excited. "And do you still have the notes you took?"

Diderot raised a placatory hand. "All in good time, Mr. Quayle. Indulge a long-winded old man his little pleasures. Like telling a story in its proper way, which is to say—with a beginning, a middle, and an end."

"I'm sorry," Quayle said, smiling. "Please go on."

And he did: "I was covering that extraordinary meeting President Mubarak of Egypt held with Jordan's King Hussein and Saudi Arabia's Prince Fahad, the most unlikely trio imaginable to meet in such a friendly atmosphere. It had been announced as a Trade Summit, with half the world's press there to report on how well they all agreed with each other."

He held a little piece of lobster in his mouth to savor it before swallowing it down. "Delicious, and the sauce is pure nectar..."

He went on: "That's what first struck me as being very puzzling. You and I both know that the Arabs *never* agree with each other, it's almost a matter of personal honor with them to say that the other fellow is absolutely wrong, to talk themselves into a state of high dudgeon and then stalk out of the room with their retinues. So when I heard, and heard again and again, nothing but: '*Yes, I agree*,' or '*How very right you are, my brother*' or '*Why don't we all do exactly as you say*,' I began to smell a rat of very interesting proportions. Now, have stringers in Cairo, people who've worked for me for twenty years or more, and I made a few discreet enquiries, and I soon found out that all that talk about trade was nothing more than a cover. Once each day's meeting was over, and the delegates returned to their hotel—all in the same one, the Shepherds, I'd have you know, which in itself is a little suspicious—they were meeting again clandestinely in one of Prince Fahad's suites. And their talk, I was told, was now not only far more acrimonious, but it wasn't about trade at all. It was something to do with Prince Fahad's desire to get Jordan and Egypt on his side in a concerted effort, which I learned was military, against Iran, a country of which Saudi Arabia is mortally afraid. Afraid? The Princes are all scared stiff that Khomeini's export of Muslim fundamentalism is going to topple them from their thrones sooner or later, as it will, eventually."

He fell silent again for a while as he enjoyed his lunch, and an Quayle wisely held his peace.

Diderot said at last, "Well, one of my informants has a daughter who works as a maid in Shepherds, and it was easy enough to get a cassette smuggled in there... I got only an hour's talk before the tape ran out, and it wasn't as clear as I would have liked, but clear enough for my purpose."

"And do you still have..." Quayle began excitedly, but he quickly broke off and smiled. "I'm sorry. Go on, this is fascinating stuff."

"For my purpose," the old man said, "which was confirmation of what I had learned on the grapevine. I had the tape translated and transcribed by a man I trust, and as a working journalist I was in seventh Heaven. And then, to fill my cup to overflowing, that bomb went off in the Saudi Arabian Embassy. Obviously, someone else had learned what those meetings were really about, someone who was actively working for Iran, the only possible deduction."

Casually, the old man picked up the bottle as though to pour himself another glass, but put it down when he saw that it was empty.

Ian Quayle promptly ordered another, and he said, "This time, I really must interrupt you, while we wait for the *sommelier*. What are you saying is that there really was a great deal more to the story than appeared in your paper?"

Diderot nodded. "As you will learn."

When the wine had been brought and poured and the waiter had gone, he continued: "As I said, a journalist's dream. Now, one of my stringers here...well, he's not exactly a terrorist himself, but he deals in arms, smuggles guns to anyone who'll pay him for them, so he gets around a bit. For a very large sum of money, he agreed to arrange a meeting for me with the man who planted the bomb—Abu Jildi himself."

Quayle felt his scalp tickling, but he said nothing and just waited.

"It wasn't easy," the old man said, "and not very profitable either, considering the huge amount of money it cost *Le Monde*. I was blindfolded, taken by car to, I think, Maadi, or perhaps somewhere else along the Nile, I could hear the sails of the *feluccas* flapping, and the creaking of heavier boats' timbers. Yes, twenty minutes from my hotel. It must have been Maadi, a small dark room lit only by a single candle, it might even have been just a shed. I had prepared a long list of questions for him, but he simply took the sheets of paper from me and tore them up. He said: '*No questions. You will listen, only.*' And then he let loose with the longest political polemic it's ever been my misfortune to sit through. He told me what merciless pigs the Americans, the British, and all the other Westerners are, recited every imagined crime the western governments have committed in the last twenty years, nearly forty minutes of it. Cold, calm, and quite eloquent, none of the fire and gesticulation you'd expect, hardly a movement of any sort. It was like a robot reading a prepared speech written by the Hezbollah, which is Iranian-led, as I'm sure you know."

The old man smiled suddenly. "And now," he said amiably, "question time. First of all, I am sure, you're going to ask me what Abu Jildi looks like. And it pains me to tell you I have no idea. He sat quite still behind a bare plank table, dressed in a long black *gallabiah*, which is almost certainly not his normal dress. Over his face, he wore the black ski mask we've all seen so often on terrorists' heads, and even his eyes were not really very visible."

"Well," said a frustrated Ian Quayle, "that's a great help."

"But when I did see his hands," Diderot said, "when he tore up my papers...they were the hands of a man not possibly over forty, and surprisingly...delicate. The nails were very well manicured."

"Ah...! Confirmation that he's not a peasant then, that's already immensely valuable. What about the tape? Can I get a copy or a transcription?"

"More frustration, I'm afraid," Diderot said gently. "The moment the tape was returned to me with typescript, I locked it all in my briefcase. When I went to see Abu Jildi, I left it for safe-keeping with my translator, a man I'd trust with my life. When I recovered it, checked of course, and everything was just as it was supposed to be. From that moment on, it never left my personal possession for a moment. Only...when I finally got home—and I left pretty hurriedly after my meeting, I can tell you—I opened up the briefcase and found a blank tape and blank typing paper, twelve blank yellow pages in place of my notes."

Ian Quayle scowled. "But if it never left your possession...? How do you think they managed it?"

Diderot sighed. "There's only one explanation. My trusted translator must have pulled a switch on me. They're very clever at that sort of thing, the Egyptians. They're all *gully-gully* boys. They're the kids who amuse the tourists by barehanded and bare-armed plucking day-old chicks from their pockets or their purses. Their wallets too, half the time, it's a skill they grow up with. My guess is that somebody got to him."

"And that, of course, accounts for the cutting of your story."

"Of course. Twelve hundred words reduced to a short

paragraph, the Editor wouldn't sit still for unconfirmed reports from stringers he didn't even know. He had to have solid confirmation, he said, or the story would have to be killed. I can see his point of view, it's *Le Monde* I work for, not some gutter rag. But it's a shame, isn't it?"

"It sure as hell is. But tell me more about this manicured terrorist Abu Jildi. What language did you speak?"

"French."

"He spoke it well?"

"Immaculately. It could have come straight out of the Sorbonne."

"Does that suggest a Lebanese? Or a Syrian?"

"Either. They both have French backgrounds. And his speechifying was pure Hezbollah, Iranian propaganda filled with Khomeini clichés. The Satan America, capitalist vultures, Godless mercenaries, that sort of thing. And I haven't been much help, have I?"

Ian Quayle frowned. "More than you think," he said thoughtfully, "I came to you with very little to go on, but now...what do we know? We can assume, I think, that he comes from the upper classes, probably has a university education, is more at home in French than in English, is calm rather than given to hysterics, and that he's extremely cautious about betraying his identity. While almost every other important terrorist we know of seems to like having his photo in the papers, Abu Jildi goes to great lengths to hide his face. What does that mean? Does it perhaps mean that his face is well-known and that he doesn't want to reveal his true identity?"

"If anything at all, it could simply be a matter of good judgment," the old man said.

"True."

Quayle was lost in deep thought for a while, and he said at last: "His speech was pure Hezbollah, you said, and yet...you know about the bombing of the Five Ports Hotel in Dover two days ago?"

"Of course."

Abu Jildi claimed responsibility in the name of the Swords of God, not the Hezbollah."

"Yes, I know, we got it on the wire service."

"But he's still financed, presumably, by Iran."

"And that is a deduction we simply cannot make. Furthermore, it's quite untrue."

"Oh?"

Diderot chuckled. "I hate uncorroborated evidence almost as much as my Editor does, a matter of my long years of experience separating fact from rumor. Remember that word—*uncorroborated*! But my arms smuggler friend tells me that Abu Jildi is desperately trying to get financing from both the Ayatollah Khomeini and from Colonel Khadafi, both of which gentlemen are apparently sitting on the sidelines, presumably waiting to find out if he's worth the millions he's asking for."

"And meanwhile?"

"Meanwhile," the old man said, "he's found an extraordinary means of raising a great deal of money very quickly. I'm sure you know that—openly or clandestinely—slavery is very common still in most of the Arab states. And in the harems of the Arab sheiks, a European or American woman is the ultimate status symbol."

"Oh my God! Are you talking about white slavery?"

"*White* slavery," Diderot said, emphasizing the 'white', "not your everyday Somali, Ethiopian, or Arab woman, but what they consider a woman of quality. Do you know what such a woman will fetch on the open market?"

"You mean they still have slave markets?"

"Let me list some of them for you, Mr. Quayle. First of all, both Mecca and Jedda hold them almost monthly, conducted quite free of governmental interference as too ancient a custom to be suppressed. There's a small one in Riyadh, one in Medina, a very busy one in Buraimi Oasis, the one in Suakin deals only in very young girls, the one in Timbuktu is wholesale only, if you please. There's one in Raifa, another in Daugua, and the one in Mt. Marra in Sudan is run like a school for concubines. The women there all get a month or so's training before they're sold. Of course, we're dealing here mostly with native girls. But a white woman is said to keep her looks longer than the Arab women do, so she doesn't have to be thrown out of the harem and put to work in the fields after just a few years to make way for better stock... So, do you know what a white woman can fetch?"

"No..."

"Twenty thousand petro-dollars is a fair sort of price for your average European girl—if she's skinny and not very young. But a really attractive young girl who can be fattened up to Arab standards—she can fetch as much as ten times that, even more."

He raised an expressive hand. "I could talk on this subject for hours, but...well, January last year, I wrote an article on the subject for France Dimanche." He grimaced. "Under another name, of course, I called myself *Passe-Partout*, a highly respected reporter from *Le Monde* is not expected to write for scandal sheets. But, a few extra francs always seem to be very useful. If you wish, I can dig up a copy for you."

Quayle shook his head. "Thank you, but don't bother. The British Museum will have it, I'll have to spend a lot of time there anyway." He thought about it for a moment, and then: "So he's actively engaged in white slave traffic, which tells us something about him too."

"Four European women have disappeared in Cairo alone in the last two months. Kidnaping, abduction, call it what you will. The Egyptian police are very worried at the lack of ransom demands, but..." There was that eloquent shrug again. "What better way for his little gang to pass their time in between bombings than in kidnapping pretty women for sale to the highest bidder?"

"Little gang?"

"My informant tells me," the old man said, "that he's sold Abu Jildi's buyer a total of thirty-four assorted guns—Uzis, Kalashnikovs, and handguns. But also a huge supply of *plastique* explosives. That presupposes not only a lot of bombing contemplated, but also a relatively small force."

"Unless he has other suppliers as well."

"My informant thinks not. He could be wrong, that's uncorroborated evidence as well. But I tend to agree with him, we're dealing at the moment with just the beginnings, aren't we?"

Quayle grunted. "It only takes one man to sneak a bomb into a hotel. So far, we've had one bombing in Cairo, one in Dover. Do you know if he has a base of operations? Tripoli, perhaps, or Damascus?"

"I've no idea. At a guess, I'd say Cairo would be the most logical place, if only because communications are better there, bad as they are, than in Libya or Syria. In Egypt, admittedly, he won't enjoy the benefit of Government support, but does he need it? And I see you haven't heard yet of the latest bombing?"

Quayle thought, *oh God no*, and said nothing, and Diderot went on, looking at his watch: "Seven hours ago, a car-bomb; just like Beirut. Only in Berlin. The car was parked right behind a Mercedes that belonged to Colonel Weiss-Histermann, you know who he is? *Was*?"

"The number two man in West German Intelligence. They got him?"

"And fourteen other people as well. *Fourteen* others dead! Something like thirty-seven wounded, some critically. And within an hour—Abu Jildi was calling the press, claiming the credit. Fifteen people killed just to get one man! Yes, they got him."

"And it's just the beginnings, you said. I think you're

right."

He called the waiter and settled the bill, wondering if he could get away with charging it off; Mrs. Bloody French liked to check on his expenses once in a while, and he could imagine the ice in her voice. "*Must* you spend nearly seventy pounds for lunch, Mr. Quayle? I'm sure sandwiches and coffee would have been quite adequate..."

They went out into the light drizzle that was falling on the Place de l'Odeon, and it seemed that the Left Bank had never been noisier nor more crowded. They made effusive farewells with promises to get together again, and Quayle streaked his Mini in and out through the furious traffic, over the Seine and on to St. Denis, heading north at speed along Route N1 that led to Beauvais, Abbeville, and finally to Boulogne for the six-thirty Hovercraft.

He was held up, cursing, just outside Montreuil, where two enormous *routiers* loaded down with produce for the market in Paris had tangled with each other, causing the world's worst traffic jam on this major route. He sat fuming in the little car for half an hour of no activity before swinging round and finding the little side road that led to La Touquet.

There, his luck was better; the ancient converted wartime Dakota that took passengers and their cars on, the twenty-minute flight over the channel was just readying for takeoff. They were beginning to roll away the ramp that led to the plane's rectum; and Ian Quayle leaned out of the Mini's window and screamed: "Hold it, I'm coming...!"

He floored the pedal and hit the brakes as the little car soared over the gap and landed in the Dakota's belly, bumper to bumper with a late-model Rolls, in a furious panic stop. There were shouts of anguish everywhere.

"If you don't mind, sir," the lugubrious attendant said, "we like to drive the cars aboard ourselves..."

"Well, how very accommodating of you," Ian Quayle

said. "Next time..."

And by the time darkness was falling, he was already streaking along the friendly country roads of Kent on his way to Surrey and his cottage.

The grandfather clock in the hall was striking ten-fifteen as he opened his front door and went straight to the Louis Quattorze sideboard in his living room that served as a bar to pour himself a very large cognac.

Augier Freres, the oldest cognac distillers in France; and their product was worth its weight in gold.

He stretched out on the sofa and called Wendy at her London Mews flat, feeling somehow that he hadn't spoken with her in months.

"I just got back," he said cheerfully, "and it's been ages. How are you, my sweet?"

"I'm fine," Wendy said, "and how was Paris? How was your family?"

"My family was at the seaside, dammit, I left them a note. But I had a fantastic meeting with a man named Paul Diderot, the reporter from *Le Monde*."

"You did?"

"Fantastic! He gave me a lot of information, and a number of ideas too."

"Great."

"So when can I see you?"

"Tomorrow. You have a ten o'clock meeting with the Director pro tem of the department."

"Oh God! Not Mrs. Bloody French?"

"Who else? She's even working out of Robin's office while he's in hospital."

"The bitch."

"A gold-plated bitch, you're right. But we always knew that, didn't we?"

"Any news on Robin?"

"I called the hospital, he's coming along just fine. They say he'll be on his feet in a week."

"Dinner tomorrow night?"

"*Chez-moi*. I really have to get rid of that leftover stew. It should still be okay, maybe."

Quayle sighed: "Love you," he said, and rang off.

He finished his cognac, soaked for a while in the tub, and when at last he fell asleep he was thinking: "Slowly, a *person* code-named Abu-Jildi is taking shape. Will I have to meet him face to face one day? Or will he just become a dossier and nothing else?"

CHAPTER 5

In her early forties, it was thought (no one seemed to know her exact age), Mrs. French could only be described as stunning.

She was tall and svelte, with hair the color of chestnuts, and quite startling pale-blue eyes. She dressed well and very expensively, and she considered careful grooming to be of the utmost importance.

But it wasn't only her great beauty that immediately struck anyone who met with her for the first time; it was the sure knowledge that this was a woman of fearsome intellect and savage temper. The high forehead was imposing, but the line of the lips said to watch out, and she was cordially hated by almost everyone who had the misfortune of working for her.

"That bloody woman," her boss Robin Harris would say. "If only she wasn't so damnably efficient."

And efficient she was...

She had begun her career as a cipherine, and had been given control of this most important department in less than a year. She had reorganized it, (firing a third of the staff in the process,) and had brought it to a peak of efficiency that had never been dreamed of before.

"Speed," she would tell her staff, "is of the essence. A Field Officer can be dying, and if it takes you an hour to decipher his call for help, then you're no good to me at all."

They quickly got the message that they were expected to memorize as many as two hundred key five-digit numbers, even though the cipher books were changed at first weekly—at her insistence—and then every third day.

Everyone knew, without looking it up, that in the present book '*05369*' meant '*urgent*,' that '*75841*' was '*next word is plural*,' that '*33296*' was '*negative*,' and it was easy enough to memorize perhaps fifty of them, given the constant flow. But two hundred? It was impossible, even if it meant their jobs.

And the young Betty French, as she was then called, could boast of as many as five-hundred within twenty-four hours of the new book's issue.

She moved after eighteen months to Ops. E, taking full charge of operational equipment issued to the people in the field, and it was she who introduced the so called L-Tablets, five grains of cyanide in a tiny capsule that could be held under the tongue almost permanently; a hard bite down on it meant instant death for anyone who felt himself (or herself) to be in danger of torture, a common enough occurrence.

Three years later, she was made head of Operations Q, the sub-department that oversaw all details of Field work, decided who should do what, and when it should be done.

Before her time in this crucial post, the chances of success in any dangerous operation had been estimated by a committee, consisting of all the staff concerned, each one voting his or her percentage figure. And if the mean figure came out at less than seventy-five percent, the operation was usually scrubbed or at least modified. But it was Mrs. French who decided that this figure was ludicrous, and had lowered it, first to sixty and then to fifty-five, (at which figure the Director himself—Robin Harris—balked and had set it back to seventy.)

She had countered by scrubbing the committee method altogether, disdaining this time-honored system as plain foolishness, and had promptly been reassigned to Head of Personnel, where she couldn't do any damage.

But Mrs. Bloody French, as she was now generally known, was not the kind of woman to take such cavalier treatment lying down; she knew a great number of very influential men in the House of Lords, and was back in the saddle within three months—this time as First Deputy Director of the whole shebang.

Everyone hated her guts, and she was perfectly content that it be so. She was a virago, and a bitch, but under her skilled deputy directorship, the Continental Liaison Board was the envy of every other cover for the legendary Secret Intelligence Service known as MI6.

She was dressed now in a cool blue linen suit that matched her eyes exactly, and wearing tiny star-sapphire earrings set in gold to complement the bracelet on her wrist. Her blouse was the usual white silk, open at the throat, and altogether she looked like a million dollars. On ice.

She said, unsmiling, "Sit down, Mr. Quayle, Miss Hayworth," and then went on with her paperwork for a moment or two as if they just weren't there.

They were in Harris' own office, where the plaque on the desk said 'Director,' and Ian Quayle hated it.

He made a mental note to call Robin at the hospital, or maybe go see him and cheer him up. Robin would know, of course, and would typically make nothing of it, just shrugging it off like the gentleman he was.

She looked up at last, glancing at her watch as though to indicate she didn't have too much time to waste on the likes of Ian Quayle. "Well? What do you have for me?"

"Nothing," Ian Quayle said amiably, and Mrs. French stared at him.

"Nothing? Are you telling me your trip to France, without my express permission, I might add, was a waste of time?"

"I'd hardly call it that. I did pick up certain information, but so far it's, er, uncorroborated. I'd rather get verification before I go public with it."

"And I'd hardly call reporting to your superiors 'going public,' Mr. Quayle. So, if you'd be kind enough..."

"Yes, Ma'am. Well, if this man Abu Jildi really heads the Swords of God, isn't just one of their flunkies, then he seems to command, at the present, no more than fifty followers or so..."

"Which can grow overnight to hundreds..."

"Of course. He's probably a Lebanese or a Syrian, probably young, probably has a university education, certainly has nice nails..."

"I'm sure that's very important," Mrs. Bloody French said, and he answered at once. "In spite of your sarcasm, yes, it really is important. Nice to know we're not dealing with a mere *fellah*."

"With a *what*?"

"That's Arabic for peasant."

"Oh."

"He's trying to get financing from Libya and/or Iran, and till now he's been making do in the white slave traffic while he's waiting for Khadafi and Khomeini to get off the fence, where they're watching to see how he makes out. He's also calm and not given to hysterics, and I'm sure that's important too, it cuts down the Arab field very considerably. I mean, how many unflappable Arabs do you know personally?"

"I personally know no Arabs at all, Mr. Quayle"

"And I insist that all of that is not yet verified. I hope it will be soon."

"It's not very much, is it?"

"No, it's not. Is that all? I have an important call to make."

"That's all for the moment. You will report to me personally on a daily basis now."

"No, I will not," Ian Quayle said mildly. "My standing orders from the Director himself are to report, always, only to my case officer, no one else except him."

"You seem to forget," Mrs. Bloody French said tartly, "that the Director is not in charge now, *I* am."

"Not as far as I'm concerned. It'll take more than a lump of concrete in his gut to allow Robin Harris to step aside. Especially if he knows *you're* taking over. Good-day, Mrs. French. Been a nice chat."

He looked at Wendy, sitting there and looking acutely uncomfortable. "Coming, luv?" He was grinning broadly.

"Miss Hayworth will stay," Mrs. French said furiously. "You may go. You are dismissed! And I expect to hear from you again tomorrow! This time, with something more important!"

"When I have something important, I'm sure Miss Hayworth will pass it on to you. See you."

He swept out, content with a kind of victory, and he said to the girl in the outer office, "When Wendy gets out of there, tell her I'll be round to her place for dinner tonight. Will you do that for me, Jackie?"

Jackie was Robin Harris' own secretary, and she hated what was going on. She was bright, bright, *bright*, with more degrees from London U than you could shake a ten foot pole at—History, Math, Economics, Languages, you name it, she had it. She was in her early thirties, mouse-colored hair all over the place, lousy with her make-up but still somehow attractive; maybe it was her bedroom eyes, dark hazel, that looked you up and down and seemed to wonder how good or bad you'd be in bed...

The office rumor was that there wasn't a single male in the Department she hadn't shacked up with, a matter of principle, *I want all of them...*

Ian Quayle had bedded her once, but no more; he never found out what it was about her that put him off.

"That cow," she hissed. "How dare she take over the Director's office? All right, I'll tell her." She smiled suddenly. "If she's still all in one piece. The monster's in a foul mood today."

"Isn't she always? Take care, luv."

"You too."

He drove around to the British Museum, and found his good friend Sonia Walenska in her little cubicle, poring over a large pile of Bulgarian newspapers and looking very pleased with herself indeed. "Good news," she said in answer to his question. "In the Bulgarian Press, there's quite a bit about your Swords of God, the most important of it by a top-notch reporter named Brun Slonimski. It seems that an Egyptian member of the Hezbollah, who strangely enough never seemed to be actually with them in Beirut, just...*guiding* them from Cairo, even controlling them to a certain extent, left them—with the Ayatollah's blessing, apparently—to start up a group of his own, your Swords of God. He's calling on men from el Fatah, from the Black Sunday people, and from Egypt's Muslim Brotherhood to rally to his cause, which he describes as 'the destruction of the infidel's nerve-center, and the establishment of Moslem Fundamentalism worldwide.' He's also calling for funds from Iran, Syria, and Libya, without very much success. And then only three weeks ago, there was a further report of the bombing of the Saudi Arabian Embassy in Cairo, for which the same group claimed responsibility."

"Good, that's exactly the sort of stuff I need."

Sonia opened the desk drawer and pulled out a thin sheaf of foolscap pages. "Here, I've got it all typed up for you. The early stuff is more of an article than anything else, the Cairo piece looks like a wire-service report. And Brun Slonimski doesn't give his sources. Does that matter?"

"Under the circumstances," Quayle said drily, "he was probably well-advised."

He started skimming through the pages. "Does he tell his would-be followers how to get in touch with him? I suppose that's too-much to hope for..."

"And you're right. But one terrorist shouldn't have too much difficulty in locating another, I imagine."

Quayle sighed. "True. They have safe-houses by the dozen, every capital in all the countries of the Middle East, Europe as well, America too. And for all we know, in Outer Mongolia as well. How far back are you?"

"In Bulgaria, five and a half weeks. I'll be starting on Romania first thing in the morning."

"Good."

He thought deeply for a moment, frowning, and he said at last, "This is Middle Eastern stuff, so why the hell can't I read the Arabic papers too? But that's not one of your languages, is it?"

Sonia shook her head again, vigorously. "No, but we have a man here who heads the Arabic Department, we could try him..."

"And we have a translator in the office too."

He didn't want to talk about possible leaks, about the hidden double agent who named himself after the Persian Kings, so he said, "But she's at home sick just now, all kinds of stuff piling up on her desk. And I don't think I ought to give this to someone I don't know."

Sonia Walenska smiled, a wearied old face brightening up. "But this man," she said, "he's not a Muslim; he's an Israeli, a Yemenite Jew. And the Swords of God will be his natural enemies. If we impress on him that this is all hush-hush..."

"Alright then, but don't tell him more than he needs to know. All I want is every report he can find in the Arab Press about the Saudi Arabian bombing. Particularly the Saudi Arabian papers themselves, plus the press releases from the Egyptian Police, that's most important. Don't mention the Swords of God to him, or the name Abu Jildi, just tell him it's the bombing we're interested in."

Sonia nodded. "But in time, you'll get to trust him, I'm certain. He's really a sweet old man." She laughed suddenly. "Ever since my husband died, five years ago, he's been after me to marry him! I told him he'd have to become a Catholic, but he said no, I'd have to convert to Judaism. Stalemate!"

Prematurely old even for sixty-five, Sonia Walenska was actually blushing.

"As long as I get invited to the wedding," Quayle said, meaning it sincerely.

The dinner at Wendy's was a great success, and the stew was hardly sour at all, a little flamed cognac fixed it quite nicely, a few tablespoons from the bottle he had brought her.

And the Mews, he thought, was such a wonderful place to be, just a couple of small rooms with a bathroom and kitchen over what had once been a stable for the carriages of the gentry. There was honeysuckle climbing wildly all aver the timbered exterior walls, with potted peonies and geraniums and masses of azaleas in white-painted window boxes.

The flat itself was well furnished with carefully chosen antique pieces bought very reasonably at auction sales. There was a wonderful old walnut-dresser from the early eighteen-hundreds, which Wendy kept in shape with almost weekly applications of linseed oil, two huge and somewhat overstuffed armchairs upholstered in old-fashioned flowered cretonne with a sofa to match, what they used to call a "Chesterfield," a very good Persian carpet on the oak parquet floor, and bronze standard lamps to make up for the lack of conventional lighting in the ceiling. The walls were hung with paintings—some good and some not so good, but all pleasing to look at—done by her friends around town.

There was a small escritoire on which stood a rather formal photograph of her father, His Excellency Sir Richard Hayworth, British Ambassador, to the United States of America. She'd grown up with him in Washington after her mother's death, and was more American than English, at least in the way she thought—always brushing aside the trivia and getting things done now rather than a week from Tuesday—and she adored him. There were other photos there too, mostly of old colleagues from way back in her days as Confidential Secretary to various British Ambassadors in France, Italy, and Germany; she liked to keep in touch with her old friends, finding they could be very useful once in a while.

She drew the yellow velour curtains now, and put a tape of Saint-Saens First Piano Concerto on the Teac reel-to-reel, and said, "Well, that's finally the end of the stew, and it wasn't so bad, really, was it? I do have some Tums, if you'd rather be careful. Like, just in case ptomaine poisoning sets in."

Ian Quayle was busy pouring drinks at the sideboard, Spanish brandy, (but one of the good ones, Carlo Primiero), into rather nice Bavarian snifters.

He said thoughtfully, "I've been thinking about that bombing at the Saudi Arabian Embassy. I've got a man at the Museum checking into the Egyptian press reports for me, but the press is pretty well controlled there, isn't it? We might be getting only what the Government allows to filter down through the censor. We must have a rep there who could do some digging for me if I need it. As I almost certainly will."

"Sure we do. And she's very, very bright."

"She?"

"Women always make the best agents, didn't you know that?" There was a gentle mockery in her voice, and Quayle grunted. "How do I get in touch with her when I need her? Not using the office?"

"Because of Bahram?"

"Exactly. We don't know who the hell Bahram is, all we know is that he's passing info on to Abu Jildi, witness the matter of the Five Ports bombing."

"You've got a point there," Wendy said. "But that's no problem, she has a scrambler-phone hidden away someplace. You have to call the number and use the identity phrase: '*Jefferson and Hubbard.*' All you'll get is a machine, so you leave a number where she can call you. It's as simple as that."

"So what number do I call?"

"I'll have to look it up," Wendy said, "I never had occasion to memorize it."

As she eased herself more comfortably, she put her feet up onto her sometime lover's lap, and she said, musing, "Her name's Aida, and she's a dancer at the nightclub in the Mena House Hotel, right beside the Sphinx and the Pyramids. But she's also a very high-class courtesan..."

"Does that mean a whore?"

"Not quite. I suppose the term is 'enthusiastic amateur.' She's much in demand in very high-class circles, Ministers and other plenipotentiaries... It gives her easy access to a lot of very useful people in and out of government. What about your source at the Museum, have you checked him out?"

He felt a little guilty about it, but he wondered silently if he were perhaps getting paranoid about the security bit. "Not at first hand," he said, "but Sonia recommends him, and I think that's enough. He's a Yemenite, and Jewish, but brought up in the world of the Arabs..."

The ringing of the phone interrupted him. He took it from its cradle and handed it to Wendy, heard her pleasant "Ah, good evening, Chief, how are you?"

He saw her frowning darkly as she listened, and he knew that the news was not good. For a very long time she said nothing at all, just shaking her head once in a while, and then at last: "When was that exactly, the date seems very important... And my God, four of them...? What about a watch on the airports...? Yes, I've heard that...so there doesn't seem much that can be done, does it? Well, thanks for letting me know anyway."

She put down the phone, and her face was tight with anxiety.

"First of all," she said slowly, "they got a search warrant for 307 Marlborough Towers, and yes, the tenant of record was your Sheik Najir Mohammed, but he's gone, no sign of him at all. They found his passport."

"Ah, then that means he's still in the country..."

She shook her head, frowning still. "No, you haven't heard the rest of it. The Chief says a lot of these Arabs carry several passports in different names, it's almost a pattern, so once the name on that passport is blown, he could use another one—Syrian, Iranian, Egyptian, whatever—with no trouble at all. The assumption is that he has left the country, because they found arms there which he normally would have taken with him if he were just moving to another safe-house, and not flying off some place."

Her face tightened. "And you want to know what the arms were? There was a sniper's rifle, an Uzi machine pistol, two one-kilo boxes of C-4 explosive, and worst of all—a Stinger. You know what a Stinger is?"

Ian Quayle nodded. "Yes, I do," but she told him anyway. "A shoulder fired missile-launcher that even an idiot can handle. Just point the damn thing in the general direction of your target, and its own infrared seeker takes care of the aiming for you, it's a terrorist's dream! And it seems that this missile was one of four stolen from the U.S. Arms Depot in Aldingham only last week. One recovered, three still missing; it doesn't look good, does it?"

"How the hell." Quayle said, scowling, "can missiles be just...just *shoplifted*, for Christ's sake?"

"The Chief says the whole thing weighs only thirty-four and a half pounds, and if you remember there was this huge demonstration in Aldingham last week, what was it, nearly ten thousand people protesting. A lot of violence, fences broken down in the excitement..." She broke off and shook her head in frustration. "I don't know, the Chief doesn't know! It just happened, is all."

Ian Quayle was in one of his moods, and he said sourly, "I just wish I could get stinking drunk tonight."

Wendy turned away and refilled his glass. She knew it wasn't news of the Stinger that worried him so much, but instead, the growing realization that he was on the death list of every competent and ruthless enemy. She said quietly, "No reason why you shouldn't. You can sleep over tonight, you know that."

But he shook his head. "No, I can't, I've got to get round to my flat and really study the press clippings Sonia gave me. A lot of very interesting stuff there. I have to go through it over and over again, see what I can find between the lines, how much of it is truth and how much is speculation. And I have a lot of thinking to do."

He looked at his watch. "Ten fifteen," he said, "I must leave by eleven at the latest. Three or four hours of work before I get to bed."

He sighed, and held her in his arms. "You know how much I'd prefer to stay! But every hour on the hour I keep wondering just how much time we have. There may not be very much before the next calamity."

"Yes, know."

His hands were running gently over her breasts, and she held the snifter up for him, to his lips, and he sipped as he stroked her, then smiled and took it from her.

"All right," he said, "I'm running scared, and I don't care who knows it. After that damned last time, in Italy, I swore I'd never put myself in such a vulnerable position again. But it seems that I've done just that. Without even leaving home And I hate it."

Wendy too was worried. "Maybe you should ask for police protection? I'm sure a call to Robin would do it."

He shook his head, grinning wryly. "Don't take me literally when I say. I don't care who knows it. You, I don't mind. But not anyone else. So let's just sit and hold hands, and drink our cognac together...and listen to music."

"Mozart," she said. "I feel like Mozart now."

She changed the tape to the *divertimenti* and country dances that the great Amadeus had written in Chelsea at the tender age of nine, and they clinked glasses as they sat like the lovers they were on the sofa, her head on his shoulder and his arm around her.

For a long time, no one spoke, and when Big Ben's distant thirteen-ton bell sounded eleven, Ian eased himself gently out of what had become almost an entanglement, and he whispered to Wendy, "Time to be on my way, darling..."

Half asleep, she sighed. "When will I see you again?"

"Soon."

"And from now on...you will be very careful, won't you?"

"Of course."

He kissed her, and held her tightly for a moment, and when he left her and went out into the mews, the night seemed unaccountably cold. He clambered into the Mini and drove round to his little flat on Flood Walk and parked in the rented garage there. He walked up the stairs, and when he went into the rather functional living room, so lacking in the charm of his Surrey cottage, he pulled up short in shocked surprise, even in alarm...

There was a man standing by the French windows that led onto the tiny veranda, and there was the biggest damn German Shepherd on a leash that he had ever seen, not growling or baring its fangs but just looking at him alertly as though waiting for an order to attack.

He began to bluster "What the hell...", but the man, smiling gently, was holding up a card that was hard to make out in the dim light of a single floor lamp.

The man said awkwardly, "Sergeant Merrick, sir, and I must apologize for the intrusion."

"Apologize my ass," Ian Quayle said angrily. "How the hell did you get in here? And let me see that card..."

As he moved forward, he saw the dog tense, and now it was showing its teeth.

"*Friend*, Betsy," the man said. "*lie down.*"

The dog did, and the man said as Ian took the card, "Orders from the Deputy Chief himself, Mr. Quayle. He told me to let myself in if you weren't at home. And if you'll take my advice you'll get better locks on that door. It took me ten seconds to open them, and anyone else can do the same."

"Well, that's very interesting. The Chief had his reasons, I suppose?" He was passing his fright off as anger now.

"Indeed he did, Mr. Quayle," the Sergeant said gravely. "Something to do with someone taking a shot at you the other night, down in Surrey, something perhaps to do with the terrible bombing down in Dover, he told me to look for a bomb here too. So I brought Betsy along best sniffing dog on the team."

"I see."

It was taking a little time to get over the awful sudden fear that had grabbed, if only momentarily, with such a savage pull at his stomach. He felt a little foolish, but he said amiably enough, "I have to admit I was startled. I mean, it's not often you walk into your flat and find a copper waiting for you. Not with a damn great dog like that."

"Betsy?" Sergeant Merrick grinned. "Why, bless you, sir, Betsy wouldn't hurt you, she's gentle as a kitten." The grin broadened. "Not unless you were carrying a stick or two of

69

dynamite in your pocket."

"And I hope you haven't found anything..."

The grin was suddenly gone, and Merrick said seriously: "I wish I could say no to that, but I can't."

For the second time in a few minutes, Ian Quayle felt the blood draining from his face; he hoped it didn't show. There was a little silence, and Merrick went to the stereo and picked up the cassette player, disconnected now. He flipped open the back where the emergency batteries were held to show that it was empty.

"In here," he said, "a neat little packet of C-4, you know what that is?"

Quayle nodded, not quite trusting himself to speak, and Merrick said slowly, "About six ounces of it. Not much, is it? But that's about the equivalent of about a dozen sticks of dynamite, enough to blow you straight through the walls of the building and leave half of this floor in ruins. And I'll tell you something, we're not dealing with an amateur here. The package was wrapped in surgical gauze that had been soaked in something, and it took me a while to figure out what it was. You know about aluminum hydrochloride, Mr. Quayle?"

Quayle was puzzled. "Only vaguely..."

"You have some in your bathroom cupboard," Merrick said, "a spray. Underarm deodorant. Our bomber had soaked the gauze in this stuff, even though C-4 really doesn't have much of a smell. Not for you and me, that is. But you can't fool Betsy."

"Jesus Christ! I have a lot to be grateful for, haven't I?"

Merrick nodded gravely. "It was set to explode the moment you touched the play button," he said. "Not the kind of music you'd like."

Ian Quayle wondered if he was actually trembling, and he covered by picking up a bottle from the bar. "Can I offer you a drink?"

The Sergeant shook his head. "Not that I don't like a drop

once in a while, Mr. Quayle, but not on duty. Though I thank you."

"And is that damn bomb still around?"

"I had the Yard pick it up at once, we might get lucky. C-4's a plastic, like soft putty, and it picks up beautiful fingerprints. It's not likely our bomber expected it to be found, so he might have gotten careless."

He snapped the cassette's casing shut. "I had to cut a couple of wires in the player, but the boys fixed it, so it's all right now. And the rest of the night one of our men will be prowling around this floor and over the roof. You won't see hide nor hair of him, but he'll be there, and he'll be relieved in the morning, eight-hour shifts now. And for your information, there's another team on its way down now to Austel-in-the-Woods to take a look at your cottage. One man will stay on there. Next time you go down you'll see him messing around in your garden. His name's Reynolds, Constable Harry Reynolds. He's a bit of a gardener himself, took first prize for his roses at Chelsea this year, so he won't do much damage."

"Well, it's a comfort, I must admit."

"And one more thing..."

Merrick took out a card and laid it down on the cassette player. "That's a number for the Deputy Chief. He wants you to call him personally at the first sign of anything suspicious, anything at all, even if it looks like trivia. That's a day-or-night number, they'll put you through to him at once."

"More comfort still..."

"And by your leave, sir, I'll be on my way. You have my word there'll be no more trouble here, so...a good night to you, Mr. Quayle. Sleep well."

"And a good night to you too, Mr. Merrick. I can't thank you enough."

When the officer had gone, Ian Quayle got on the phone to Wendy and told her only that, unexpectedly, he had police protection now. He said nothing about the bomb, but instead: "I'm sorry if I woke you up, love, but I thought you might be lying awake and worrying. Everything's fine."

He set his papers out on the desk, and went to work.

CHAPTER 6

"Three or four hours' work," Ian Quayle had said, "before I get to bed."

But the incident of the bombing attempt had left him wide awake, with no thought of bed at all, and so he spent the night with innumerable cups of coffee and a certain amount of cognac too, reading and re-reading the tear-sheets Sonia had given him, searching out the truths and the half-truths that lay behind the cold, wire-service facts.

And when the doorbell rang, he was astonished to see that it was already nearly eight-thirty in the morning.

It was Wendy, and she was shocked at his disheveled and unshaven appearance, not the Ian Quayle she was accustomed to at all. "Oh God," she said, "don't tell me you've been up all night..."

He grinned at her. "And don't tell me you've never seen me unshaven before." He ran a hand through his tousled hair. "Yes, I've been up all night, but it was worth it."

"And why didn't you tell me last night about the bomb?"

"So you know about that..."

"Of course! How long did your think you could fool me?"

"I didn't want you to lie awake all night. I figured I was worried enough for the two of us."

"That's what I thought, and it was sweet of you. That's a very nasty business."

Even thinking about it seemed to distress her, and she threw up her hands. "There's got to be an answer, that's twice in four days they've tried to kill you Ian, I'm so very worried..."

"Yes, me too. But I think a man named Brun Slonimski just *might* have given me a slant on that."

"Brun who?"

"Slonimsky, he's a Bulgarian journalist who—for reasons I don't know but can only regard as suspicious—chooses not to divulge his sources."

He picked up one of the tear-sheets and waved it at her. "He's written quite a lot about the Swords of God, a very interesting article. He doesn't mention Abu Jildi by name, but he says..."

Ian Quayle rubbed at his red-rimmed eyes and read: "*A senior officer in the Hezbollah has broken away from that organization, which he seems to have run*—get this—*at long distance, from Cairo, almost never going to Beirut which is where most of the Hezbollah operate.* I find that very interesting. It suggests that Abu Jildi has some business or other which keeps him mostly in Cairo. It suggests that he's not even his own boss not free to move around that much..."

"What kind of business." Wendy asked, knowing what a foolish question it was, and Ian answered her, exasperated: "How the hell should I know? You want me to *guess*? Okay, he's a bank teller. Or maybe Chairman of the Board at the Egyptian National Bank. No, he's a red-cap at Cairo's airport. Or maybe General Manager."

"Keep your shirt on, Ian Quayle..."

"Okay. But the important thing is that he left them claiming that they refuse to understand who their natural enemy really is..."

He looked up. "That's point one, bear it in mind. Now,

much further on in his article, he mentions the disappearance of an Egyptian Intelligence Officer, who was later found floating face down in the Nile with his throat cut, that's point two. No direct mention of the Swords, but the inference is there, because it's the Swords he's writing about, agreed?"

"Tenuous," Wendy said, "but okay, *maybe*."

"Point three is the bombing of the Five Ports, when a whole slew of Intelligence Agents, the top brass, was attacked *en masse*. Point four is the murder of Weiss-Histermann. You heard about that?"

"Yes, of course I did, go on, I still don't get your drift. Maybe I'm dumb."

"Well," Ian said emphatically, "doesn't that all suggest to you that when Abu Jildi talks about the Hezbollah not knowing who their natural enemy is, he's not talking about people at all, he's talking about an *idea*, a *concept*?"

Wendy frowned. "The concept of worldwide intelligence?"

"Exactly! Look at it like this. Who's been killed by the Hezbollah? Marines, Christian Arabs, Shia Muslims, even each other. And what good does that do to what they like to think of, rather muddily, as their 'cause'? Sure, it hurts *us*, but does it do *them* any actual good? Of course it doesn't! And I'm beginning to think that this is precisely what Abu Jildi is up to. He's declared war not on that poor bastard at MI5 who was killed, not at the European Intelligence Officers, not at Robin Harris, but at the *whole idea of an intelligence network*. Because it is, after all, the intelligence coterie, worldwide, that points their individual governments in the right direction, the anti-terrorist direction. In other words, the hell with the hand that holds the gun, he'd rather go for the nerve-center itself. Sever the nerve, and the governments are powerless. Am I making sense?"

"W-e-l-l..." Wendy was very unsure, but: "I have to agree, it does make a crazy sort of sense."

"And there's a nasty corollary."

"Which is?"

"The intelligence community shows the governments where to look, and act. But who shows *them*? Without research about the terrorists, the terrorists would have a very much easier time. That lumps me in with the rest of them. So, knock the poor bastard off with a sniper's rifle, or put six ounces of C-4 *plastique* in his bloody cassette deck. Or what'll the next attempt be, I wonder?"

Wendy's voice was hushed. "Ian, I'm so scared for you..."

"So how do you think I feel? I've got police protection now, day and night, it seems, and they're pretty damn good. But so's the other side."

He told her about the attempt to thwart the explosive-sniffing dogs with aluminum hydrochloride, sprayed out of his own dispenser, for God's sake!

He ran a hand over his face again, and muttered, "And I've just made a startling discovery, which is...being scared half out of your wits doesn't help at all! Suddenly, research has become a Field Officer's job. And I hate it!"

Impetuously, he took her in his arms and he said, trying to lighten his voice, "And I haven't even said good morning, have I? Good morning, my love, and how did you sleep?"

"Better than I'm going to sleep tonight," Wendy muttered, "that's for sure."

"So why don't you nip into the kitchen and make us some breakfast? Two or three eggs apiece, and there are some beautiful bangers in the frig. I'll go and get cleaned up."

"Okay."

She forced the fear to the back of her mind. "We have an eleven o'clock appointment, with Robin Harris."

Ian Quayle looked at his watch. "Then we don't have much time, it's a long haul to Dover. Not to worry, we'll push it a bit."

"Not Dover. Cadogan Place. Robin's back home."

"What?" He stared. "For Christ's sake, they can't have discharged him already! What is it, five days?"

"Six. But he discharged himself. Seems like he hauled his own doctor down there, and between them they bullied the hospital into letting him finish his recovery at home. He called me at five-thirty this morning, positively gloating. Well..." She shrugged. "You know him well as I do. What Robin Harris wants—Robin Harris gets."

Ian packed up his papers and locked them in his desk drawer. "Bangers," he said "and scrambled eggs. There are some tomatoes too from the garden at the cottage. I have to get cleaned up."

As Wendy began pouring boiling water over the tomatoes to skin them prior to the frying, she switched on the kitchen radio and paid it no attention at all until the BBC announcer said, in nicely-modulated tones: *"We must break into our regular programming at this time to announce a major disaster. A transport aircraft of the Royal Air Force has crashed into the English Channel, and everyone on board is presumed lost. Although this was a military, not a civilian aircraft, we have learned that the passengers aboard were diplomats from France, Italy, and West Germany..."*

"Ian...!" Wendy screamed, "come! Quickly...!"

In moments, Ian Quayle was there, dripping water all over the place, a bath towel around his waist. And they listened together as the voice droned on:

"...we do not know at the moment. Presumably, there are valid reasons why European diplomats should be travelling on other than civilian aircraft, and we are now seeking some sort of elucidation of this puzzling aspect of this disaster. The cause of the crash has not yet been officially communicated

to us, but meanwhile, we have an extraordinary interview for you with one Major Gordon Redick, an American Marine Corps Officer who is touring Britain now and was sailing in the channel at the time of the disaster. Our ship-to-shore telephonic communication is not as clear as it might be, but what Major Redick has to say is startling, to say the least."

They both waited, as the crackling came on, and a disembodied voice, and then an improvement as someone, somewhere, twirled dials or pushed buttons:

"...Yes, that's right, I'm a Major in the Marine Corps, and my wife Beulah and me, we've been cruising the English Channel in this rented yacht, it's called the Boadiccea, seems like that's the name of one of your Queens, I don't know, maybe four, five hundred years ago. Anyway, this motorboat like overtook us at a very high speed, passed us less than a thousand yards off our port side, and this sonofabitch on the deck had a launcher on his shoulder, I had my binoculars on him and I saw him fire. Yes sir, I saw him fire. It was a Stinger, that's a shoulder launched missile, one hell of a lot better than the SAM them Russians have, all you hafta to is kinda point it, and it locks on target. I gotta tell you, that's one hell of a missile. The plane exploded in midair, debris all around us, no way anyone could have survived, no way..."

The nice voice took over again from all that static, and said:

"We must apologize for all that interference, caused by static-electricity in the atmosphere. To wrap up, a Royal Air Force transport plane carrying an unknown number of European diplomats back home to France, Italy, and West Germany, has been apparently shot down over the English

Channel, possibly by an Arab terrorist organization, though we can't be sure of that yet. And perhaps it was destroyed by an American missile called a 'Stinger.' As we have reported before, four of these deadly Stinger missiles were stolen from the American arsenal in Aldersham recently. And now...more on the football riots that have so far claimed eleven lives..."

Wendy switched off, and she said tightly, "So. They got them after all. Every man jack of them."

She went to Ian and put her arms around his bare shoulders, and she whispered, "I'm so confused... On the one hand, want you to back out of all this, because they're after you too. And on the other... I know there's no one who can find out who these monsters are faster than you can."

He held her tightly. "How can I find out about them? Wendy, my job, the one thing I'm good at, is *research*. You want to find out about Black Sunday, which began nearly twenty years ago, yes, I can research them for you. The Hezbollah? Only twelve years old, but they already have a history of sorts, they've been written up in every major newspaper in the world, and I can find out everything you want to know about them. But the Swords of God? Wendy! They were born *yesterday*, for Christ's sake! It means that the whole fabric of research just isn't there yet for me to look at! Try me in ten years' time again, when they have a history! And twice they've tried to knock me off, even before I've really unearthed anything at all."

"Don't think I'm not worrying about that too," Wendy said miserably. She broke away from him and set about her chores with the controlled movement of a robot, to the frig for the breakfast fixings, to the dresser for the plates and the cutlery, to the cupboard for the coffee...

Quayle went back to the bedroom to finish dressing, and when he returned, there it was on the table all ready for him. He took her hand and said lightly, "I'm honestly going to have to marry you one day. What do you say?"

"That'll be the day," Wendy said. "Sit down and eat, for Christ's sake, there's nothing like a full stomach to drive the demons away."

She even washed the dishes when they were through, and Ian looked at his watch and said, "Okay, let's mosey over and see Robin. We have to stop on the way at Julia's?"

"Julia's?"

"I want to send some flowers to Sonia at the Museum."

"Ah yes..."

They went down the stairs to the garage and walked to where the Mini stood in its allotted space.

Close by, in someone else's bay, there was a Volvo station wagon with three men in it, and Quayle froze...

But Wendy said quietly, "They're from the Yard, it's okay."

She walked over to them and leaned down to the window. "We're on our way now, to see Mr. Harris, you know where that is? Cadogan Place?"

The man at the wheel nodded. "Don't take the normal route, Miss Hayworth. Take Flood Walk to Chelsea Manor Street for a right turn to the Embankment. Then along the river to Chelsea Bridge Road all the way to the Gardens, got it?"

"Got it. We have to stop off just for a moment at Julia's Flower Shop, that's on Margaretta Terrace."

"Oh. Very well. Then take Oakley Street to the Embankment. You may not see us, but we'll be right behind you."

"Okay."

"And don't worry, Miss Hayworth. From now on, for the foreseeable future, Mr. Quayle's not going to be unobserved for one moment, day or night."

He was suddenly covered with confusion, a nice guy, and he said, tending to stammer, "That is to say, until we know he's safe..."

"Good. I'm glad of it."

She went back to wriggle herself into the Mini, and for a brief moment Ian wondered if his beloved little car would blow up the moment he turned on the ignition...

More paranoia, he thought, and switched on, and drove off sedately as Wendy gave him the new route, and turned onto Margaretta Terrace for the flowers...

"I always send Sonia roses," he said. "But why don't we find her something more original? Come and give me a hand."

They found one of the rare parking places only fifty yards or so away from the flower shop, one of London's best. It was run by a very large lady who smoked a constant pipe even in the hallowed cool area where all the best blooms were kept.

The hell with walk-in refrigerators; Julia had half a dozen of those old-fashioned ice blocks delivered to her shop every morning, and played an oscillating electric fan over them all day long, the best cooling system ever dreamed up by a manic iceman.

She embraced Ian Quayle like a long lost son and glared at Wendy, and she said, in heavily-accented English, waiting for him to switch, as he always did, to Italian, "Roses again, I think, no? Why you never changing your mind?"

"*Questa volta*," Ian said happily, switching languages, "this time, yes. Something different." He made the introductions: "My associate, Wendy Hayworth, Julia, er, Julia. Wendy will do the choosing this time."

Julia looked her up and down, and wasn't impressed. "No she will not," she said, and that was the end of that; you just didn't argue with Julia when it came down to choosing suitable flowers. "I choose what you want for your *innamorata*."

In fifteen minutes it was all over, and when they went outside again, Ian Quayle looked at his car, parked up the road, in the acutest dismay...

With a longhaired, very blond young man at the wheel, it was taking off, at speed. He saw it scrape the car ahead of it, with a horrible grinding sound, and he thought instinctively of all the good work old man Perkins had done on it, bringing the paintwork back to its original pristine luster...

And then the unmarked police Vauxhall was slamming to a stop right beside him, the tires screeching, and the Sergeant shouted, "Someone stole your Mini, Mr. Quayle! But don't worry, we'll get him..."

The Vauxhall took off, and Ian just stood there like a bewildered idiot, staring after them.

"That's all I need," he said furiously, "some bastard stealing my car... Come on!"

He took Wendy's hand and dragged her to the corner of Oakley Street, and there was the Mini, grid-locked in the world's worst traffic jam, with the unmarked Vauxhall only five or six cars behind it.

He saw two of the cops get down and run forward, and then...

Some hidden instinct told him to look up, and there on the roof of the Foster Building on the corner a man was standing in full view... There was a ski mask on his face, and there was a long metal tube perched on his shoulder. In a moment of absolute shock, Ian Quayle recognized it as a bazooka, and he yelled: "Wendy, down...!"

The warning was not enough, he was sure, and he hurled himself at her and carried her to the ground with him, covering her body with his own against the awful mayhem that, he knew, was imminent now.

He shouted to her, "Lie still! Don't move...!"

But then, he saw that the bazooka was not aimed at them, but at the little Mini. He saw it explode violently, saw pieces of twisted metal flying through the air to land, almost in slow motion, on the nearby rooftops.

He saw too that the unmarked police car had cut in front of the Mini to force it to the curb, and was now just a flaming wreck, with the burned and decapitated body of the driver still incongruously at the wheel. Of the two other Scotland Yard men who had been aboard, there was no sign at all, and the screaming that rang through the narrow street was intolerable.

There were wounded bodies lying about, some of them clutching at mangled limbs as they screamed, and a great deal of blood everywhere. He saw a dazed and wounded child trying to struggle to its feet, saw a woman running unsteadily to pick him up.

Two other cars nearby were on fire, and the street was littered with shards of plate-glass from shattered storefronts. There was mayhem and there was chaos all around them.

CHAPTER 7

The main bedroom of the elegant Cadogan Place apartment, just off Sloane Street, had almost been turned into a hospital ward, though it looked now like an office with a bed in it.

The long walnut refectory table from the dining room had been moved in here and set neatly with pads and pencils, and both Mrs. French and Jackie, the Director's Secretary, were there, poring over their notes.

Present were also Detective Inspector Morrison, liaison with Scotland Yard, a dour professional cop to whom nothing came as a surprise; Arnold Burla, a whiz kid of only thirty-one who was head of the Continental Liaison Board's Ops. G, and a guard who stood at the door with a Sterling submachine gun under his arm; it was the chopped version with only a four-inch barrel; nice, you could almost stick it in your hip pocket, thirty-four rounds in the mag, not bad at all.

Robin Harris, showing almost no sign of wear except for a heavily bandaged left hand and a rather drawn look on his very aristocratic face, was propped up in bed against a mass of pillows, with Wendy seated solicitously beside him, while Ian paced back and forth impatiently, quite ignoring Mrs. Bloody French's terse, "Oh do sit down, Mr. Quayle..."

A nurse was there by the bed fussing around with her

work, pushing buttons and adjusting wires and getting the computer readout for pulse, heartbeat, temperature, condition of the liver, all kinds of other crap in digital readouts and wiggly lines which she seemed to understand perfectly; but then, she was just a kid, so it was easy for her.

She made all kinds of marks on her graph, and she said at last, sensing the atmosphere: "Well, everything seems as it should be, so I'll leave you now."

The guard opened the door for her only at a signal from the bossman; this was the most carefully protected apartment in all of London, the artsy-crafty outside window-shutter, adjustable oak slats, were actually made of high-tempered steel that could break up even a bazooka shell.

Robin Harris nodded his thanks and patted her tight little bum as she smoothed the covers for him. "Oh," she murmured, "you're really making a very fast recovery, aren't you..."

And when she had gone, he said, "So, we all know what this meeting is about. Ever since that Air Force Transport jet was shot down with half of the Western Union's Intelligence community on board...we've had considerable pressure from the office of the Prime Minister herself. Our liaison with the Yard is at a very high level now, and I want to start with an update on the latest tragedy on Margaretta Terrace. Mr. Morrison, if you'd be so kind..."

Detective Inspector Morrison, a thickset, burly man with tousled gray hair and a drooping moustache, cleared his throat and shuffled his papers.

"Well, sir... we're all agreed at the Yard that this really was indeed an attempt on Mr. Quayle's life, for reasons only the Chief seems to know about. At any rate, he hasn't seen fit to enlighten the rest of us."

"Go on, Morrison," Mrs. French said coldly, and there was that bronchitic throat-clearing again as the Detective Inspector continued:

"From the top of the Foster building, where the assassin had taken up his position, there's a clear view of Mr. Quayle's garage, but from that height he wouldn't have been able to see clearly enough whether there were two people on board or only one..."

"And the question seems to be," Robin Harris said, "why didn't he fire his bazooka then and there, as soon as Quayle drove out? Every minute on top of that building, armed with a bloody weapon he wouldn't easily be able to hide once he had it ready, must have been a major danger for him."

"Quite so, sir," Morison said, "but we think we know why he didn't do that. A witness reported to us that he saw someone he thought was an Arab on the corner of the Terrace talking—'very furtively' the man said—into a small radio. Now that looks suspiciously like an accomplice, saying something like 'Stand by,' or 'Here he comes now...' So, our man couldn't fire right away for fear of getting his buddy blown up along with his intended victim. And there's a better line of fire anyway where he did actually press the button."

"Casualties?" Ian Quayle asked. "We saw a lot of dead or wounded bodies lying around."

Morrison nodded and checked his papers. "Three of our own men in the Vauxhall, the young punk who stole the car, three men and four women bystanders killed as well as one five-year-old child; and fourteen wounded, some of them seriously, mostly by flying glass. The thief was a man named Bernie Halpert, a known car thief who works with a ring centered in Paddington, they steal specialized cars, cars they've already got a buyer for. And Mini Coopers have always been high on their list. But we got the assassin."

"Ah..." Wendy said, "that's what I wanted to hear."

"An Arab," Morrison said. "Seems that to get up onto the roof he found his way through the basement of one of the shops there and took the service lift. Several people saw him carrying his long wooden box, but..."

Morrison shrugged. "There's some remodeling going on up on the third floor, and he just looked like one of the workmen, so no one challenged him. But when he came down again, well, that was quite a different matter! The service lift's motor was blown by the force of the explosion, and he had to take the stairway. He found himself in one of the showrooms of Amel Fils, the jewelers on the corner, and one of their guards..."

He was smiling thinly now, and looking over his notes again. "One of their guards," he said, "is a young woman named Pamela Weston. She saw him running through their very secure property and tried to stop him. He made the mistake of knocking her down, something he didn't ought to have done. Because she's trained in the martial arts, and she tells us..."

He sighed. "A young slip of a girl, can't weigh much more than a hundred pounds. But she flipped him over her shoulder with no trouble at all, then picked him up by the scruff of his neck and his, er, his testicles, begging your pardon, ladies, and hurled him across the room into a plate glass showcase. And it must have been quite a throw, because she broke his neck. And he's dead."

"And that's quite a story, Morrison," Mrs. French said, "I'm sure we're all very grateful to you."

"Oh, it's not finished, Ma'am, not by a long shot."

He peered at his papers again and looked at Robin Harris. "The Chief," he said, "wanted me to be sure to tell you two things. We ran down the, assassin's fingerprints, and they're the same prints we found on some plastic explosive taken from Mr. Quayle's apartment, he said you'd know about that."

"I do indeed," Robin Harris said.

"And secondly, the Chief wanted you to know that they're the prints of a Lebanese construction engineer named Ali Kabbaj, though he has more aliases than you can shake a stick at. And one of those aliases seems to have been Sheik Najir

Mohammed el Afwan bin Sousa, the Chief said you'd know the name."

"Score," Ian Quayle said sourly. "Us, one. Them, God alone knows how many. As yet, I wonder how long we have to keep that ratio up?"

"And if that is a subtle suggestion that you should be taken off your current assignment," Mrs. Bloody French said, "kindly submit it to me through the proper channels and I will take it under advisement."

"Mr. Morrison," Robin Harms said loudly, "do we have any further news on the downing of that Air Force transport over the English Channel?"

"No, sir, nothing you don't already have. We know it was shot down by a Stinger missile fired from a rented launch at sea. It was rented by a group of three men we're told looked like Arabs, but the identification they gave was fictional, addresses that just don't exist. One of them had a driver's license in the name of Abdul Mohammed, but there have to be a thousand Abdul Mohammeds in England, it's a very common name. The launch was found abandoned at sea, they must have been picked up by another boat. No survivors on the plane, of course, and we don't even know who the victims were."

There was a touch of suspicion, even of hostility in his voice: "It's a police matter, Mr. Harris, sir, but we're under orders not to ask what civilians were doing onboard an Air Force transport, not even to ask who they were."

"For good reason, Mr. Morrison," Robin Harris said gently. "Please take my word for it. Matters of State. But to return for a moment to the question of the car thief, Bernie...?"

"Bernie Halpert, sir."

"Ah yes, Bernie Halpert. What about the press? Do they know who was actually killed? Do they know that it wasn't Mr. Quayle?"

Ian Quayle found his restrained temper bursting out of its

confines. He was even angry now with Robin Harris, who wasn't only his boss but a good friend as well.

He said seriously, "For Christ's sake! You want me to play dead, is that it? No! It's never going to work! First of all, my family would have to be informed, and what are you going to tell them? 'I'm sorry, but Ian's been killed...?' Or are you going to say, 'We're just pretending he's been killed?' Either way, I won't allow it."

"Patience, patience, Ian," Robin Harris said. "We're waiting for Mr. Morrison's reply."

And the Detective Inspector, wondering what had brought all this on, was nodding his head. "They know," he said.

He grimaced. "A gag order came down from the Chief, but it was a little slow filtering down to the lower ranks. So the late afternoon edition for the Evening Standard will be carrying a profile of Bernie Halpert, a professional car thief cut down in the prime of life, by mistake."

"Well," Ian said, "Thank God for that."

Robin Harris ignored him completely. Instead, he said to the Detective Inspector, very mildly, "That would seem to wrap it up, Mr. Morrison. I can't thank you enough for your help, which has been considerable."

Morrison loosened up a trifle. "I've got this feeling, Mr. Harris," he said slowly, "that I'm moving around on the outskirts of something very, very important, not knowing what's there on the inside of... of what you might call the inner circle. Matters of State you said, sir; And I just hope I've been able to assist in some small way?"

"You have indeed, Mr. Morrison, and I thank you. Good-day now."

"Good-day, sir..."

When he had gone, Robin Harris thought that perhaps the time had come to put Mrs. Bloody French in her place, at least for the moment. He'd made very little fuss when she'd taken over his office in such a cavalier fashion, but it still rankled; and he decided to hit her hard, below the belt...

He said with deceptive mildness, "Perhaps now we should return to the very important question of Ian Quayle's predicament." His eyes on her, ice-cold, he said: "How did you put it? Something about a subtle suggestion..."

He raised a hand as she began to answer. "No," he said, "I'd like it verbatim, Jackie?"

Jackie could hardly hide her secret pleasure as she read her shorthand back to him. "And if that is a subtle suggestion that you should be taken off your current assignment, kindly submit it to me through the proper channels and I will take it under advisement."

Mrs. French was squirming, in a fury, but she said nothing, and Robin Harris murmured, almost apologetically, "The proper channels you refer to are from Mr. Quayle himself to his Case Officer, Miss Hayworth, from Miss Hayworth directly to me, and then from me to you, in as much as I will expect you to implement my decision, I hope that's quite clear to you?"

She was not the kind of woman to go down without a fight. She held back the murder in her soul and said tightly, "Of course. But during your present most unfortunate indisposition, Mr. Harris, I felt I really should take as much of your workload off your shoulders as I can. It seemed the only decent thing to do."

"Ah how nicely put, and that's very thoughtful of you. So let's hear what our potential victim has to say Ian...? What's your view? Do we go for the white and take you off the case...?"

"Which might be of no use," Ian said, and Robin Harris nodded. "Precisely. We can promulgate it in orders, which Bahram, whoever he may be, will undoubtedly see and pass on to Abu Jildi. But we can't be sure that Abu Jildi will buy it, it's going to look too much like a ploy to get him to hold off.

Alternately, we can hit the red head on and throw you to the lions, with all the protection we can muster for you, which can be very considerable indeed. So, what do you think? It's your life at stake, no one else's at the moment."

"Let me make a point," Wendy said slowly, "to put this danger into perspective. Ian's own point, we talked about it a couple of days ago."

She began gesticulating, searching for clarity, and she said, "All the Western Governments are banding together now, at last, thank God, to fight terrorism together, and it's already beginning to pay off. But Abu Jildi seems to have decided—and I think he's right—that the police, paramilitary and military forces of those Governments are not what he thinks of as the real enemy. The *real enemy*, for him, is the Intelligence establishment that points the military forces in the right direction. And these are the people he's declared war on. And who points Intelligence in the right direction? The researchers. In our case, that means Ian Quayle. Okay, you put it nicely, Robin, white for cowardice, and red for danger. But let's explore the murky area in between before we go any further. There may be another color there."

"Cowardice," Mrs. Bloody French said. "I was wondering when someone would actually enunciate the word. Are we going to allow the Arabs to scare us away from what we have to do? Do we surrender to terrorism? Isn't that what the problem's always been? It took the damned Americans to show us the way, all right, I can stomach that. What I *can't* stomach is that when we're faced with danger we should throw up our hands and cry uncle. If it comes to a vote...then I say we don't back out, we forge ahead. Mr. Quayle, admittedly the best man in the business in spite of his arrogance, will continue finding out just who Abu Jildi and his Swords of God are. And when the mass of his research is sufficient...then we tell our own Government, as we're expected to do under our mandate, just where to point the military."

A little silence followed, and at last Robin said: "Well, your point is well taken, Mrs. French. Though I must confess I've never heard MI6's mandate interpreted in such an extraordinary fashion. Wendy?"

Wendy Hayworth said bluntly, "I want Ian Quayle off this case with immediate effect. I agree, it may not work. But what I'm convinced *will* work is keeping him on it."

She erupted, and said wrathfully, "Three attempts on his life in six days! Okay, they've lost their first assassin, does that mean they don't have any more to call on? Of course not! They'll even have suicide bombers, we can be sure of it! Someone sitting next to him on the bus, in a restaurant, standing beside him in his favorite pub over a pint of bitter, and the sonofabitch has a pocketful of C-4 with a timer embedded in it! Suicide bombers are a dime a dozen now, a short cut to Paradise!"

Her emotion was rising, and she said, biting her lip, "Unless we realize the danger he's in. I give him just a few more days of life. And then...everyone in this room will be at his funeral, and we'll all be wondering where we went wrong."

She reached out and took Robin Harris' hand, and she said stubbornly: "I want to throw an A-3 at him, Robin. It's the only answer."

An A-3...

A-3 was the ultimate Field Officer response for a man who was in immediate danger of extinction but was far too valuable to be wasted.

Suddenly, with no notice at all, he would be whipped out of the field, not even knowing what was happening...

Sometimes, three or four men would simply bundle him into a car that would then speed off to destinations unknown. Sometimes he would find the naked girlfriend in bed beside him slapping a palm-needle into his bare shoulder, with complete coma coming in less than four seconds.

Sometimes it was less dramatic, just a heart-to-heart with a longtime friend. And sometimes it involved heroic rescues with blazing guns...

But always, Agent X would be removed from the immediate danger and put on ice, with or without the consent that always seemed to come to him in the course of time.

Families and friends would learn that he was dead, and would weep for him, and this was hard to take. (Often, an elaborate death would even be staged by the experts to add substance to the farce.)

And then, two or three months later, Agent X would surface again under a new name, a new identity, just as deadly as ever.

The A-3 affairs were always remarkably efficient, though not greatly loved by their victims, most of who would rather have sweated the whole thing out and taken their chances.

But now, Ian Quayle was beside himself as he rounded on Wendy. "You can go to hell," he said furiously, "I am not going to sit still for an A-3 or anything like it! There has to be another answer, somewhere, for Christ's sake! And we have to find it, isn't that what this meeting's about?"

"Calm down, Ian," Robin Harris said patiently. "And I'm still waiting for a suggestion from you, that might, I hope find an answer in the murky area. Wendy spoke of. So think what you want to say, and then say it."

For a long time Ian Quayle did just that. He began pacing again, and he said at last: "'*All the protection we can muster,*' you said. And I've seen it at work. A good man with a bright dog foiled one attempt on my life, the first one failed because the assassin was not as good a shot as he's supposed to be, and the third...three men were killed protecting me, a lot of others killed just because they happened to be around... And if anything at all is certain in this bloody mess it's that Abu Jildi is going to make damn sure that the next time he's going to succeed. Or the time after that, or after that, or after that. He can keep this up indefinitely. Can we? I doubt it."

"The answer is *no*," Robin Harris said, "and very well, you've given us the background and it's a true picture, of course it is. So, in your opinion, what's the solution?"

Ian Quayle sat down at last; it felt good to be put in this judicial position, and it gave him strength.

"Wendy is right," he said, "in her estimation of my chances, though in nothing else. '*A few more days of life*,' she said, and yes, I agree with her. So it's those '*few more days*' we have to worry about. In any event, they'll give us *time*, something we badly need, to come up with some better ideas, perhaps even with a solution of sorts. Okay, there is an answer."

He leaped to his feet again, not at all happy with just sitting there, and began waving his arms around as he so often did when he was excited.

"It's all predicated on *protection*," he said, and with a very hostile glance at Mrs. French, "And it has nothing at all to do with cowardice! How much good to the Department am I in a bloody coffin? I'm talking pragmatically now! So... A great deal of the research material I need is in my London flat, on Flood Walk, not a good place to work because there's just too much coming and going, hordes of people living there, some of whom can only be classed as undesirables. Let's not be racist, but what I have in mind is a surfeit of Middle Easterners who aren't really happy unless they can carry a machine-pistol around with them on the streets. Great in Beirut; but not in London... And piles of research stuff are already in place in my Surrey cottage, background material to the origins of Arab terrorism, patterns of behavior, terrorist profiles, all kinds of interesting papers I'll have to study over and over again."

He broke off suddenly, and he muttered, scratching at the top of his head. "I want to continue doing what has to be done. I want to do it under conditions of maximum safety. That means the cottage. It's a million miles from anywhere. A stranger in the village—even a strange car—is suspect. And if I can have an armed police officer practically living in my kitchen, another in a prowling car, we've got it made. I'm expecting tear-sheets from the British Museum, which I'd normally go and pick up myself. Okay, a police car can get them for me and bring them down to me. And then... It's a sort of holding operation, isn't it?"

"It all makes sense," Robin Harris said, "so let's go with it. I'll have a police car parked permanently outside your cottage, to show the flag, so to speak, and I'll have an unmarked police car; two officers on board, prowling the neighborhood. And I'll have another officer in the house with you permanently, never letting you out of his sight."

"Perfect."

Ian Quayle thought about it for a moment, and then said, "The man by my side. Can I pick and choose?"

Robin Harris nodded. "You can."

"And can we raid the bomb squad at the Yard? A Sergeant named Merrick, he has an explosive-sniffing dog named Betsy. I met him once, I have a great deal of confidence in him."

"I'm sure it can be arranged," Robin Harris said. "The Yard's under as much pressure from high authority as we are to get this thing settled. The office of the Prime Minister is twisting all of our arms now, understandingly so."

And so, it was decided, to Mrs. French's acute satisfaction and Wendy Hayworth's equally acute distress...

Ian Quayle was to continue with his work, but only at the cottage, never once leaving it without a heavy police escort.

Armed police would patrol the grounds, prowl cars would keep watch on the winding country lanes, a Command Post would be set up in the village...

And Robin Harris said at last, "Short of a thousand-pound bomb dropped from a high-flying aircraft, you'll be safe,

Ian...and we'll keep this up as long as we have to."

"It's a state of siege, isn't it? Am I really worth all this bullshit?"

"You know the cliché," Robin Harris said amiably. "'A dead agent is a bad agent.' We'll go to the end of the earth to keep them alive...and working."

He knew at once that it was a mistake, but Ian Quayle got there first. "True," he said sourly, "and how often do I have to remind everyone that I'm not a Field Officer? For Christ's sake, I'm just a bloody clerk!"

"Of course, forgive me if I give your work more importance than you do yourself. We depend upon you to... what's your phrase? To point us in the right direction. I know it, Mrs. French knows it, Wendy knows it, the whole Department knows it."

"How very true," Mrs. French said caustically. "I do hope it doesn't frighten you too much, Mr. Quayle? It shouldn't, you now. After all, you always have your Wendy to hold your hand."

Ian Quayle turned his cold eyes on her and tried to stare her down, but he didn't get anywhere at all.

"Bloody woman," he said, "I often wonder if you know, *really* know what a fucking bitch you are! If it weren't for Robin here, and yes, for my Wendy too, I'd have quit a long time ago."

"Language, Ian," Robin Harris said plaintively. "In front of the ladies..."

And Mrs. French said nothing; her thin smile said it all.

Ian Quayle caught Jackie's eyes, and there was nothing but delighted mischief in her eyes; she had the hots for him anyway, and didn't care who knew it.

But Arnold Burla, facts always at his competent fingertips, said quietly, "My Department feels that the Swords of God can be snuffed out if their leader, Abu Jildi, can be killed. Obviously, this is not directly a matter for the Department, but we have to point the way for the people who can do that. It means that Mr. Quayle *has* to continue with his research. If it should come to a vote... I have only one thing to say. I want to know who this Abu Jildi is. Others can take it from there. Me—I want him dead. There've been far too many assaults, in far too short a time. In all of our long history we've never before had to face so ruthless an enemy."

He smiled at Ian Quayle, a humorless smile that never reached his eyes.

"Go to it, Quayle," he said. "Find him for us."

CHAPTER 8

For the next four days the cottage was truly under virtual siege; Constable Harry Reynolds, a natural-born gardener, was its only visible aspect as he pottered around pruning everything in sight, (but very expertly indeed).

But it was not as bad as Ian Quayle had feared.

A police car brought him enough groceries to last for a lifetime, the bar was already well-stocked, and all visitors—Albert from down the road, Eddie Forbes from London with his model Melancholie Melanie come to make amends—were carefully vetted before being allowed entrance.

"I don't believe it!" Melanie said. "I mean, what the hell's going on, Ian? There was this cop, *a cop* for Christ's sake, he had this mike sort of thing and he stuck it right up under my skirt, I mean, a lady has to have a smidgen of dignity left, wouldn't you say? It was pinging away there like crazy, I practically had an orgasm right there. He said: 'You're clean, Madam, go ahead.' '*Madam*?' Christ, I haven't been called Madam since was seven years-old! Isn't a madam someone who runs a whorehouse?"

In spite of these interruptions, Ian Quayle threw himself into his work with a vengeance as the pile of tear-sheets on his desk grew almost hourly. The police were bringing him the museum stuff now, and the translations from the Arab Press were sometimes worth their weight in gold in all that between-the-lines material.

But not always...

"I don't give a shit about Arafat," he would say to Wendy, "Or George Habash either. Abu Nidal? Well, maybe, he just might be Abu Jildi under a new name. But Kanafani? Abu Jihad? Abu Sharif? I don't give a damn about these arseholes..."

Almost hourly, the profile he was preparing was taking on the flesh to fill out the bare bones he had started with, and he sat that evening—in great satisfaction and with a glass of Augier Freres beside him—poring over what he knew would be only the first of his Progress Reports to Robin Harris, via his Case Officer Wendy Hayworth.

It meant little to him that he was a prisoner in his own house; the hell with it, he was coming along just fine.

Making small corrections here and there, he read:

Subject: Abu Jildi.

Because subject's terrorist group known as The Swords of God is new to us, it may be that we have fallen into the trap of assuming that their leader is a newcomer too.

This is not so.

There is a certain amount of speculative evidence that he was one, at least, of the masterminds behind the Palestinians' 'Black September' massacre of eleven Israeli athletes at the Munich Olympic Games, (September 5, 1972). This would tend to put him in the over-35 age group, a fact of which there is other—and more compelling—evidence. It may be that he was one of the founders of the Black September group, together with Wadi Haddad, Hassan Salameh, Abu Daoud, and the others who are too well-known to comment upon.

It is certain that he was also a member of the Hezbollah, perhaps even one of its founders, and that his main function at this time was the funneling of funds from Iran into Lebanon, and their allocation. It seems that he was highly skilled at juggling money in the various Beirut banks, and I choose to believe, for the moment at least, that he might as well be a financial wizard of sorts. (A brief comment in the Egyptian Alhazar refers to him sardonically as a frustrated 'money-man.')

He is undoubtedly Lebanese, though perhaps of Iranian heritage, and he is a Shia Muslim. His English is fairly good, his French immaculate, and he also speaks Palestinian. Arabic (which is very close to Lebanese.) and has been able to pass, on occasion, as an Egyptian, with no dialect problems. He speaks Farsi fluently, a little German, and has a smattering of Russian. He also seems to be a family man, of sorts, with only one wife, who either lives in London or has been staying there for quite some time. It seems that they have a teenage daughter about whom absolutely nothing is known, and perhaps also a much younger son who is being educated in Switzerland. He also seems to have somewhat of a reputation as a ladies' man, though this aspect of his character might well be a confusion with someone else.

Above all, perhaps, he is very secretive. While most known terrorist leaders eagerly seek out media coverage at the personal level, subject goes to great lengths to hide his true identity. The inference, I feel, is obvious—this is a man who is well-known in other circles and wishes to hide his activity as a terrorist. He is no Arafat, no Habbash, no Abu Nidal. He might even be a Government Minister, a University Professor, a financial tycoon, or just a whatever-face that everyone will instantly recognize.

This is a speculative report, more details will follow.

Ian Quayle leaned back in his chair and put his feet up on the desk while he thought about what he had typed. Thought too, about Wendy. Would she be coming down this evening? It was Friday evening, no office tomorrow. He needed her, needed her badly, but all day she hadn't called.

Or had she?

All this time, his phone had been playing silly-buggers, ringing and then cutting off at once, and he knew what it was; *someone* had tapped into his phone, probably the office.

Or was it some damned Arab with six passports in his pocket?

No, they'd have told him.

Or would they have?

And why should they monitor Wendy's calls? It worried the hell out of him, but he could be philosophically-inclined when he wanted to, and he knew that it was part—a stupid part, perhaps—of the price he was paying for his safety.

He turned his attention back to his report:

Subject: The Swords of God.

Almost nothing has been written, as yet, about this nebulous organization, except that it is the brainchild of one Abu Jildi—see above—who has turned this terrorist organization away from the usual haphazard terrorist objectives, and aimed them at the western world's Intelligence Establishment; this in itself is a reflection of Abu Jildi's thinking, which is above average by a very considerable measure. Abu Jildi has decided that his enemy is the nerve-center of anti-terrorist activity. We ourselves should adopt the same philosophy: Destroy Abu Jildi—and we have blunted, if not broken; the Swords of God.

He thought that was very nicely worded, and began to worry about Wendy again; where the hell was she?

He sipped his cognac, and began reflecting on this very strange relationship. A woman of the most exciting sensuality whom he took to his bed sometimes, always for the wrong reasons...

She was a woman of very superior intellect who was technically his boss but was (only on occasion, he was sure), as desperately in love with him as he was with her. A woman he fought with all the time, but wasn't that what love was all about? Fighting?

And then, there was a stylized knock at the front door, the one-one; one-two-three that meant it was the amiable Sergeant Merrick with his dog Betsy.

Poor Betsy, vegetating now in the country with no explosives to sniff at! But there were stoats and weasels, and badgers too, and the caged Horace the ferret to worry about. And Betsy, off her leash most of the time, returning to it when she was needed like the pro she was, was having herself a ball.

This was the kind of country she was spawned in, and it was glorious for her.

Ian Quayle threw open the door, the deadbolt newly installed, and yes, there was Constable Merrick, holding up a red-bordered envelope.

"Special Delivery," Merrick said. "And it's all right, Mr. Quayle, we checked the delivery man out, he's kosher."

Ian Quayle took the envelope from him, "And is everything quiet out there?"

Betsy was leaping all over Quayle to show how much she loved him, and Merrick said sternly, "Down, down, you want to disgrace me, you dumb dog?"

He grinned suddenly. "Nothing she hates more, Mr. Quayle, than being called a dumb dog! Yes, everything's quiet. One of the patrol cars found a van in from Guildford, but it was just a poacher, a man the local police know very well. He was told to go and poach in someone else's forest."

"And it's a nice night, isn't it? Nights like these, I sometimes wonder why I spend so much time in my London flat.

There's nothing, but nothing, like the serenity of the country."

"Yes, it's true. Good-night, Mr. Quayle, sir."

"Good-night, Mr. Merrick. And thanks. For everything."

He was suddenly aware that he had a Special Delivery envelope in his hand, and Special Delivery always meant a certain importance. He wondered if he's been drinking too much good cognac this evening, and he said aloud: *"Where are you, Wendy, when I need you?"*

He found his letter opener, a Spanish stiletto, and slit open the envelope.

It was a letter within a letter, which meant that its final contents were confidential, not to be perused by any Tom, Dick or Harry at the Special Delivery desk. And it had come from *Messages Internationales*, a delivery outfit headquartered in Paris.

From his mother Claudine, then, or perhaps from his lovely daughter Pia...

He tore open the inner envelope, and he stared in astonishment at the array of letters there:

LASTN UPSRY QTPLU XSR3Y TGKPF KPLYR REQUY...

The letters went on and on, for more than a dozen neatly-spaced lines, but it was the first group that intrigued him, LASTN...

It stood for '*Last Night...*' and it was an indication that this was his own personal LMT code. And who the hell outside the London office knew his personal code?

Who the hell *in* the office knew it, for that matter?

Wendy, of course, and Mrs. Bloody French, and Robin Harris; and Ops. G., may be Ops. E as well, though he wasn't too sure about that...

And, of course, most of the cipherenes who spent their days and nights decoding messages from the field.

Last Night...

How long was it since he'd last used his LMT? He couldn't even remember when; in his safe stay-at-home job it wasn't necessary. But Mrs. Bloody French, in one of her rare good moods, when she wasn't aggravating everyone she came in contact with, had said, all charming smiles, "You never can tell when a P.C. might come in handy."

"A P.C.?" Ian Quayle had asked mildly. "No, don't tell me, let me guess... It stands for *Personal Code*, I'll bet... Right?"

She hated this loathsome man, but if she waited to continue manipulating him—then just once in a while she had to smile for his benefit.

And when Mrs. French smiled, this most ruthless and thoroughly evil woman in the whole of the Intelligence Establishment, she radiated life-giving sunbeams. You just automatically figured that she adored you, that she was your sister, your daughter, your mistress all rolled up into one. And sometimes it took an effort of will to remember that five minutes later she'd happily stab you in the back or cut off your testicles, to be grilled tomorrow morning for breakfast, probably, devilled with herbs and mustard and a touch of vinegar too.

Now he struggled to remember his key: one word wrong could be hell.

He said aloud:

'*Last night, ah yesternight, between her lips and mine...*'

No, god dammit, it was berwix her lips and mine! Or was it? Yes; it was *benwix...*

'*...betwix her lips and mine*
There fell thy shadow, Cynara...'

He found a sheet of yellow paper and quickly drew the squares.

And what the hell was today? Friday, the sixth day of the week; the sixth letter in the phrase then... He wrote it all out in the horizontal, placed the letters in the vertical, and then, when he read the final horizontal he was ready to explode with shock, with anger, and: with sheer terror.

He read:

PERSONAL LETTER TO MR. IAN QUAYLE, SALAAMS. FOUR DAYS FROM TODAY, WHICH IS WEDNESDAY NINETEEN, YOU WILL BE REPORTING TO ME PERSONALLY AT HOTEL SEMIRAMIS, CAIRO, EGYPT, AT MIDDAY EXACTLY. I AM DEEPLY REGRET THAT CANNOT GIVING YOU MY ATTENTION IMMEDIATE, BUT I AM HAVING IMPORTANT MATTERS FOR FEW DAYS. YOU GOING TO SUITE 702 ALONE. REPEAT ALONE, AT MIDDAY EXACTLY. IF YOU ARE NOT DOING THIS, SO FEW DAYS LATER YOU ARE RECEIVING EARS OF YOUR DAUGHTER PIA DELIVERED TO YOU PACKED NICE IN COTTON. AFTER THAT, THERE IS FINGERS ONE BY ONE, AND MAYBE LAST, IS HER HEAD TOO.

The letter was signed with a flourish, in fine disregard of any security: "*Abu Jildi, a name you are knowing.*"

Ian Quayle stared at it, and he felt the dreadful physical effect of the blood draining from his face and leaving him white as a sheet loomed from the finest long-grained Egyptian cotton.

CHAPTER 9

It was riot a time for hysterics.

Hysteria would perhaps have been understandable now, but it would serve no useful purpose whatsoever; and so, by an effort of will, Ian Quayle forced himself to sit down and think, because thinking was all that mattered now.

His beloved daughter kidnapped? Carted off by masked men to destinations unknown?

No, not unknown...

He thought of his talk in Paris with the journalist Paul Diderot, and of the temporary financing of this operation with the white slave traffic. And for the sweet, lovely, and innocent Pia to be sold to one of the Arab Sheikhs as a harem status symbol? Like the Rolls Royces they bought by the half-dozen?

The hysteria was mounting, and he fought it; but he could only fight it halfway.

He picked up the phone and dialed Paris, knowing that his line was tapped by his own bloody office, and the hell with it. And the phone was picked up at the first half-ring.

Claudine was there on the line, the mother he loved so dearly, and her habitual *sangfroid* had left her completely; she was close to the hysteria that Ian had so carefully consigned to the back of his mind, knowing only that a cold assessment of the situation was all that mattered now.

"Thank God," she said emotionally, "thank God you called, something terrible has happened..."

She was switching between English and French in her distress, a word or two thrown in of her native Hungarian, and Ian said urgently: "Wait, Maman, I know what this is about, we must speak only Hungarian now..."

It seemed she hadn't heard him, and she went on, speaking almost incoherently: "We came back from the seaside, and there were three men in the apartment, with masks on their faces of devils... In the most execrable French, they told me they had come to take Pia away. I fought them, of course I fought them, and so did Pia. But they knocked me to the ground, and for *quelques instants* I was unconscious. When recovered myself, they had gone, and they had taken Pia with them. I summoned the police, and they came at once, and I've been trying to call you all day, but there is something wrong with your phone..."

Something wrong with the phone?

He knew it, the new computers at the office taking over and screwing up. He switched languages himself, and said as calmly as he could, in Hungarian, "Listen, Maman, my phone has been tapped, this call is being monitored. But they won't have a Hungarian translator on duty now, so we can talk privately for a while. Okay, in time, the tape will be translated for them, but time is what I need now. Can you hear me clearly?"

"Yes, yes I can..."

"Good. I am coming to see you, at once. It will not be as quickly as I would like, it's a little, well, complicated for me now, there are people, my own people, who will try to stop me."

He was speaking very quickly now, wondering what the girl on the machine in the office would be doing; she'd heard enough already to start the ball rolling, and he thought he knew what she'd do...

An emergency call to Case Officer Wendy Hayworth while he was still on the line, a call from Wendy to the command post in the village, a screeching police car driving furiously up to his front door to make damn sure that he stayed put...

He said, "*Les flics*, the cops, are they still there?"

"No, they've gone, I can call them back..."

"No! No, don't do that, Maman! You must do nothing now, you understand? Nothing now, just wait for me. I'll be there just as soon as I can."

He put down the phone and stared out into the garden. Constable Harry Reynolds was out there, washing down the hoe and the spade he'd been using and running a quick file over their blades like the passionate gardener he was.

But there was no sign of Sergeant Merrick with his dog, and it was Betsy he was worried about now. Would she bark when she heard him moving through his own garden? He thought perhaps not, and then wondered if he were selling her short, the damn dog had all the natural instincts of a professional cop herself.

It was twilight, and he hated the thought of another hour, at the very least, before darkness set in.

He took his passport from the desk in his study, and pulled Volume Three of Larned's splendid 'History for Topical Reading' from its place on the top shelf of the wall-length bookcase. Behind it, there was an envelope containing what he thought of as emergency cash, and thumbed through the bills, four twenty-pound notes, six tens and a couple of fivers, it would have to be enough.

He turned on a few lights in the house against the coming darkness, tuned on the cassette deck and slipped in two sequential tapes, then went to the kitchen and quietly opened the back door.

He stood there for a moment looking out at the masses of rhododendrons, their colors brilliant in the evening light.

Closing the door behind him, he sauntered toward them casually, his eyes alert and looking for any sign of life; there was none.

But then he heard that damn dog bark, and suddenly, there was Sergeant Merrick with Betsy on her leash, rising up like a ghoul in the twilight from the cover of the gooseberry bushes, not more than forty feet away.

"Everything alright, Mr. Quayle?" Merrick called, and Quayle turned and smiled. "Everything's fine, Mr. Merrick."

"Something you need, sir?"

"No, not really. Just thought I'd move Horace's cage into the old stable."

"Horace? Ah yes, the ferret. Want me to give you a hand with it?"

Ian Quayle laughed. "What, you and Betsy? I don't know which of them would kill the other. No, it's not heavy, I just have to make room for it, that's all. Thanks anyway."

He sauntered on past the flower border and the big onion patch to the side door of the stable and went inside. He let the door swing shut behind him and ran swiftly to the window on the other side. He clambered through and dropped down at the edge of his property where the woods began, and ran fast down to the little stream there and along it till he came to the first of Albert's fields, where five Jersey cows stared at him morosely.

He hurried along the hedgerow till he came to the farmhouse, and there was Albert Ray, a good neighbor and friend, peering through his kitchen window to see what the dog Charlie was kicking up such a shindig about.

He threw open the door immediately, beaming, and said, "Well, I was wondering when I'd get to see you, Mr. Quayle. You've been down here three days already without once dropping by... It's something to do with all them London cops, is that it? Never saw so many cops at one time in all me born days."

"No time to explain, Albert," Ian Quayle said, "but I've been under police protection ever since I got here, it means I can't leave the cottage without a bodyguard in tow. And just now...there's something I have to do that I can only do on my own."

"Well," the gruff old man said, "I was wondering what it was all about..."

"Can you drive me into Godalming, Albert? In a hurry? I have to be there like half an hour ago."

Placid old countryman or not, Albert could leap to it when he had a mind to. "Let's go," he said. "Godalming? Take us fifteen minutes."

"I don't know how far out the police blockade is, it might be quite a way. Is there something in the back I can hide under? A tarpaulin, maybe?"

"A whole pile of potato sacks there."

"Great. And if you're stopped, Albert, you haven't seen hide nor hair of me, okay?"

"Just leave it to me, Mr. Quayle. I ever if you about the time I escaped from a POW camp in Germany? World War Two, I was an old man already..."

They were stopped only once on the road.

A flashlight beam cut through the darkness, and Ian Quayle heard a voice he recognized, the *basso profundo* of Austel-in-the Woods' Sergeant Tim Berry, deeply disturbed now.

"Hello there, Albert, where you off to?"

"Godalming, Tim, if it's any o' your business. And isn't it high time someone told us local yokels what the hell's going on down here these last few days? I never seen so many coppers in one place at the same time in all my born days."

"And all of them from London town," Tim Berry said darkly. "It's them Arab terrorists, Albert, you heard about them?"

"Only what I read in the paper."

"Seems they're trying to kill our Ian Quayle. And why would anyone want to do a thing like that?"

"You tell me, Tim."

"And maybe they got at him last," Tim Berry said.

Albert stared. "They did what?"

"We just got word, Ian Quayle walked into his stable, right under the nose of one o' them bright boys from Scotland Yard, and he never come out again. So, either he took off for reasons of his own, which don't make sense to me... Or, they got him at last. So, you see anyone suspicious wandering about...you jump 'em, Albert, and let me know. Just be careful, I see you got Charlie in the back there."

"And he takes good care of me, Tim, don't you worry."

"So be on your way, Albert."

"Good-night, Tim..."

At a quarter to eight, they pulled into the Avis place in Godalming, and by seven fifty-two Ian Quayle was speeding towards London Town, heading for the ten o'clock Air France flight to Paris.

He just abandoned the rental car there, double-parked for the police to worry about, and at eleven twenty-two precisely, Madame Constant, concierge at the St. Cloud apartment of his mother, Claudine Andrassy, pushed the button of the elevator that led to the upper story.

And to Ian's surprise, and initial annoyance, Police Inspector Pleyer was there, a man he had met before, and—to be fair—who was probably very good at his job.

At *both* of his jobs.

He was an Inspector of some seniority in the Surete, but for some years now he had also been, secretly, the representative in Paris of England's MI6.

But it was his mother Claudine who attracted his immediate attention, as always. The awful bruise under her left eye cut him to the quick as he hugged her, moaning, "And you've been hurt too..."

"*C'est rien*," she said, "It's nothing. We have more important problems on our hands now."

111

At the age of sixty-three, Claudine Andrassy still reflected the great beauty she'd been blessed with as a teenager when she'd been a *prima danceuse* fresh out of school and already showing the kind of talent that occurs only once or twice in a generation.

By the age of twenty-seven, Claudine Andrassy's fame had spread worldwide, and to balletomanes everywhere she had become a Goddess, a *Prima Assoluta* like no one before her, not even the most famous of the Russians.

Until, that is to say, that damned Russian defector, high on stuff he should never have even sampled in his new, free society, dropped her and cracked her kneecap.

She'd finished the ballet, dancing in the most acute agony, and she'd not collapsed till the final curtain had fallen after the most interminable time, a time of standing ovation the like of which London had never seen before in the whole of Covent Garden's long and honorable history.

They knew, out there in the audience; they *knew*.

Grown men were unashamedly weeping; and when the thunderous applause simply would not stop, the Stage Manager had said quietly, hoping that no one would see that he was crying too, "All right, final curtain, *final*, you hear me? And get that stretcher on stage, now...!"

Sixty-three years old, and still fabulous...

Claudine was slender, even whispy, tall and lithe as a hazel sapling, with long dark hair that was often piled up in studied carelessness over a very handsome forehead.

She had the most enchanting eyes, rather larger than usual, and neither gray nor green but something in between. Her cheekbones were high, with the tiny wrinkles at the sides of a full and sensual mouth which said she smiled very easily.

But now, there was not very much to smile about.

She turned away and picked up a framed photograph, dark and piercing eyes, a long, hooked nose, a lantern-jaw; the late Harry Quayle, Shakespearean actor *par excellence* whose ripened voice dripped twenty-four carat gold, a voice—and a talent as well—to rival those of Gielgud, Richardson, Evans, Olivier, and the other incomparables.

And still...a *failure*.

"Blame it on Sir Richard," he used to say in his more sober moments, which became more and more rare as time rolled on.

And by 'Sir Richard,' he meant the Richard Burnett who made the finest of all the English gins.

Harry Quayle was dead now, long gone; but the pain was still there.

Claudine hugged the portrait to her breast, and turned to stare at her son, a disconcerting habit she had. "I lost my husband, your father, Ian," she said quietly. "Now, have I lost your only child too, my granddaughter? Have we lost her too?"

"We have not lost her," Ian said steadily. "I swear to God I will bring her back."

"Unharmed?" Claudine's voice was pure ice.

And there was a little, very heavy silence.

And then Ian Quayle said stubbornly, biting his lip, "I said only that I will bring her back. And I will."

He turned to Inspector Pleyer at last and took his hand. "Inspector...we met once before, if you remember?"

Pleyer inclined his head. "I remember. Then, too, they were trying to kill you."

"Yes, it's becoming a habit, isn't it? And I hate it. Will you tell me why you are here?"

Pleyer hated explanations, but he said courteously, "When we learned of Mademoiselle Pia Mancini's kidnapping, then my office automatically put a tap on this telephone, waiting for a ransom demand, you understand? Instead, they overheard your conversation with your mother, which put an entirely new color on this whole matter. My office suggested that I come here to meet with you, perhaps to find out what you know that could be of importance to us."

"In exchange for which...can I count on your cooperation?"

"You can," Pleyer said emphatically, "absolutely. I have the feeling—call it, if you will, the instinct of an experienced investigator—that this is not entirely a matter for the regular police."

Quayle nodded. "And you are right."

He hesitated, and then: "I find myself in the awkward position of talking to you as one MI6 man to another, even though at this moment my office and yours are desperately looking for me, in the hope of dragging me back to London by my ankles. For the last three days, I have been a virtual prisoner in my own home, what they think of as 'protective custody,' even though they never use so insulting a phrase. When I heard what had happened, I chose to escape. It was easy enough, but I'm aware that they'll be hard on my heels very soon, if they're not already."

He looked at his watch. "I have very little time..."

But for more than five long minutes, he told the Inspector everything that had happened in the last six days, beginning with the bombing of the Five Ports Hotel, moving on to the three attempts on his own life, on to the kidnapping of his beloved daughter, and finishing with the special delivery letter from Abu Jildi.

He saw the whitening of Claudine's face when he quoted the phrase...'*her ears packed in cotton*,' but he would not pull the punches now.

He said slowly, "The love of a father for his daughter is what we are talking about now. And we must not forget that same man's love for his mother. It is my intention now to rescue Pia. But if I do so, and find that I have left my flanks unprotected, and come home with her only to find that now my mother is gone...? Do I make myself clear?"

The Inspector smiled thinly. "I was a fighting man myself once, M'sieur Quayle," he said. "World War Two, in the Resistance. I was nine years old when it all began. Yes, you make yourself very clear."

"And..."

"And you have my word that in your absence, your mother will have all the protection generally afforded only to the President of the Republic. We used to call it 'securing the rear before you advance.'"

Quayle looked at his watch. "In forty-five minutes I have to be at the airport, I can't make it, can I?"

"You can," Pleyer said. He turned to Claudine and murmured, "If I might use your phone, Madame?"

"Of course..."

The Inspector dialed and spoke very briefly; and in less than three minutes Madame Constant the concierge called up and said, positively awed, "There are three motorcycle policemen here, Madame, together with a patrol car. Something to do with catching a plane...?"

Ian Quayle embraced his mother, and he said to her quietly, "She will have been hurt, Maman, we must accept it. But I swear to God that I will bring her back to us before the damage becomes irreparable..."

"Ian, *mon fils*..." There were tears in her eyes. "You too, be careful. What you do now..."

"What I do now," Ian said harshly, "is what has to be done."

The Inspector was on the edge of an exchange that was emotional in the extreme, and he said with great diffidence, "If you would tell me your plan of action, Mr. Quayle, perhaps I could help in some way...?"

Ian Quayle released Claudine's fragile body and turned to him.

"My plan of action?" he said heavily, "I don't have one. All I know...all I know is that I have to go to Cairo and find my daughter."

Inspector Pleyer was pulling rank, and for thirty-five minutes the police car, escorted by a pair of siren-wailing motorcycles, tore through the streets of the City of Lights.

And by the skin of his teeth, Ian Quayle found himself a last minute seat on Air France Flight 142, destination—Cairo, Egypt.

Four and a quarter hours later, in the moonlit night of the glorious thirtieth parallel north, Ian Quayle found himself in one of the noisiest and most tumultuous cities in the world.

Cairo...

It was one o'clock in the morning. But the city was still awake.

"Mena House Hotel," he said to the taxi driver. "Let's try and make it before their nightclub closes down for the night, okay?"

"Thirty dollars," the taxi driver said, and Quayle answered coldly, "I have ten pounds English, take it or leave it."

You were supposed to change your currency at officially-accredited exchanges, but taxi drivers, waiters, and pimps preferred the unofficial rate.

"Okay," the driver said, "fifteen it is."

"Ten."

"Twelve."

"Ten. And if they're closed already when we get there...only five."

The taxi sped off.

CHAPTER 10

Mena House under the moonlight had never looked better.

It was still perhaps one of the five most attractive hotels in the world, with not only comfortable suites and bungalows, and an excellent cuisine, but also one hell of a nightclub (given, of course, the moral restrictions of a rather uptight government; the belly dancers, by law, were required to be covered from neck to ankle, but somehow, they managed).

The nightclub area was entirely open under the cold moonlight, a first class Italian orchestra (of second class citizens), playing for the dancers under a semi-canopy of wildly rampant jasmine, honeysuckle, and bougainvillea in both red and purple, clambering over every trellis in sight. Potted geraniums splashed color all over, interspersed with the brilliant blues of lobelia; and there was the scent of English lavender everywhere.

Altogether, the broad patio of the Mena House's Oasis nightclub was one hell of a place to be.

"*Champagne, M'sieur?*" the waiter asked, as Ian Quayle watched the gyrating dancer. And he nodded "Yes, please. Is that the famous Aida?"

"*Non, M'sieur,* Aida will come very soon now, after this number."

He swept away, and soon returned with a bottle of Veuve

Cliquot, vintage 1969, and Ian sighed; it promised to be a very expensive evening.

And then, a roll of the drums called for awed silence, and the announcer took the spotlight and raised his arms high, and shouted, *"Et maintenant, M'sieurs et 'Dames...la fabuleuse Aida...!"*

The spotlight swept to an arbor which till this moment had been quite dark; and there she was, a woman of extravagant beauty and sensuality, tall, dark-haired, black-eyed, not as plump as was normally expected in Egypt, but full-breasted and round-hipped to a very delectable degree.

In the momentary semi-darkness, she appeared to be almost naked. But as the dimmer came up it could be seen that she was legally covered in black chiffon, with cut out hands over her breasts and an exaggerated fig leaf over the pubic area, a sop to the law and a condemnation of it at the same time...

She snaked her way from the arbor to stage center and went immediately into a Sarabande, its original Seville version, with the orchestra valiantly tackling the strange triple time, three minims to the bar. But soon she was moving out of its slow stealth and speeding up till she reached a fury of agitation, and then, with a signal to the bandleader, slowing down to a slow, slow exhibition of the pure eroticism for which it had been famous in 16th Century Spain.

And when at last she was finished and the drums rolled their overpowering climax, the audience—mostly Government functionaries by the looks of them—was on its communal feet and cheering as Aida swept away, and Ian found his Cross and the 5x3 cards he habitually carried, and he wrote,

Just loved your dance. Would you honor me with your company for a glass of champagne?

There was a moment of panic when he found he had

forgotten the identity-code that was so necessary now... What was it? Palmerston-Something? What was the mnemonic, *Cat-in-the-cupboard?* Yes, there'd been a cat back home named Jefferson... when he was a kid.

He signed the note: *Jefferson Hubbard*, and gave it to the waiter, along with one of his ten-pound notes, nothing like playing it rich...

"Kindly give this to Mademoiselle Aida," he said.

"Will you see that she gets it at once?"

"*Bien, M'sieur...*"

The waiter was gone with the message and his money, and Ian Quayle settled down to watch her encore, sexy as hell in spite of—or perhaps because of—the black chiffon.

He watched for a sign from her, but there was none at all, not even an exchange of glances, and he was furious; there was so little time left before the deadline that damned Abu Jildi had imposed on him...

And where was his Pia now? While he was drinking vintage champagne in a goddamn nightclub...?

He found that he was trembling, and fought for control.

And still no sign from the damned Aida...!

The waiter came with the check, and it was time for a showdown. Ian. Quayle said belligerently, "Did you give her my note, or didn't you?"

"Good night, sir, *bonne nuit,*" the bloody waiter said, and with a quick bow he was gone.

Quayle picked the champagne bottle out of the elegant silver cooler:

Empty. Had he really drunk all of it?

Well, at least it was good. And at seventy quid a bottle it damn well ought to be...

He got to his feet and went out through the scented portico and onto the street. From here, you could see the Sphinx towering up under the moon in the most awesome dignity imaginable, coming out of the remote past to tell the modern world what a pile of shit they had to put up with these days.

Awesome wasn't the word, the true word had not yet been coined for this moonlit majesty...

The taxi drivers were crowding him. "My car, *Effendi*, air-conditioned... Only five dollars to Cairo, *ya siddi*, five dollars..."

And then, suddenly, for no reason at all, they all seemed to just melt away...

Now, instead of the crush, there was just one man there, black as the ace of spades, a Sudanese from his dress, perhaps even a eunuch; he was huge.

He said quietly: "Mr. Jefferson? Mr. Hubbard? Your car is here, sir."

Ah so all was well, after all...

Or was it?

Someone opened the rear door of a taxi for him, and as he found a seat there, two other men appeared out of nowhere and sat beside him. The Sudanese sat in the front by the driver, and after they had gone for four or five miles, he turned around and said, amiably enough. "You will not mind, will you, if we blindfold you now...?"

"Just so's I get to meet with Mad'moiselle Aida," Ian Quayle muttered, and for the first time now, he suddenly realized that this might not be what they had in mind.

He let them bind a black cloth over his eyes, and with no thought of resistance at all; how could resistance help now?

The taxi was old and decrepit, and it seemed to be held together with baling-wire. It apparently had no horn, so that the driver was obliged to hang one arm out of the window and bang ferociously on the door when someone or something was in his way...

The upholstery was in terrible shape, and a piece of broken spring from the seat was pressing into his butt. There was an indefinable smell there too, and he wondered about it for a long time before deciding that what the hell, it was just the smell of unpleasantness.

But soon it came to a halt, and he let them guide him out, stumbling over a sidewalk, and a voice said quietly. "Over here, please...."

He let himself be helped into another car, and when the motor turned over he knew that he was in something very much better. The smell now was of leather and very pleasing, and when he leaned back into the seat he found it comfortable in the extreme, with room to stretch his long legs without obstruction.

A limo, then, perhaps a Mercedes or even a Rolls; the motor was almost silent. And did it matter?

On mature reflection, he thought, yes, it did. Perhaps only subconsciously, he'd been a mite worried about meeting with the legendary Aida, mistress of Ministers and other potentates, in a cab that stuck broken springs into his behind.

But in a little while—and he figured that by now he was maybe twenty miles from Mena House—the luxury car purred to a halt and once more he was helped out.

He was guided up a single flight of stairs, and he heard, still blindfolded, a stylized knock on a door, hear the door open. He was gently pushed inside.

The door closed behind him, and now, at last, the black rag over his eyes was removed.

He found himself in a nightmare of art deco rubbish, and very expensive rubbish at that.

The hall he was in was vast, and a marble floor nearly twenty feet across, quite devoid of any carpeting. There was an *haur-bois* in one comer in which a single skull—plastic, he thought—was over-illuminated against a black velvet background. The ceiling was very high above his head, and painted in the most awful colors he had ever seen in his life— startling reds, deep blues, and swirling yellows that made his mind swirl with them; he almost wanted to vomit.

The three men just seemed to melt away, but the big Sudanese took him by the arm and led him across the monstrous hall to a door that seemed to be covered with a shining yellow sheet of plastic, a disaster.

He threw it open, and said quietly, in French, "He is here, Madame..."

Now the ambiance was entirely different, a certain amount of taste visible for the first time.

It was what back home he would have called a 'bed-sit', so large that the king size divan bed was almost lost in it. An oak parquet floor with a huge and very good Karmanshaw rug on it, one wall entirely of beveled mirror glass which he thought probably hid a walk-in closet, a tapestry on one of the walls depicting the disastrous (for the British) attempt to occupy Egypt's Alexandria.

When was it? Ian Quayle stared at the tapestry and racked his memory. Yes, 1807, General Frazer's humiliating defeat...

There were three fairly decent cabinets scattered around, not exactly antiques but made in the old days when dovetailing in furniture was important and 'gorm' was a common word to describe the polish... There were a couple of ottomans, three armchairs, four coffee tables scattered around, a very good sideboard-dresser serving now as a bar (well stocked, he noticed), and there was still enough room left to house the Bolshoi Ballet at its most ebullient.

But he turned his attention to the woman seated at the long and elaborately carved dressing table, staring at herself— and at him—in the mirror there, and at their multifaceted reproductions in the beveled mirror wall; there was something very surreal about it all.

She was taller than he had thought in the club, and perhaps more...what was the word? Stately?

Her spine was very straight, and she held herself well,

and her eyes were the largest he had ever seen, almost black and very slightly slanted, as though there were perhaps some Mongolian blood in her somewhere.

Had the Mongolians ever ravished Egypt?

Ian Quayle wondered about it; he didn't know the answer, he only knew where he could look it up, and that was what research was all about—not necessary knowing the answers, but knowing where to start searching...

She was undoubtedly very lovely indeed. Flowing black hair down to her waist that she was methodically brushing with the mandatory one hundred strokes of Middle Eastern childhood. Her skin, devoid of make-up now, was flawless, a light coffee-colored, almost like good cappuccino, the cheekbones high and well-defined.

She wore a man's terrycloth robe, half-open almost down to her waist, which was infinitesimal, and a leg was exposed as though she were posing for a G.I. poster.

But nonetheless, Ian Quayle realized at once that there was a certain quality about her. Perhaps it was in the way she held herself, like a queen rather than the whore he knew she was.

She said now, glancing at him obliquely over her shoulder, "First, you will tell me your name. Jefferson Hubbard, you said."

"Hardly," Ian Quayle said tartly, "the kind of name you'd pick out of a hat."

"But I have to be sure. The wrong people might know it too. Are you the wrong people? If you are, you will not leave this place alive."

"I'm the right people, God dammit!"

"Then tell me your name."

"My name is Ian Quayle," Ian Quayle said.

"And your case officer's name?"

"Wendy Hayworth."

"And her boss's name?"

"That's a name I won't give you."

"Very well, I accept that."

Her English was immaculate, scarcely accented at all, and she said, beginning to smile a little now, "Her boss's name is Robin Harris, and that's to make *you* feel more comfortable. I spoke to Mr. Harris this evening on my scrambler phone. They're very worried about you, Mr. Quayle? They were supposed to stop you in Paris, but something went wrong. So they called me, with a very important message. It says... Go home, Mr. Quayle, go home! They tell me that you're too vulnerable here! Wendy Hayworth came on the line, terribly agitated, and she suggested that if you remain in Cairo...you probably have less than twenty-four hours of life left in you."

"Nice to know," Ian said sourly, "that she worries about me. But I have more important things than my own life to worry about. Did she tell you why I'm here?"

Aida was frowning, a dark and angry scowl that changed her looks altogether. "She told me it was about Abu Jildi and his Swords of God. I've been working on that myself for some days now... But Miss Hayworth sounded a little confused, all she had to go on was an intercepted phone call you made to your mother in Paris. Something to do with your daughter? She's disappeared? Then why should she be in Egypt?"

Ian Quayle took Abu Jildi's letter from his pocket and gave it to her, and when she read it the scowl was darker still, and at this moment Ian Quayle decided, in spite of the awful anxiety that was clutching at his stomach, that Aida was not a woman he'd ever wish to tangle with...

But then, she did an extraordinary thing; she put the note down on her dressing table as though it were burning her and virtually ran to him, putting her arms around him as though he were an old and dear friend she'd known from childbirth, and she whispered: "*Ya Allah... Mon Dieu*, Oh God! Will you accept that I bleed for you? Will you accept that I will do everything I can to bring your daughter back? Do you love her as you should?"

"Yes on all three counts," Ian said quietly. "It's not my life that's at stake now. It's Pia's. Will you listen to me for a little while, if I tell you?"

Aida turned and leaned back against the dresser, grasping its edges with her hands, and stared at him, her intriguing eyes wide with expectation.

"I will listen," she said quietly. "I too once had a father who loved me dearly. He died at the hand of a terrorist."

Her eyes followed him as he began prowling, the habit he always just dropped into when he was agitated, gesticulating wildly once in a while, a residue, perhaps, of his mother's Central European blood.

He told her now, some twenty years ago, he'd fallen so desperately in love with a fellow student at London University, an Italian girl named Carlotta Mancini who was studying, of all things, *criminology*, (he hadn't even known that there was a chair in this recondite subject), simply because her father was a cop in Rome.

Not just a cop—a very senior police officer...

There'd been a frantic love affair, two kids who were always on the verge of marriage; but where the hell was the money coming from to support a family? Ian Quayle was still a student, earning a little here and there by doing research for the British Museum, and his father, Harry Quayle (who was perhaps the greatest Shakespearean actor of his generation), could never afford even to pay for the rent on their Bloomsbury flat.

Claudine was still the highest paid—and the most loved—prima ballerina in Europe; but in those days it wasn't done to live off the earnings of your mother, however famous she was, and so it was always a question of very-soon-now-let's-hope...

And then he told her of that awful day when he'd gone round to her bed-sit, to be met by the landlady with the lugubrious comment: "She's gone. Paid me the rent and left."

All there was in her room was the pile of 78 rpms he'd lent her, the great Leonard Warren recording of Rigoletto, and the Deruta ashtray he'd bought her for her birthday, just because it matched her two-person coffee set.

"And I never knew why she'd left me," he said now. "At least, not then."

Aida was watching him, a stationary feline who already knew the answers, and Ian Quayle nodded. "Yes, I know, it's foolish, isn't it? But I was just a kid in those days, not even knowing that *coitus interruptus* doesn't necessarily work once in a while. But it wasn't until, my God, twenty years later that I discovered I had a daughter."

It was hard to control his emotions.

But he went on. "And then, it was too late to rediscover her mother, the Carlotta I believe I still loved. No, not *believe*, I know it! Because the Red Brigades in Italy had chosen to murder her father, who by now was a General, the head of Rome's anti-terrorist squad. They wired a bomb to his car, and General Mancini was dropping his daughter off at the dressmaker's, all I ever saw of her was charred bones, splattered over Roman roof tops. *That* was when I found my daughter."

He rubbed a hand over tired and red-rimmed eyes.

"Do I love my daughter as I should?" he asked bitterly. "Yes, I do! There was some talk about her future. She was studying ballet in Rome, and what better tutor could she now have than my mother, the greatest *Assoluta* in history? And so, it was decided that for at least a few years my Pia would be better off studying under Claudine Andrassy...than digging vegetable patches at my Surrey cottage, which is all I could have done for her. It was a hard decision for me, but it was the right one. But then, after three failed attempts on my life, Abu Jildi found an easy answer..."

"Wait, wait!" Aida said urgently. "Three attempts on

your life?"

Ian Quayle told her of the 'poacher' down in Austel-in-the-Woods who'd put a rifle bullet through his living room window and wounded him, though very slightly; of the frightening business with the explosive in his cassette recorder; of the attack on his little Mini, foiled only by the one chance in a million car thief.

Aida listened in silence till he was through, and she said at last, "It's obvious, isn't it? He can't kill you in England, so he's brought you to Cairo, by the simplest device in the world—a gambit he knows you *have* to accept! You do know, don't you, that the moment you meet with him face to face, all you'll see is a silenced revolver aimed at the bridge of your nose? And that's the last thing you'll *ever* see? I hope you are not a fool, Mr. Quayle. I never like to do business with fools, they tend to put my own life in danger."

Ian Quayle was not often lost for an answer, but he said nothing, knowing that what he was doing now was indeed foolish in the extreme. But what was the alternative?

The alternative did not exist.

And then, there was a tap on the door, and in answer to Aida's "*Ta'al*, come..." the big Sudanese was there. Showing off his good manners in front of a guest, he spoke French instead of Arabic. "It is four o'clock, Madame. The BBC."

"*Ah oui...*"

Aida went to the big console and touched buttons, and she said to Ian Quayle, "In all the years I've been working for Robin Harris, I've never been able to find out where the overseas service of the British Broadcasting Corporation gets its information. But they get it first, and they're the most reliable. I want to find out about that aborted bombing attempt."

"Oh? What attempt was that?"

"Didn't you know?" She turned the sound down as the news in Arabic came on, and said drily: "Cricket. New Zealand is giving India a very bad time, it seems..."

Looking up, she said again: "Didn't you hear? The ten p.m. flight of Egyptian Air 413, Cairo to Rome."

"No, I didn't hear. I was flying myself at ten o'clock, and a bombing attempt on another plane is not exactly the kind of news they'd feed you. What happened?"

The sound, turned very low, was still the exciting news about the bloody cricket, and Aida said, turning it even lower: "Flight 413 was very close to take-off time. There was a passenger named Marie-France Pages, a young Frenchwoman, twenty-eight years old and not very bright, it seems. At the very last moment, a taxi driver hurried in with her carry-on, which she'd left behind, and she was about to board with it."

She broke off, and then: "Wait, here it is now."

Aida slid the sound over, and listened carefully for a moment. She turned the sound up a little more and moved away, and said, a little absently, "I'm forgetting my manners, aren't I? Will you have champagne?"

"The mood I'm in now," Ian Quayle said tightly, "anything, anything at all."

"Ah! Then in that case..."

She turned to the servant. "Cognac, Suleiman."

"*Hadr, ya sitt...*"

He poured a Delamain cognac, the one with the smoky flavor, into two marvelously thin tulip glasses as Aida watched the set and listened to the fine classical Arabic of the BBC Overseas Service, which only the most highly-educated Arabs understood, not many of them around these days...

She switched off at last and sipped her drink, and she said thoughtfully: "Interesting. I wish I knew where they get their information, but I told you that already, didn't I? It seems that Marie-France Pages is in protective custody, and saying nothing at all. But the Egyptian police, who are not entirely fools, believe her story."

"Which is...?"

"That she simply did not know that her carry-on had been tampered with. She just did not know she was carrying a bomb. They believe her. God alone knows why, it makes no sense at all."

Ian Quayle shook his head, vehemently. "No," he said, his research mind dropping the pieces into place. "A year or two ago there was a case like this. An Irish girl who had an Arab boyfriend, he gave her a bomb to smuggle aboard an El Al plane. It happened once, it can happen again."

Aida stared. "But she too would have been killed...!"

"Yes, of course. And isn't that a nice way to get rid of a lover you're tired of, and make a political statement at the same time? We're not dealing with nice people here, we're dealing with savages, Aida. And is this the Swords of God again, or not?"

Aida went to the bed and put her beautiful tulip glass down on the bedside table. She lay down on her back and arranged the bathrobe just so, and she stared up at her reflection in the mirrored glass over her head.

"So far," she said, "no one has claimed credit, and Marie-France is keeping silent. All we know is that she had twelve ounces of an American Army explosive known as C-4 in her bag, which had been sprayed with some chemical or other to disguise whatever smell it has. The Egyptian security at the prodding of America, is getting to be a little more sophisticated now. They have these dogs at the airport.

"Wait, wait, *wait*," Ian Quayle said urgently. "Sprayed with what?"

Aida, confounded, shook her head, "I don't know. Aluminum something-or-other, they said."

"Aluminum hydrochloride?"

"Maybe. Yes, I think so, something like that. Does it matter?"

"It matters one hell of a lot," Ian said; "it's what Abu Jildi's man used when he tried to blow up my cassette recorder, me with it. Who was on that plane?"

Aida stared at him. "Who? Something like a hundred and fifty passengers bound for Rome."

"And one of them's important to us. Can you find out?"

"Just tell me a name," Aida said and Ian Quayle answered at once: "Not a name, a profession. If there was someone on board that plane who's even only fairly high up in the world of Intelligence... If there was, Aida maybe the whole bloody thing's opening up for us."

He told her at length of his favorite theory—that Abu Jildi had declared his own personal war on the Intelligence Establishment, and she listened to him in careful silence.

When he had finished, she picked up the phone and dialed. The phones in Egypt weren't the best in the world, and it took her more than half an hour to reach her party.

Suleiman the servant came then and just automatically refilled his glass with the wonderfully smooth Delamain cognac, and he waited in patience.

And then, at last, Aida was in deep and earnest conversation in Arabic, a conversation that seemed to go on forever. Her grave eyes flickered to Quayle once in a while, and when the arguing was over she put down the phone and looked at him with a strange kind of admiration.

"Did I almost suggest you were a fool, Mr. Quayle?" she asked. "If so, it was a mistake. You have the natural instincts of a first class Field Officer..."

"I'm not a Field Officer!" Ian Quayle said furiously. "I do research in London, and that's *all* do!"

"The right instincts," Aida said, insisting. "One of the passengers of Flight 413 was Gerhardt Grolmann. He was dressed in drag, for God's sake, and calling himself Elsie Braun, just to make sure no one knew who he really was. With a

Panamanian passport! You know who he is?"

Ian Quayle nodded, and he said tightly: "Yes. Yes, I know who Gerhardt Grolmann is. He's not only the West's brightest Intelligence Officer. He's also the most dangerous."

CHAPTER 11

Gerhardt Wilhelm Klaus Grolmann, Number Three man in West Germany's GSG-9, was probably, from the terrorist point of view, the most feared Intelligence Executive in the whole of Western Europe.

It was he who, calling himself by the simpler name and title of Hans Mannheim, Ambassador-at-Large Pro Tem, had addressed a lethargic (but still suspicious) meeting of the United Nations at which important nations like Libya, Yemen, Zambia, Mozambique, and Upper Volta had shouted him down when he had proclaimed, in a speech that would go down in history: "Half the so-called Third World, a euphemism for countries whose Dictators never even heard of Berlin—let alone know it's importance in global affairs today, or even where it is—half of that Third World supports international terrorism merely because, in their half-baked philosophies, anything that is fought against by the civilized western world—yes, I say again, the *civilized* western world, is anathema to them! It's time we stopped paying our subsidies to nations that scorn us! Where is our dignity? What happened to it? Why do we keep pumping money, without which they'd all die of their own lethargy and foolishness, to Governments that seize on every opportunity to spit in our faces? Has common sense left the dream world of the United Nations altogether? I suspect that it has..."

Gerhardt Grolmann wasn't much liked for his speech; at the very least it suggested that he knew rather too much than was good for worldwide terrorism, and there were people gunning for him now.

"I never met him personally," Ian Quayle said, "but I know more about him that his wife does. That isn't saying very much, incidentally, she's a cow, both physically and intellectually. Has it ever occurred to you that you can look at a woman's face—or a man's—and instantly come up with what is often a very accurate assessment of his or her psychological characteristics?"

"What you are saying," Aida said without any venom at all, "is that fools look like fools?"

"Er...yes, I suppose that's true. But Grolmann's official title is Director of Research Intelligence to the Grenz-schutzgruppe Neun, commonly called GSG-9. It makes him my equivalent—maybe at a somewhat higher level—in the German anti-terrorist forces, one hell of a trophy if they could get him. A very logical target for Abu Jildo. Did he make it?"

"Yes," Aida said, "he made it. After a two-hour delay, Flight 413 took off. Grolmann is on his way to try and change the Italian philosophy about Arab-sponsored terrorism. Lots of luck..."

And then, the phone rang again. There were two phones in the room, in a country where it took a three-year wait and something like three thousand bucks slipped into the right palms to get just one.

This one was the red phone, discreetly hidden, and Aida was there at once, leaping off the bed like a Doberman that heard a distant footstep in the dark...

She slipped back the little sliding, door and took out the receiver and said into it; "*Mishmish*, apricots," an identification.

And then she listened, not saying a word, and once again those dark and lustrous eyes glanced at Quayle once in a while.

For a long time she listened, and the scowl was darkening all the while.

She said at last, "*Ana fahim*, I understand..."

She put down the receiver, and carefully did back the concealing little door, and she looked at Ian Quayle and said softly, "That was my informant in the Police Department again. They just found the body of Marie-France Pages, a suicide in her prison cell. She hanged herself."

Ian Quayle stared. "She did what?"

"She hanged herself," Aida said, "on strips of cloth torn from her mattress."

There was a long, long silence, and Ian said at last, very quietly and wondering if he were perhaps forcing a point, "Is it my imagination, or is hanging a very strange way for a *woman* to kill herself."

There was a certain hesitancy...

Did women poison themselves and leave the hanging to the men? It made no sense at all.

Trying to cover, he mumbled: "The aesthetics of that broken, elongated neck... Am I being stupid? Perhaps I am..."

Somehow to his surprise, Aida shook her head. "No, that's not stupid, it's a very good point. But are you suggesting she was murdered?"

"Is it possible? Is it even probable?"

Aida went back in silence to the bed again, and stretched out her body, a jaguar in repose. She began massaging her forehead with her fingertips, and she said, "Yes, it's possible. Somebody gave her a carry-on that had been packed with plastic explosives, a tiny detonator that wouldn't show up on any scope. But she still wouldn't say who tampered with it, absolute silence. But when the realization really hit her that someone was trying to destroy a plane and kill her off at the same time—how long would that resolution have held out? How long before she'd be ready to tell everything she knew? Turn on the fan for me, will you?"

The Cairo night was excessively hot, but there was one of those Indian fans in the bedroom's ceiling. Quayle pulled the cord and set it rotating, and watched Aida as she loosened her bathrobe about her body.

He sat on the edge of the bed beside her and said, "Tell me about Marie-France Pages. Did you know her?"

Aida shook her head. "I never met her, but I know all about her. Ask questions."

"Age?"

"Late twenties."

"Looking like what?"

"Looking like a million dollars. Very blonde, long straw-colored hair, pale blue eyes: A size six going on eight. A little too plump, but that's the way the Egyptians like their women."

"Ah...then she had an Egyptian boyfriend?"

"One after the other, mostly nonentities, trash people. But lately, she seemed to have settled down a little. With someone who was looking after her very nicely indeed, thank you. She'd always drive a Volkswagen, but recently she was seen driving a red Ferrari convertible around town, you know what a car like that costs in Egypt?"

"Great," Quayle said, "it's almost all I want to know about her! Who was her new boyfriend? Someone I can find, and talk to?"

Aida sighed. "No, no one knows, it was all very secret."

"Other friends," Quayle said, insisting. "Anybody who was close to her. She must have held down a job, for example. Co-workers?"

"This yes," Aida said instantly. "She was a ticket clerk at Air France. She had a small house in Maadi, down the river, which she shared with a friend."

"And can you give me her name?"

"*His* name," Aida said. "Steven Madian, who was her

immediate superior."

"Two boyfriends at the same time?"

"Off with the old, on with the new," Aida said drily.

"Ah, like that."

"Yes, like that. Does it disturb you? Are you the sexless English prude we are all taught to laugh at?"

"Probably not," Ian said mildly; "but I was wondering about the name. *Madian?* Is he an Arab?"

Aida shook her head. "No, he's French." She hesitated, frowning. "But come to think of it, Madian might also suggest an Iranian background somewhere in his ancestry. I don't speak Farsi, but I do know that there are several towns in Iran called Madian This, Madian That... I've never thought about it too much."

"He speaks. Arabic?"

"Of course, like a native."

"English?"

"In his job, he'd have to."

"How well?"

"I have no idea. I've never spoken to him, never even met him." She shrugged eloquently. "And even if we were to meet, we'd both naturally speak French. The language of the upper classes here."

But something was worrying Ian Quayle, and he couldn't quite figure what it was; an improbability there somewhere, something he couldn't immediately put his finger on.

He thought about it for a long time, and suddenly found himself wishing he had Wendy here to discuss this with; but she was far, far away, and there was only Aida.

But Aida was a woman who listened well, and responded even better, sparking ideas of the kind that couldn't easily come from one mind alone, and he said at last: "The precedent—that Irish girl and her Arab boyfriend, it's sticking in my mind, and maybe I shouldn't allow it to."

Her eyes were on him, probing, and he went on impatiently, feeling a little awkward under her stare: "In that case, what did we have? We had an Arab terrorist who wanted to destroy a plane and get rid of a mistress at the same time. Okay, do we have the same thing here?"

Aida said promptly: "I've never thought of Abu Jildi as— what do you call it?—a copycat killer. The psychology's wrong."

"Maybe."

As he thought about this some more, he found to his surprise that he had taken hold of Aida's hand, and was holding onto it quite strongly. He released it at once with a feeling of guilt, and he said, "Steven Madian...has he ever been married? Does he have any kids?"

Gossip was Cairo's life's blood, and Aida laughed softly. "I have heard it mentioned," she said, "that he has a whole brood of children in Paris. Whether he was ever actually married or not—that's an entirely different matter. And it may not be true, it's just one of the things women talk about at cocktail parties."

"But we can assume that he was indeed Marie-France's lover, not just a roommate."

Aida shrugged. "I'm sure we can. She was a very attractive woman, if you like that type, and he's always believed that he's God's gift to every woman in town. Yes, he must have been her lover."

"Good. So where can I find him?"

"In his office, where else?" Aida said. She looked at the solid gold Cartier watch on her wrist and said, "Five o'clock in the morning, and his office opens at nine. We have four hours before you can proceed any further. What shall we do? For myself...I will sleep now. If you wish to sleep beside me? It can take away the pain, Ian."

He swiveled himself around and propped himself up on one elbow to stare down at her, a bronze goddess. One breast was half-exposed, and he pushed the robe aside gently with his fingertips and caressed her, then cupped the cappuccino ivory, firm and yet soft, cool to his touch yet sending a current of fire through him. He leaned down and kissed it, lingering with his tongue on the tiny nipple, hard as a diamond now.

"Nothing I can do," he whispered. "Surely the most desirable woman I ever set eyes on, and for the moment at least—I'm impotent."

"Your daughter Pia?" Her voice was a zephyr.

"Yes, Pia, my daughter. Can you... can you try to understand?"

"I understand perfectly."

"It doesn't make sense, does it?"

"It makes all the sense in the world! So sleep. Take off your clothes and sleep beside me. I will be there if you need me, and if not...so be it."

It was hard to find the words. "For something like, I don't know, thirty hours seem like an eternity, I've had to force all thought of Pia's sufferings away from me, encased in carbon steel at the back of my mind, to be used only when the time comes, to be used only when I have to kill... Meanwhile, I'm... I'm *crushing* all my thought into a different mold, I have to be cold, and callous, and skillful, and determined—I can't afford passion now! And it's not easy, I don't know how long it'll be before...before I bloody explode!"

"So sleep," Aida said. "Have you slept since you received that letter?"

"No."

"Then try it. Ideas come in sleep, and sometimes... sometimes solace too. Come, sleep beside me. I'll wake you when the time comes, one way or another."

After a little hesitation, Ian Quayle peeled down to bare skin, folding his clothes neatly and setting them down on the chair before, feeling a little foolish at first, stretching out beside her.

There was a certain comfort in the thickness of the terry cloth that separated them in parts, more comfort still in the touch of that firm, up-pointed breast under his palm.

He awoke in the night, hard as an iron rod, and tried to force himself to sleep again. And he slept indeed, but in subconscious worry that kept the pleasure of sleep away...

He dreamed erotic dreams that made no sense at all until, in a half-awake moment, he realized that the wall of Jericho that was the fragile terry cloth between them was no longer there, maybe swept aside and out of the way in someone or other's heat.

And when the gentle tap on his wrist awoke him at the first sign of the dawn, he could not be sure whether he had taken her this night, or not.

"*Kahwe, ya Effendi,*" Suleiman the servant said, "Coffee. And will you have cardamom seed?"

Rubbing the sleep from his eyes, Ian Quayle muttered, "Cardamom? Well, er, yes please."

Suleiman took one of the seeds, to be crushed with the teeth, and dropped it into his tiny china cup."

"*Sucre, ya Effendi?*"

"No, no sugar, thank you."

The eunuch smiled. "Ah, *sadr* then, sour. The way good coffee was meant to be taken."

He poured from the narrow spouted *jezveh* into a glazed cup no bigger than half an eggshell; and beside Ian Quayle, the lovely Aida was stirring.

"Ah," she murmured, "the scent of coffee to awake to! What did mankind do before he discovered coffee?"

She was instantly wide awake: "And this morning, you have to see Steven Madian at Air France. Shall I call him for you? An introduction?"

Ian Quayle shook his head. "No, I'd rather go in cold."

"Before he has time to prepare his answers?"

"Something like that."

"Yes, it's always better. Will you come back here afterwards?"

"I would like to. But I was brought here blindfold, I don't know where the hell we are..."

"When you were brought here, you were a stranger, you could have been an enemy. No more. The address is 162 Butto Street, in Heliopolis. Would you like one of my drivers to take you where you have to go? Yes, I think it would be better. These days, we can never know who the enemy is."

"Well...if you say so..."

"What will you have for breakfast? I don't have kippers, I'm afraid, but I do have ham and eggs. Or croissant with butter and marmalade."

"Did you say ham?"

There was a thin smile, and then: "I am a Christian Arab, Mr. Quayle, not a Muslim, nor a Jew, which means that I have none of those foolish dietary restrictions: I believe in Christ the Father, the Son, and Holy Ghost—and ham and eggs for breakfast is a taste I acquired in London."

"Ah...then in that case?"

Suleiman was called in, and somewhere in the depths of the vast apartment a kitchen began functioning. Nameless servants were there, four or five of them, who never ever left the hallowed quarters that were centered on a wood-burning stove that ran the whole length of a twenty-foot wall. Made of cast iron, the whole surface of the stove was polished every morning at five o'clock with old-fashioned stove-black, stiff and soft brushes, and finally with a cloth, till you could look into its surface and practically see your own reflection.

They had breakfast together, and Aida watched in astonishment as Ian Quayle went surgically to work on his twin eggs; with the point of his knife, he divested the yolks of first one and then the other till he had eaten every miniscule portion of the whites, leaving the two yellow yolks there in the center of the white porcelain plate (the ham already eaten now too, just to get it out of the way...) and then stared down at their naked beauty, and murmured: "Perfect..."

He found a minute portion of white adhering to one of the yolks, and clicked his tongue in impatience, and severed it...

Aida stared as he slipped his fork very carefully under the first of the yolks and lifted it up to his mouth and dropped it with infinite care onto his tongue. He held it there for a moment; and then there was a look of absolute ecstasy on his face as he crushed it against the roof of his mouth...

He saw Aida shaking her head, and he looked down at the second pristine and naked yoke, and knew that there was a certain sacrifice to be made here...

He hated it, hated giving up the results of such patient, surgical care.

But Ian Quayle was, above all else, a gentleman, and for a gentleman of the old school, no sacrifice was too great.

He slid his fork carefully under the second yolk, and held it out to an astonished Aida. "Try it," he said earnestly, "try it just once, and that's the only way you'll ever eat a fried egg again."

Slowly, Aida opened her mouth, and he gently slid the egg in. "Hold it there for a moment," he said, a teacher to a pupil, "and then—press your tongue to the roof of your mouth to break it. Feel it leaking down your gullet when it bursts."

Aida did as she was told, and the smile on her face was all the reward he needed.

An hour and a half later, he was hammering on the glass doors of the Air France office, one minute after opening time.

"I wish to see M'sieur Steven Madian, *s'il vous plait*," he said to the dragoman. "My name is Alain Rogers."

CHAPTER 12

The Air France office was an airline office and nothing more, just a half-dozen rooms filled with male and female clerks busy at the things they best knew how to do.

There were posters everywhere depicting the French culture—picture-postcard shots of the Eiffel Tower and the Champs Elysees, sunsets over Bora-Bora and all the other tourist lures interspersed with quite excellent reproductions of Chagal, Picasso, Seurat, and the ubiquitous Paul Gauguin.

And Stephen Madian was something else again...

He was a giant of a man, tall and muscular and ferociously bearded, a ferocity that reflected his temper. There was something in those dark and brooding eyes that indicated impatience.

And with what?

With fools? With people who only wanted to waste his time?

But he was a handsome brute, with a wide and high forehead that maybe suggested an equally high intelligence, with a strong jaw that must have driven all the women crazy, with an air about him that said one word...*strength*.

But now, the professional at work, he was all smiles. Ian Quayle thought the smile was just a little forced.

"*M'sieur Rogers*," he said affably. "How can I help you?"

142

"Well," Ian Quayle said, "first of all I should tell you that I am here not for your benefit, but for mine. I came hereby Air France, I'll take Air France back to London, where I belong, so yes, I'm a customer. But I am also a journalist, M'sieur Madian. I'm a freelance, and an associate of Paul Diderot of *Le Monde*. I imagine you know him, is that true?"

There was already a guarded look on Madian's handsome face.

"Paul Diderot? Yes, I have had certain dealings with him. A man of the utmost integrity. A quality I have found to be very rare in journalists."

Ian Quayle ignored it. "I'm sure you can guess why I'm here."

There was a little moment of thought, and then: "Yes, I think so..."

Steven Madian leaned back in his chair and stared at his interrogator, and he said slowly, not trying to hide his distaste, "You are about to ask me *why* my friend Marie-France committed suicide. Yes, I heard about it already, through channels that need not concern you. And my answer is...I do not know why."

"No," Ian Quayle said, "that was not to be my question. My question was why was she *murdered*? No. I already know the answer to that. So let the question be: *who* murdered her?"

"Murdered?"

That strong bass voice had become a whisper: "*Murdered*, you say? You're mad...!"

"I'm the sanest man you ever met in your life, so listen to me! *Someone* smuggled a carry-on packed with explosives to her moments before she boarded that plane..."

"A taxi driver!"

"Yes! But who give it to the taxi driver rather than deliver it himself? Someone who packed it with skillfully deodorized C-4 plastique. *That* is what I want to know."

But Steven Madian was still staring out into space, and shaking his head. "No," he whispered, "I will not believe that she was murdered."

"Then will you believe that she committed suicide? By hanging herself?"

"No. I cannot believe that cither."

Ian Quayle stared. "Are you telling me that you think she's still alive?"

Madian had buried his head in his hands, and he looked up now; Quayle was astonished to see that there were tears rolling down his cheeks.

"I don't *know*!" he said in desperation. "All I know is that the report of her death came to me from a police informant whom I have always regarded as reliable. But now...there are matters here, *M'sieur Rogers*, of politics at the ministerial level."

He pressed a button on the desk and said briefly into the speaker phone: "No calls, no interruptions," and then leaned back in his chair, only a trifle more relaxed, and said quietly, "When I received word of her death, reported to me as a suicide, yes, I will confess that I wondered for a moment if it might have been murder. But only for a moment. Because I very quickly realized that yes, she had reason to kill herself. And that I was responsible."

"I have to know what it was that prompted you to decide that," Ian Quayle said at once, and now Steven Madian was not in a mood to hold anything back, anything at all.

"Because I had...broken off with her," he said, not even aware of the arrogance. "We had lived together for more than two years, and there was a time when I think that I truly loved her. But lately, she was becoming cooler and cooler toward me as the time went by, even though I was still servicing her better than ever before."

That awful arrogance again: "I must tell you in all modesty, Mr. Rogers, that I know what it is that women want more than anything else in the world. And that I am very, very good at giving it to them. Never, since I was an immature youth of seventeen, have I slept with a woman who did not, during the night together, enjoy more orgasms than I did myself. It has become almost a matter of pride with me. And yet...here was this stupid woman..."

"Marie-France?" Ian asked politely, and Madian nodded. "Yes, Marie-France! I had always treated her like a Goddess! And then I found out that she was sleeping around with some damned cop, a *flic*, and coming home to my house in Maadi and saying she was too tired to make love! Until..."

Steven Madian was on his feet now, looking for someone to knock to the ground.

"Until," he said, "one day I found her VW parked on the street outside the house, and in the garage there was a brand new Ferrari..."

Echoing Aida's own comment he said wrathfully, "You know what a car like that costs in Egypt?"

He went on. "I asked her whose it was, and she told me it was hers, she'd bought it with all her accumulated savings. Balls! Even though she wasn't paying anything at all to the costs of running a very nice little house, I even had to buy the groceries, she could never have saved that kind of money in a lifetime!"

He was getting mightily agitated now as Ian Quayle sat still and listened, something he was expert at, and he was waving his arms around in a fine display of Middle Eastern volatility.

"But even so," he shouted, "I still let her live with me, in the full knowledge that sooner or later she'd realize how well off she was with me! And give up this damned new lover she'd found!"

He quietened down a little, and said with a certain calm, "Undignified? Yes, of course, I know it. There was my woman screwing around with another man, and still I didn't throw her out like a discarded sandal as you might have expected, or even beat her. But that's the kind of man I am, *M'sieur Rogers,* tolerant and forgiving. I like to think of myself as one of nature's gentlemen."

"Yes of course," Ian Quayle said. "Just kindly tell me the name of the man who took your girl away from you."

Steven Madian shrugged. "How the hell should I know? He was a cop, that's all I know. That's all I want to know! Now that she's dead... He can have her."

Ian Quayle rose to his feet, he'd had enough. But...

"To set your mind at rest," he said, "she didn't kill herself for love of you, someone murdered her before she could change her mind, when all the pieces settled into place, and blow the whistle on whoever it was tried to blow-up a plane with two hundred people on board just to get rid of...of *her*, and perhaps another enemy too. And for a while, I thought that just might have been you, M'sieur Madian. But our little chat has changed my mind for me. But even so..."

He was at the door, opening it and turning back.

"Even so," he said, "I swear to God I'm going to find out who killed her. It's just the first step in something far more pressing."

"And when you do," Steven Madian said urgently, "you'll let me know, won't you? Won't you?"

"Perhaps," Ian Quayle said cruelly, "Perhaps. I'll think about it."

He was over the threshold, the door half-open, and all the girls in the outer office had looked up from their work.

Ian Quayle said deliberately, "You really are a shit, M'sieur Madian, aren't you? Not only an arsehole, but a *shit* as well. Good day."

He was gone.

The chauffeur took him back to Aida's apartment, a

taciturn sort of man who was happiest when he had nothing to say.

There was a security guard there, but the chauffeur passed through him with little more than a grunt, and he walked up the stairs to the apartment which had become his temporary home.

He pushed the button on the hideous plastic door, and there was Suleiman to welcome him, with even perhaps a sly smile on his world-weary face...

"*Nurak sa'id*, may your day be peaceful," Suleiman said. "And you have a visitor, *Effendi*. A lady from London."

"Oh God."

He threw up his arms in despair, and muttered: "Oh well, it had to come sooner or later. And I think you for warning me, Suleiman, you're a good kid, you ever stop to think about that?"

"Within the restrictions of my duties, *Effendi*, I like to be as helpful as possible."

"And you do it marvelously well... Don't tell me her bloody name; it's Wendy Hayworth, isn't it? And I'm in dire trouble, Suleiman. The direst trouble."

"If you say so, sir..."

Suleiman just wasn't going to get himself involved, and he held out an arm. "This way, sir, please."

"I know where the bloody living room is," Ian Quayle said, and strode to the door there.

And when he flung it open, all his worst fears were realized...

There was Wendy Hayworth, his Case Officer and his sometime mistress, the woman who—at the urging of her boss in London, Mrs. Bloody French, held him back or urged him on as circumstances required...

Many years ago, when Ian Quayle had been quietly moved from Grade Six to Grade Five, Mrs. Bloody French had called in a very junior Case Officer named Wendy Hayworth and had said to her: "A man named Ian Quayle, Miss Hayworth, who does research for us. I want you to monitor him for me."

There was probably no one in the office who hated Mrs. French as much as Wendy did—except, perhaps, Ian Quayle himself. But the boss man, Robin Harris (who didn't care for her very much either), had once described her as "frighteningly competent," and he was right.

"*Monitor* him," Mrs. French had said. "I have a feeling that he's probably good field material, though he'd be the first to deny it, and that's something that's very hard to find these days."

"I'm not quite sure what monitoring means," Wendy had said uncertainly; and then there'd been a blunt and callous talk which made her blood run cold. There was a reference to her own personal file, including names, names of her past lovers—Willie Slocombe-Brent, Lord Horley (right under Lady Horley's nose,) Jerry Heston, and then—an event that Mrs. French dwelt on at length—that disastrous liaison with one Cecile Deschamps, which was an experiment more than anything else that only lasted for a couple of months...

There'd been a twisted sort of smile on Mrs. French's gorgeous face, a smile that turned it into a mask made of polished and undiluted venom: "I'm not trying to turn you into a whore, Miss Hayworth. I'm just trying to make your established lifestyle work for us."

For two weeks she had studied Quayle's personal file, till she knew every damn thing that had happened to him, that he had done, since the day he was born. Thank God, she found that they had an enormous amount in common, and to her astonishment she found that even before their first date—an innocent theater-and-dinner together—she was almost falling in love with a man who, up to this moment, had only been a hundred and thirty-five pages of typescript.

They'd soon become lovers, but only of the most casual sort; though in the course of time the relationship had become much more cemented—lovers half of the time, and the rest of the time hating each other's guts.

It was a very symbiotic sort of relationship, disturbing to him when he thought too deeply about it. But when he'd made the point with Wendy, she'd smiled gently and had said, "Don't knock symbiosis, lover. There's nothing like rhythmic contradictions to put a little spice into what would otherwise be a rather irksome sodality."

She liked to talk like this once in a while, just to annoy him.

Ian Quayle was quite prepared for one of their fights now, though you never knew with Wendy. She tended to work by the book, and she had no time at all for even the slightest departure from the rules. He, on the other hand, thought that rules and regulations were formulated only to confine a spirit that wanted to be free.

And one of those rules was—you just didn't go traipsing off to a place that was off limits, like Cairo, without as much as a word at least to your own Case Officer, Quayle knew the trouble he must be in at the office, not with the hated Mrs. Bloody French, but also with Robin Harris, a man he greatly admired.

And so...he was ready for an explosion.

It never came.

Instead, Wendy ran to him as soon as he opened the door, and threw her arms around his neck, hugging him like a long-lost child.

"You poor darling," she whispered emotionally, and there were tears in her eyes, with no attempt to suppress them at all.

He returned her embrace, and saw over her shoulder that Aida—thank God!—was no longer wearing the robe she seemed to prefer for lounging around, a robe that was always open clear down to the navel, with glimpses of the pubic triangle whenever she moved; he wondered why this seemed so important to him, but he dismissed the thought at once.

"Wendy..."

"Are you all right?" She held him at arm's length. "My God, you look as though you haven't slept since I last saw you. And it's been, what, a week?"

"Just two days since I left home..."

"And have you made any progress?"

Ian Quayle said glumly: "I've just come from a man I thought might well be Abu Jildi. But he's not."

"I wasn't thinking of Abu Jildi."

"Pia?"

"Pia."

Quayle found himself shuddering. It was only two days since that dreadful letter had arrived, yet it seemed like a lifetime.

He said tightly: "There is nothing in the world more important to me than Pia. But I know one thing with absolute certainty, and that is—I can never find my daughter till I find the man who is holding her prisoner. You think I haven't worried myself half to death about this? But the only key there is...is Abu Jildi himself. When I find him—I will have found Pia. And that's when the trials and all the anguish will begin."

Wendy nodded. "I know it. I just...just wasn't sure that you were strong enough." She sounded confused. "No, that's not true, I know how strong you can be sometimes. But this... I know how terrifying it is. Terrifying! Have you heard about the ransom yet?"

He was startled. "*Ransom...!*"

Aida held up a slip of paper and said: "From Mr. Harris, it arrived an hour ago," and Wendy said: "Robin's own idea. He wasn't at all convinced that it would do any good, but...he's as concerned as you and I are, Ian."

Ian Quayle took the paper from the Egyptian girl and read

it slowly. It was the LMT code, with the quadrations all there for him to see, and the decoded message scrawled across the bottom:

DIRECTOR TO OPERATIVE 405 URGENT AND EYES ONLY STOP USE ALL EFFORT TO PASS WORD THAT HER MAJESTY'S GOVERNMENT IS PREPARED INSTANTLY TO PAY ONE HUNDRED THOUSAND POUNDS REPEAT POUNDS ONE HUNDRED THOUSAND FOR SAFE RETURN OF PIA MANCINI STOP NORMAL CHANNELS STOP PAYMENT TO BE MADE ON LONDON AUTHORISATION THROUGH YOUR OFFICES BY WHATEVER MEANS ACCEPTABLE TO OTHER PARTY MESSAGE ENDS.

"Robin's own idea," Wendy said again, "GA's raising hell about it on grounds of principle more than anything else, but Robin says if they won't put up the money, then he'll damn well find it elsewhere."

"And you and I both know that Robin's not a rich man..."

"And it will never become necessary," Aida said quietly. "Abu Jildi can get more than that for her on the slave market."

She reached out and touched Ian's hand, aware of her own harshness. Wendy saw, and turned away, but it was only a very brief instant of what might have been hostility.

She said heavily, "Aida is right," and Ian said bitterly: "A *million* wouldn't have been enough. Sure, he needs money, but in this case, it's me he needs. Not money, not my daughter. *Me.*"

"And thank God you're aware of that," Wendy said. "What we have to make sure of now is that you never get to meet with him, face to face, as he wants. Because if you do..."

"We're wasting time," Ian Quayle said roughly, and turned to Aida: "We may just be on the last leg of the journey. How many Ferrari dealers are there in town, do you know?"

"Two," Aida said at once.

"Do you know them?"

"Do I have to? Tell me what you want to know."

Ian Quayle sighed. "Marie-France's new car," he said, "was given to her by a cop. '*Un flic*,' her other boyfriend said, speaking French, and what the hell is a '*flick*'? It's a cop, that's all it is! But no damn copper on the beat is going to lay his hands on that kind of money quite so easily, to my mind it presupposes a fairly senior cop, someone who's got maybe a Swiss bank account or whatever. Okay. What I want to know is...who paid for it. Can you find out for me?"

"Of course, it's very easy..."

"*Not* through your police contacts, he may have covered his tracks."

"Ah... Very well, it can still be done, it will just take a little longer."

"How long?"

"Two days?" Aida asked, and Ian Quayle shook his head. He looked at his watch and said, "Nearly midday. I want to know by this evening at the latest."

"Then I must go to work on it myself, and at once."

"If not before."

"Very well."

She turned to Wendy, a phony little smile on her face. "As I told you, Ii do have a spare bedroom here, where Ian slept last night... Am I right in thinking that perhaps you are accustomed to sharing sleeping quarters?"

"Yes," Wendy said deliberately. "We are."

"Good. Then you will, of course, stay here. You'll not only be more comfortable than in a hotel, you'll be safer too. There are two guards here, one on the building, one for my apartment. They are both armed, they are both ex-police officers, and I pay them both handsomely. No one will disturb you, believe me."

"You're very kind," Wendy said sweetly, "and I accept

152

very gratefully."

There was a certain tension between the two women, and Ian was well aware of it; but he thrust it all to the back of his mind as not being of the slightest importance; there were far more momentous problems now.

"And I will go now," Aida said, "to talk with people who sell forty-thousand-dollar cars. If you need anything...Suleiman is the head servant. Anything at all that you might need."

She was gone. "Okay," Wendy said, "Who's this Marie-France? Another one of your paramours? Like Aida? You don't like to waste time, do you?"

"Two points." Ian Quayle said testily. "First of all, I'm not into necrophilia, and Marie-France, for me, is merely the name of a dead woman who may or may not have been murdered, and if so, maybe or maybe not by Abu Jildi. And secondly..."

The cognac was flowing again under Suleiman's competent ministrations, and Ian was getting a little didactic.

"Secondly," he said, "Aida is not a paramour either. For Christ's sake, I've only just met her!"

"And I have this impression that all she really wants is for you to ball the ass off her. If you haven't already done so."

"Oh, for Christ's sake...!"

"Where did you sleep last night? She went to the greatest pains to tell me about the spare bedroom. And as one woman to another, I can surely tell when a whore is lying."

It was getting rough already, and Ian Quayle said testily, "She's not a whore."

"Are you kidding? She goes to bed with every Minister in the Egyptian Government!"

"Which is why she's so valuable to the office!"

It was time for a showdown, and he said nastily: "Didn't Mrs. Bloody French once tell you to go to bed with me? And didn't you leap to obey her?"

"Yes I did!" Wendy said furiously. "The worst mistake I ever made in my life! Okay, I've had lovers before, I won't deny it! And you're just about the worst of them, Ian Quayle!"

"I am, am I? Worse than your bloody Lord What's-his-Name? Lord bloody Horley? Christ, he had to be bloody senile!"

"Lord Horley," Wendy said with great dignity, "was a *gentleman*, something you can never aspire to! And what's more, in spite of his age, he was damn good in bed!"

"Gerondophilia," Ian Quayle said sarcastically "Great, just great! How did he manage? Lashing it up with a toothbrush? Terrific! And what about that bloody Frenchwoman you were shacking up with? What was her bloody name, Cecile Deschamps? Don't think I haven't read your file, Mrs. French gave it to me, so's I'd know what kind of a case officer I was getting."

Wendy was in shock, and in tears too. "She...she gave you my file? Oh God! She's not supposed to do that...!"

"And there's a phrase there I just love."

Ian Quayle was going great now, quite carried away with stuff he knew he was going to regret sooner or later, and he said angrily, "One hell of a phrase. Among all kinds of crap, it said you were a '*latent lesbian*.' I love that word '*latent*,' you know what it means? It means existing but not manifest or developed, isn't that nice? Does it mean that when I sleep with you, I have to worry because you'd be happier if I were a woman?"

"You shit, you absolute shit!"

She struck out at him furiously, with all the considerable strength she had. "Why do you have to be such a goddam prude? Cecile Deschamps was *an experiment*, I was just trying it for size, learn a little something every day. And I didn't like it, so I stopped it, okay? And are your own morals so goddam impeccable? Evangelist-style, is that it?"

The blow had caught him square across the face, his reaction not as fast as it should have been, and stepping back he'd tripped over his own bloody feet and was lying there on the ground like an idiot, staring up at Wendy and wondering what she was so uptight about.

"Christ," he said, "am I supposed to say now: Thanks, I needed that? Jesus, that's one hell of a right hook you have there."

Wendy was already crouched down beside him and hugging his head to her breast.

"Jesus is right," she said. "You goddam stinker, why do you always make me so mad? Why do we always have to *fight*? You know I love you, you know you love me, so how come we're always at each other's throat, can you tell me that? Like goddam tigers!"

"Don't ask me questions I can't answer," Ian said, "it's an affront to my personal dignity..."

But he was in a good mood now, buoyed up by his first real lead to the man he so desperately wanted to find.

"I have to consider myself lucky," he said to Wendy. "Back there in Paris, when I saw Inspector Pleyer at Claudine's flat, I was convinced that Robin Harris had sent him to get me, to pick me off back to England right away."

"It wasn't luck," Wendy said. "It was Mrs. Bloody French."

He frowned. "How's that again?"

"When you disappeared from the cottage, and we'd tapped into your phone call to Claudine, she guessed where you were headed—to Cairo via Paris. Mrs. French called Pleyer and told him to do what he could to speed you on your way."

"What? I don't believe it! I'd been expressly ordered, by Robin himself, not to go anywhere near Egypt! She knew that!"

"Of course she did. And when I left, Robin had found out and was just about wiping the floor with her. He was threatening to fire her, she was threatening to resign, I have to tell you—there's merry hell to pay back at the office now. That bitch *wanted* you here, Ian. The only place, she figured, where you could work effectively."

And then, almost as if on cue, there was a discreet knock on the door, and Suleiman was there. If it surprised him to see the two of them on the floor in each other's arms, he gave no sign of it at all.

Instead, he murmured, in that deep, melodious voice, "It is two o'clock, Mr. Quayle. If you wish to take a siesta—the spare room is ready. Mad'moiselle Aida has asked me to wake you at six, by which time she will be back. I will have coffee ready for you."

"Thank you, Suleiman," Ian Quayle said, mustering what dignity he could and clambering to his feet. He was suddenly aware that he'd left Wendy lying there, and he put out a hand to help her.

"Thank you," she said, and he led her to the spare bedroom, where the mosquito-net was draped over the wide four poster bed.

With nothing more to be said, they took off their clothes and lay naked together on the bed, the big fan in the ceiling turning slowly to drive away the afternoon's heat.

He played with those splendid breasts for a while, breasts that were firm and upstanding as demi grapefruit and ten times as soft. He ran his fingertips delicately over her thighs, thighs that Solomon would have written songs about, fingering with the infinitely light touch of a pheasant's feather.

But after a long, long time, he whispered miserably: "There's nothing I can do, my love. Please try and understand. This is not the time."

Writhing, and wanting him so very badly, Wendy said quietly: "I understand, I *do*... Sleep now, Ian, it's what you need now. You do know that you look like hell, don't you? So sleep There's nothing we can do now till your Aida returns."

"*Your* Aida?"

It could have been the beginning of a new fight, but Ian Quayle was just too damn dog-tired.

A hand at her breast, a thigh thrown over hers, he was already asleep.

CHAPTER 13

It was almost seven o'clock in the evening when Aida returned; and she was waving a sheaf of papers at them, a glint in het lovely eyes that was quite evil.

Ian Quayle and Wendy Hayworth were dressed again and sitting in the vast living room as they sipped the Delamain cognac that Suleiman had served them with; the snifters were so tissue paper thin that a sneeze would have blown them to hell and gone.

Not waiting for the servant, Aida poured herself a very large drink, and she said exuberantly, "I think we struck gold, pure, twenty-four carat gold! But all my training has taught me to chase clues down into the warrens they came from before jumping to conclusions. They have to be examined from half-a-dozen points of view and evaluated, they have to be..."

"Shut up, Aida," Ian said irritably. "Okay, you made your point, we're all hanging on your words."

She threw him the kind of look that could only be called adoring, and she said, more quietly now, "First of all, Marie-France's' Ferrari was sold by Abdulla Peton et Fils, and the *fils*, the son, was apparently once one of my lovers, I'd quite forgotten. So it was ridiculously easy. The car was paid for in cash, forty-two thousand pounds, and promptly registered in her name."

"And the buyer?" Quayle asked urgently. "A cop?"

"A cop? *Un flic*? Not quite the right word."

A dramatic artist, of a sort, at heart, she knew about timing, and she waited just long enough to take a sip of her drink and to savor it. And then she said, quite sure that it was a bombshell: "He was Colonel Hassan Mifari el Afoun. You know who he is?"

Quayle shook his head, and the lovely Aida went on: "Colonel Mifari is head of the Security Police here. Not only that, he serves as Personal Advisor to the Minister of the Interior, and in that capacity sits in on most Cabinet meetings. Which makes him a man of enormous power."

"Wait," Ian said with a frown. "He's a Cabinet Minister...?"

"I didn't say that," Aida said at once, but Quayle ignored her protest and went on, "A man in a position of high authority..."

"That's correct..."

"...in a Government that has gone on record as willing to fight international terrorism wherever it shows its face?"

Aida nodded. "That is correct too."

"Then it would account for one thing, at least. It would account for his mania for secrecy."

"Correct again, though it's not enough. But I have more, much more."

"A profile? That's what we need now."

"A very detailed profile," Aida said. "I've filled it in with my own observations."

Wendy stared at her. "Does that mean what I suspect it means?"

Aida was very cool. "There have been occasions in the past," she said drily, "when Colonel Mifari and I have exchanged confidences."

"You mean he was your lover," Wendy said tartly.

"Okay, no one is questioning your lifestyle, I'm just trying to figure out if it works for us, or against us."

She was acutely uncomfortable, realizing suddenly that she was almost quoting Mrs. Bloody French, but Aida said coldly, "He was never my lover! He paid the rent on this apartment for a couple of months last year, in exchange for sexual favors. But a lover? No! A lover is not someone you just go to bed with once in a while, can you understand that? No, perhaps you can't..."

There was that hostility coming to the surface again, and Ian Quayle, quite pissed off with it, said angrily, "Get on with your profile, for Christ's sake! Abu Jildi's is already etched into my mind, with a branding iron, and I want Colonel Mifari's now! So let's get the hell organized! First of all—how old is Mifari?"

"Forty-seven," Aida said. "He looks younger."

"A ladies' man, or not?"

"Very definitely. The kind of man who has a permanent hard on, always looking for somewhere to bury it deeply, burying hang ups and frustration between friendly thighs, looking for..."

"Go on," Quayle said wearily. "Is he married?"

"A widower." She said drily, "They're always the worst."

"Okay. Family?"

"A son and a daughter. The son is seven, the daughter fifteen."

"Being educated where?"

"In Switzerland and France. And the daughter is here now, came to visit her father for the vacation."

"Her mother?"

"Her mother died seven years ago, when their son was born. Since when, Colonel Hassan Mifari has just been whoring around. Which is something he always did anyway."

Profiles, profiles, profiles, they were always so very important...

Ian Quayle ticked off in his mind the points that had been made, and he found that he was getting more and more convinced...

"Languages?" he asked. "French, of course."

"Immaculate. Part of Colonel Mifari's education was at the Sorbonne."

"His English?"

"Not very good. He knows it, of course, but he makes a lot of foolish mistakes. When he wants to tell the world how well-educated he is—he speaks French, not English."

"So far, so good," Ian said, "so let's push our luck. Any connection with Iran?"

"Another part of his education," Aida said triumphantly, "was at Teheran University, under the Shah. They threw him out when they discovered that he was secretly funneling private funds to an Iranian exile in Paris; a cleric named Khomeini."

"I like it," Ian Quayle said, restraining his excitement, "I'm beginning to like it very, very much."

But his researcher's mind, the mind of a scholar, slowed him down; there wasn't any real proof yet, just a lot—maybe a great deal—of circumstantial evidence that might or might not add up to a mess of potage.

He fell into one of his abominable periods of introspection, looking for the clincher that would turn circumstantial evidence into something worthwhile. Wendy waited patiently, knowing his moods, knowing that when he was like this there just wasn't any way he'd listen to common sense from anyone else.

But Aida was less patient. A jaguar on the prowl, she waited for as long as she could stomach it, and she said at last, reading his mind exactly: "Ian... I *have* what you're searching for. The final proof, right?"

Ian looked from Wendy to her, wondering why two very bright women were so opposed in their philosophies; wondering too in a moment of stupidity why these two gorgeous creatures had crossed his path at the same time together. He thought of the last night when—beyond a shadow of a doubt—he'd fallen asleep on the big bed beside Aida, a woman he'd only just met, a woman of extraordinary fascination.

Was it just a dream? Or had he really been kissing her breasts?

Surely she had said to him, '*I will be there if you need me...*'

He'd been tired, he remembered, desperately tired, and maybe he'd even had too much cognac.

He could recall the hardness of nipples under his tongue, the taste of salt in her navel. Or was that just a dream too? He knew that he'd never know.

And would she?

Perhaps.

But *only* perhaps; it was hard to live with.

He tore himself away from the ruminations, and he said carefully: "Yes, the final proof. The letter that was sent to me special delivery from Paris. It suggested that Abu Jildi had a few days of urgent business to attend to. The reason why, damn his bloody eyes, he couldn't give me his immediate attention. But at the time, I thought it was just a ploy, to make sure I knew how little my daughter Pia meant to him."

Wendy thought about this, and she shook her head. "No," she said slowly, "I don't think so. Sure, every day you have to suffer, as you have been suffering, wondering about her all the time...it's going to make you all the more amenable when at last you do meet. And this kind of calculated cruelty surely fits the profile..."

"But on the other hand," Aida said, "every day Ian is working against him means another day of danger for him. His war, as you've said, is with the Intelligence Establishment, and Ian is part of it. No, I believe he really did have something else to occupy his mind."

She said deliberately, "And I can prove it."

She flipped pages on her file, and she asked: "*Bien*, on what day was Pia kidnapped?"

"Friday," Ian Quayle said, "That was the fourteenth."

Was it only three days ago? It seemed like an eternity.

"And I have it here," Aida said, flipping pages. "Last Friday, Colonel Hassan Mifari was in Paris. He'd arrived there the previous day to pick-up his daughter Lilian—and take her home to Cairo for the vacation. But then...then he was called urgently by his Government for a meeting with King Hussein of Jordan to discuss—of all things—the threat of terrorism in the Middle East. And that's something he wouldn't have missed under any circumstances. He took his daughter back to Cairo with him on the Saturday, and flew on to Amman, Jordan, at once. He returns to Cairo tomorrow."

Ian Quayle found that he was trembling. "He picked up his own daughter and mine at the same time," he muttered. "How the hell did he get Pia to Cairo?"

"He has all the help he needs," Wendy said, not even aware of the wound she was inflicting. "I imagine they drugged her..."

"And packed her into a wooden crate," Ian said savagely. "That's been done before too. Three years ago, there was a Libyan exile living in London who was wanted by Ghadaffi for what is, cheerfully called 'questioning.' The cops found the poor bugger, drugged out of his wits, in a crate at Heathrow Airport, remember? The manifest said 'Hospital Equipment,' and they rescued him just hours before he would have died of suffocation."

"I remember," Wendy said, and Aida brought it all down to earth again.

"And the head of the Security Police," she said clearly, "is in a better position than anybody on the face of the earth to have engineered the death of Marie-France, let's not forget that."

"And there's another thing I like," Ian said. "I've always known that Abu Jildi had to work with the Hezbollah of his origins by sort of remote control. He always had something that kept him in Cairo instead of Beirut where the action has always been. Okay, now we know why. You don't have to convince me anymore, Aida. You've found Abu Jildi for me. Two questions. Where is he now?"

"I told you, in Amman."

"Okay. Second question. Where is his daughter *now*? What's her name? What does she look like? What kind of security does she have?"

"She'll be in her father's house, without a doubt," Aida said. "The address is Number 12, Sharia Mansour, Garden City. Here name is Lilian Mifari. What does she look like? I don't know, I've never seen her. But she's an Egyptian teenager from the upper-classes. Undoubtedly she's dark-eyed, black-haired... What, you're looking for a blonde Scandinavian student on a group tour? We do know that she wears glasses, we do know that she's seldom been seen without a pile of school books under her arm."

For a very brief moment Wendy wondered why it had taken her so long to catch up to what Ian was up to. And when he said to Aida—who seemed, goddammit, far too fond of him for her liking: "If Colonel Mifari's returning tomorrow—then I have to act today. Wouldn't you say?" she suddenly knew what was happening now.

And she exploded.

"Good God!" she said, aghast. "No, Ian! No, no, no...! I won't allow it!"

As she searched for the words, a very cool Aida said, mocking her, "You won't allow it? I have an idea, Miss Hayworth, that you're not going to be able to stop him."

And Ian Quayle said, hard as nails, "I told you, Wendy, I

told you I had to find Abu Jildi in order to find Pia. Now...I'm convinced I have found him. The rest is easy."

"No! In God's name no! That's not the way we operate, Ian! Robin Harris would have fifty fits if I allowed it! Kidnapping an innocent young girl on the streets of Cairo? That's what you're thinking of, isn't it? Isn't it?"

"Of course it is," Ian Quayle said shortly. "It's not only the best thing to do now—it's the *only* thing to do! And I'm damn well going to do it. With or without your help."

There was a little moment of silence and unspoken enmity, and then Wendy said, ice-cold, "Are you forgetting that I'm your Case Officer? Which means that you're under my orders?"

"And are you forgetting that we're talking about my daughter's life?"

He blew up. "For Christ's sake! That sonofabitch Abu Jildi is going to put her on the slave market for the harems! If he wasn't already done so!"

She reached out and touched him, just a small gesture that said a great deal. "Is Pia still a virgin? I imagine she is..."

It was very awkward for him. "I suppose so. She's twenty-one years old, brought up in Italy in the Catholic church. Yes, I think she's probably still a virgin. And this is a hateful subject..."

"We have to think of it now," Wendy said. "Abu-Jildi wants her for the slave market, where virginity is very, very important, and high-priced."

"Oh God..."

"It means that he'll keep her...*intacta*, unbroken, until he's ready to sell her."

"And meanwhile," Ian Quayle said brokenly, "let's not pull any punches. Meanwhile, they'll be teaching her..."

His voice broke altogether. "They'll be teaching her...teaching her other ways, we both know it."

Wendy would not pull the punches either. "Yes," she said, "that is what they will be doing now."

"And you want to stop me from doing what has to be done? I don't believe it!"

He had not convinced her; she had convinced herself. But there were still other ideas...

"I know that I can't stop you," she said, "with bureaucratic orders. But I have a better idea."

"Like hell you have. There *is* no better idea..."

It was not a moment to indulge the awful fears that were on her. She pushed the fear to the back of her mind and let it rest there, knowing what she had to do now. She forced herself to calm down, if only a little.

"It's a question of *time*," she said clearly, taking over full command of the situation. "*Time* is our first problem."

Ian Quayle grunted. "That's very astute of you. Time is the one thing we don't have now."

"Then we must earn it," Wendy said. "You're forgetting Robin's ransom offer. Okay, I agree, it's far too small, but the principle is there. If we can talk GA into raising the amount, quite considerably, Abu Jildi might still go for it."

"Might!" Ian said, positively snarling. "GA *might*, Abu-Jildi *might*! What the hell good is *might*? Might's a quality I have no bloody interest in..."

"Listen to me, or Christ's sake...!"

Wendy put out a hand and just touched him, conscious of the strain he was under. It was a very small gesture, but it was an assurance of the close affection that held them together even in the very worst of their sometimes brutal arguments.

She said quietly, "It's *time* we need now, Ian. And we can make ourselves some if...if we use our intelligence. Time, time, *time!*—it's all we need."

She fell silent for a moment, and Quayle felt that she was shaking just a little. She moved away from him as though to strengthen her position, to distance herself from both of them, especially from Aida. She took a long, deep breath, and she said clearly, "Hear me out, Ian, please. Please?"

"All right..."

"Abu Jildi wants you dead," Wendy said, and she added tightly, "And let's not forget that when you meet with him, face to face, all you are going to see before you die is a little round metal hole that's the barrel of a silenced handgun, okay?"

She got back, with an effort of will, to the matter in hand.

"He wants you dead, and why? Because as far as he's concerned, that's the only way he can eliminate you from the list of what you've called his real enemies. But suppose we can persuade him that there's another way?"

"There is no other way," Ian Quayle said. "You're full of shit, Wendy. I always knew it."

"Hear me out!" Wendy said furiously. "Suppose, just suppose, that you are prepared to remove yourself from that list, just...just drop the whole thing..."

"Not on your bloody life..."

"Will you listen to me, you sonofabitch? Will you give just a little thought to the idea that some of us are blessed with thought processes that aren't quite as screwed up as yours seem to be?"

He fell silent, and she went on, speaking calmly and with a great deal of assurance: "We can do it, and I'll tell you how... We can persuade him that in exchange for Pia, unharmed, you will voluntarily retire from the case, from the service itself if necessary, and if he knows you as well as I'm sure he does he'll also know that you're a man of honor who'll keep his word..."

Quayle threw up his hands. "Balls!" he said, "Balls, balls, and more balls! If you only knew how dumb you can be sometimes, how just plain stupid..."

"Have you finished?" Wendy was ice cold again now.

"Yes," he said shortly, "and so have you."

"No, I haven't. The best is yet to come."

"Oh? So there's a clincher here too?"

"There is indeed..."

Wendy took that long, deep breath again, and said quietly: "To clinch the deal, we'll make him an offer he can't refuse. *I* will take Pia's place. He'll still have a hostage for...for all the time we need to settle the matter of ransom. It makes sense, Ian. Even you must see that."

He could only stare at her and try to master the conflicting emotions that were piling up and overwhelming him. He tried to speak, but found that the words just wouldn't come. His mouth was dry, and there was a sudden wrenching pain in his gut.

In a moment, he went to her and took her in his arms, holding her tightly.

"I love you so much," he whispered, "and that's a fine, fine gesture. But even if I allowed it, which I won't, it wouldn't work, my darling. Believe me, he'd find a way to get you both, I'm surprised he hasn't tried that already."

He could feel her heart beating as wildly as his own, and he shook his head vehemently. "No. I have to put Abu Jildi over a barrel now, just like he's been holding me. Then, and only then will he be forced to do what I say. Which is...release Pia to me at once. But bless you, bless you a thousand times..."

"Sweetheart, you have to listen to reason. We can get Pia back, and then Robin can put you, and Pia, and Claudine as well, under the tightest security ever. And then, we can start over, we don't have to keep our promise to Abu Jildi, it was given under duress..."

"What do you mean, start over? With you ready to be sold to the harems? You're crazy..."

"You're interrupting me again before I finish. One more point, and I agree it's essential. That is... I can escape, Ian, I'm highly trained in this sort of thing. I can *escape*! And that's what

I'll do once I know that you and Pia are safe. End of operation."

"No."

Ian Quayle still held her tightly, knowing that Aida was watching them with a look on her face spelled amusement and a marked degree as scorn as well.

"You know what has to be done, Miss Hayworth," Aida said, mocking, "and yet, as far as the office is concerned, when it's all over, successfully, you knew nothing at all about what was going on. They'll just think you're more stupid than you really are."

Wendy ignored her completely, hating her more and more with every damn comment she made. She said to Ian, a last desperate piece of reasoning she knew would have no effect at all:

"If you go through with this, contrary to my orders, I'll have to resign. You know that, don't you? I'm just not authorized to break the laws of the country I'm working in. And they'll fire you, of course."

"We'll pretend we're Grade Two for the moment, Grade Two can do that, and I'm not about to allow any bureaucratic idiocies to interfere with me now."

Wendy was still hesitant, she'd been too long in the service, and was too dedicated to flout its rules, whatever the reason might be.

And Aida, a step ahead of everyone as always, said coldly to Ian, ignoring Wendy as though she were a piece of the furnishings, "You and I both know that she can't stop you, what's she going to do? Fight us both, physically?"

She laughed. "I have only to clap my hands once or raise my voice, and Suleiman will come running. I'll have him strip your Wendy naked and tie her down to my bed so that I can amuse myself with her while you're gone."

Now, at last, she looked at Wendy, more mocking than ever: "You don't really have too many options, do you?"

"Oh Christ," Ian said loudly. "Jesus bloody Christ..."

There was a little silence, and then: "Bitch!" Wendy Hayworth said.

Aida nodded. "Yes, I'm a bitch. Just don't ever think I'm anything else."

Quayle let out a long drawn sigh. "Okay," he said quietly, "I'm off on a course Robin wouldn't approve of, a course that would drive Mrs. Bloody French bananas if she knew about it."

He thought about that for a moment, and went on: "If she knew about it *in advance*; that is. Faced with a *fait accompli*, operation successful, she won't say a word, and I don't give a damn if she does. Because it's the only way, I swear to God. Abu Jildi has my daughter. Okay. When I have his...that's when we talk."

It was a losing battle, and Wendy gave up. "I've lost control, haven't I...?"

Quayle said, without rancor, "No. You never had any control. Not over this part of the operation."

"So let's see if I can regain at least a little of it."

She turned to Aida and said, with exaggerated politeness: "Could I borrow your cypher pad?"

Aida's eyes were hard. "If it's a message for the London office—no."

"Then I'll write it in clear and you can save me the trouble of enciphering by doing it yourself. This message—I think you'll be glad to see it."

Aida went to the sideboard drawer and took out a squared pad and a pencil and handed them over in silence. Wendy thought for a moment and then scribbled a few lines, and when she was through she gave it to Aida and said, "I won't wait for the reply, but get it off right away if you will."

Aida's puzzled frown was dark and even threatening, but she took the paper and read aloud:

C0441 PERSONAL TO DIRECTOR ONLY URGENTEST IMPORTANT REQUEST TEMPORARY REPEAT TEMPORARY ONE DAY ONLY PROMOTION TO GRADE TWO REASONS COMPELLING DETAILS TO FOLLOW ENDS

There was laughter now in Aida's handsome Egyptian eyes, and she said, admiringly, "Well, it's nice to know that if we try hard enough we can get through to you, Miss Hayworth."

"Yes, and I'm sorry I lost my temper back there for a moment. That's something honestly don't like to do..."

"Ha!" Ian Quayle said, but Wendy just threw him a glance. She looked back to Aida. "Can we be friends after all? It really would help."

"Of course," Aida said, and Wendy shot out her hand in a very British sort of gesture; Aida took it at once.

But she also leaned forward and planted a very open kiss on Wendy's mouth, the tongue probing.

Wendy was momentarily in a kind of shock, but she hesitated briefly before brushing away the hand at her breast.

Watching, Ian Quayle said, "*Tiens, tiens*, well, well. And could we get on with the matter in hand? I'll need two good men, Aida, with instructions that no one is to get hurt. Can that be clearly understood? No guns, no knives, no muscle, just tough-looking backup to inhibit any argument."

Aida clapped her hand once, and Suleiman was there immediately. She spoke to him at great length in Arabic as he listened attentively, nodding slowly once in a while. Twice he asked questions, and each time Aida nodded her head and clicked her tongue, meaning 'no': in the local custom, and there were more long explanations, more questions—this time with agreement—and even a certain amount of argument from the servant.

But at last he was gone, and Aida explained.

"He's a very good man, Suleiman," she said, "he has certain ideas of his own. Very soon now there will be two men waiting for you in a car that is not mine. They are both ex-police officers, both fired from the force in disgrace, one for attempted murder and the other for covering up a bank robbery he might have been party to. And one of them still has his uniform, it will help a great deal..."

For the next several minutes she gave Ian Quayle the answers to all of his many questions, setting out in the most minute detail just how best this could be pulled off—how, and especially *when*—as soon as the *meuzzins* would begin their call, because from that moment on a great number of people who might be paying attention to things they shouldn't be, would be kneeling and facing Mecca, caring only about their duty to Allah the Greatest...

"The senior of the two," she said, "is a man named Abdullah. His English is quite good, and before he broke into that bank he was a Sergeant. It doesn't presuppose intelligence, it presupposes only the power of authority. The other man is the driver, named Musa, who knows hardly any English at all. Don't even try to talk with Musa, he tends to start waving his dagger around if you so much as look at him. Talk only with Abdullah, he'll pass on your orders."

Ian Quayle scowled. "But Musa knows there's to be no violence?"

"He knows. That's what annoys him so much. But he'd rather suffer a flogging then offend me, so there should be no difficulty."

It was a time for persistence, for batting down the hatches and sealing all the holes. "And the cellar, how safe is it? Is it at least, well, decently habitable? Comfortable, even?"

"She'll be more comfortable there," Aida said brutally, "than your Pia probably is at this moment."

Quayle found he was trembling but he said nothing as she

told him about it...

The cellar was under a warehouse on the outskirts of Heliopolis, a very secure warehouse indeed, because it was used almost entirely for the storage of stolen goods, from cars and tractors to linens, carpets, and silverware, from foodstuffs to jewelry to building materials and fertilizers. Moreover, it was inhabited almost constantly by thirty or forty of the local thieves and their hangers-on—the lookout kids, ranging in age from eight or nine up into their teens and the 'blind' beggars who prowled the streets with their eyes open and alert under their shades for signs of any possible hit. And many of them, it seemed, were heavily, if unobtrusively, armed. And Quayle thought it was a nice little touch when she told him that there were signs posted everywhere proclaiming the storage of dangerous chemicals, complete with the mandatory skull and crossbones, just to keep the curious away.

"The thieves and the beggars," Wendy said, "they'll know at least part of what's going on under their feet. Isn't that a danger? Are you so sure that they can be trusted?"

It was a foolish question, and she knew it. "They're not likely to jeopardize their livelihoods," Aida said tartly. "What, give us away and have the police down on their heads? It's not very probable, is it?"

"Okay. What about the owner? He's presumably some wealthy landlord, most likely a Pasha. If he finds out he's tangling, eventually, with Abu Jildi and the Swords of God...we have to be sure, Aida. Certain beyond any shadow of a doubt."

Aida smiled thinly. "*I* am the owner," she said drily, and Ian Quayle grunted. "Oh. A finger in every pie, is that it?"

"Not exactly," Aida said. "A finger in *many* pies. This is just one of them."

Suleiman was at the door again in his silent slippers, bowing very slightly and saying, "*Hadr, ya Sitt*, it is ready."

Aida looked at her watch. "Twenty-seven minutes to the

call to prayer, the timing is good. Go now."

As Ian Quayle followed the servant out, he glanced back and saw that Aida's huge and luminous eyes, a faintly quizzical look in them, were on Wendy, and Wendy was turning away and trying to hide a very acute embarrassment by pouring herself a large snifter of Delamain.

He sighed, closed the door softly behind him, and set out for what was possibly the first overtly criminal act of his career.

CHAPTER 14

One look at the towering, scowling hulk of the man named Musa made Ian Quayle realize that Aida had been right.

Muttering to himself half the time, the most ferocious look imaginable on his pock-marked face, he gave the impression that he was on the verge of tempestuous eruption. His black moustaches covered almost half of his face, and it looked like his bushy eyebrows covered the other half. He was dressed in dirty white *gallabiah*.

But the ex-Sergeant Abdullah was a far more personable kind of a man, shorter but very solidly built, with a tendency to grin broadly at the slightest opportunity; a good-looking man in his fifties, he nonetheless gave the impression of being a thorough rogue, and Ian Quayle was grateful for it, just what was needed now...

The car was not bad at all, far better all-round than your average Cairene automobile, a thirty-year-old Chevy that had its full share of dents and scratches (and one rear window cracked, all of them tinted), but its motor was surprisingly quiet for a city in which most automobiles gave out more noise through their mufflers than was made by their horns.

As they sat on Mansour Street in Garden City and waited, Quayle wondered what this car was used for normally. It was in far too good a mechanical condition to have served as a taxi, it started at the first twist of the key—unheard of in this city except with the posh European cars of the very rich!—and responded like a sports car to the touch of the pedal. A bank robber's car, no doubt...

He was watching the house just ahead of them, wondering too if it were all going to be as easy as it all had sounded when he went over it with Aida.

But why shouldn't it be?

The house was tall and imposing, two and a half stories of good stonework, gray with age, but well-kept. There was a small lawn in the front yard, nicely manicured, with a few scattered rosebushes in excellent bloom, and an immense mango tree, heavy with fruit, that reached all the way up its two and a half stories, heavily laden branches overhanging the wrought-iron balconies there. A fountain played in one corner of the courtyard, and all in all it looked like a fine place to live...

A sudden distant wailing interrupted his reverie, taken up at once by another nearby, then by another and another and another all over Cairo as the *meuzzins* atop their sky-high minarets began the long-drawn drone of the call to prayer.

"Now," Abdullah said quietly and threw open the Chevy door. "*Stanna*, wait," he said to Musa, and Musa grunted.

Quayle followed the ex-Sergeant, a cop again now with all the assurance his somewhat slovenly uniform gave him, through the open wrought-iron gates to the courtyard. The guard there, kneeling on his little prayer mat, paid them only the slightest attention as he lowered his forehead to the ground.

They went up the winding flagstone to the front door, a door of very satisfying proportions, heavily constructed from solid teak with black-headed iron bolts all over it and decorative iron hardware everywhere... Quayle looked at the ex-Sergeant, perhaps for comfort, raised the knocker, and banged it three times.

Almost immediately, the door was swung open and the

Dragoman was there in all his finery—a crimson robe threaded here and there with gold wire, green cummerbund, a white turban on his grey head, and fine camel leather sandals turned up at the toes.

He was very, very old, perhaps in his seventies, but still straight-backed and strong looking, a Nubian from the distant desert to the south, where the finest Dragomen in the whole of the Middle East came from.

Dragoman, it was an illustrious title.

Strictly speaking, it was one of the many Arabic words for 'interpreter,' but over the course of time it had become to mean much the same as Major Domo, the man in charge—absolute charge—of his master's house.

The old man glanced only briefly at the Sergeant, then paid immediate attention to Quayle, recognizing, as only a servant can, a gentleman of some quality. And coming from the old, old school, he spoke halting French at once. "*Bonjour, M'sieur.* How may I help you?"

"I'm looking for Mademoiselle Lilian Mifari," Quayle said, answering in the same language. "Is she at home?"

Courtesy, courtesy, courtesy; and caution...

"If I may know your name, sir?"

"My name is Alain Rogers," Ian Quayle said, "and I have a message for Mademoiselle Mifari from the Colonel her father."

"Then if you will give it to me, sir, I will see that she gets it."

Ian Quayle smiled. "I was told to give it to her in person. And like you, I am sure, I must obey the Colonel's instruction to the letter."

The Dragoman inclined his head: "Then if you will kindly wait one moment, sir, I will see if she is at home. Excuse me."

Gently, he closed the door and left them standing there, but he returned almost at once and let them in. "Mademoiselle

Lilian will be pleased to see you. This way, please."

They followed him into the huge hall, marble-floored and carpeted in priceless Persian rugs, through two more rooms almost as large as the hall, and into a much smaller study. The old man said, still talking French, "*Monsieur Alain Rogers, Mad'moiselle.*"

He bowed as he went out, and closed the door behind him.

Ian Quayle looked at the girl there, a little startled because she was not at all what he had imagined. Somehow, he had pictured her as sweet and pretty like so many teenagers all over the world, slim and willowy and nice to look at.

Instead, he saw a remarkably sullen-looking young girl, a little under twenty years old he thought, by no means pretty, and grossly overweight for her age. She wore the most ghastly pink silk dress he'd ever seen, but it was the ill-tempered look about her that threw him, and he wondered if the speech he had prepared would be enough.

But he smiled and half bowed. "Miss Lilian Mifari, I presume?"

"Of course."

"My name is Alain Rogers, Mademoiselle..."

"I know that, the Dragoman told me. You heard him."

"Er, yes. I am an associate of your fathers, the Colonel, and he has sent me to bring you to him."

She stared. "How can that be? My father is in...he's out of the country at the moment."

Oh, the caution...! Her father's daughter!

"No," Ian Quayle said. "He has returned from Jordan one day early."

Then, a little embellishment to dress up the list. "His meeting with King Hussein was not as successful as he could have wished, so he has returned to Cairo on matters which—as I am sure you will appreciate—are of the utmost secrecy."

She was scowling now. "Then why hasn't he telephoned? You may not know how close we are, my father and I. So why hasn't he called?"

Quayle liked the insistence on the family devotion, but there was no time to gloat about it now. He said glibly. "Oh, he did! In my very presence, he spent more than half an hour trying to get through, but...you know what the phones are like in Cairo."

"Yes, that's true enough..."

"And he said to me at last. 'Go and fetch her to me, Rogers, it's essential I talk to her at once.' And so...here I am."

"Well..." There was an unexpected change of tack now. "Do you speak Arabic, M'sieur Rogers?"

Ian Quayle shook his head. "Your father and I speak French together."

"And your position?"

It threw him a bit, but the lies came easily, smoothly. "My own position? I am advisor, Mademoiselle, to the English Foreign Office official who was present at the meeting between King Hussein and the Egyptian Ministers, which your father attended in his official capacity. The Sergeant here will attest to that."

It wasn't going down very well, he sensed. And he sensed too that Abdullah was getting a little uncomfortable. And why? Were the prayers about to end, so that the whole world at large would be back about its business? And on the alert again?

He smiled. "But it's not the first time your father and I have worked together. We've become very good friends."

He saw her glance briefly at the telephone, and it was a time for desperation now. He said, very gravely. "And it grieves me deeply to tell you that your father has been hurt, quite badly."

"What...?"

Quayle said brutally. "There was an assassination attempt, he was trying to..."

But she leaped to her feet and interrupted him furiously, snatching up her purse. "Then why didn't you tell me that at once, are you stupid? Take me to him immediately. Immediately, you hear me?"

She was striding to the door like a virago. "Where is he?"

"In Heliopolis. We can make it in twenty minutes..."

"We'll make it in ten, or you'll answer to me personally."

In the huge hall, not even breaking her stride, she spoke briefly in Arabic to the Dragoman, and he hurried to the front door and swung it open for her.

She stared at the Chevy and said angrily, "Couldn't you have found a better car for me?"

"That's *my* car, I'd have you know," Quayle said, "and it'll get us there faster than anything else you can think up."

He was losing patience with the bloody young girl, ready to throw her aboard physically if she didn't move her oversized ass. But she climbed awkwardly into the back seat and sniffed the air. "Garlic," she said, "you or your driver must eat a lot of garlic. It stinks."

"It's so good for the digestion," Ian Quayle said mildly. "For the soul as well, come to that. Nature's own panacea."

She fell silent, not liking this offensive foreigner in the least, as the car sped through the crowded streets on the blasts of its horn and the sheer danger of its speed.

Soon they came to the tightly-packed complexes of Heliopolis, the most crowded suburb in a very crowded city, and the girl said sharply. "Is it the hospital we're going to? Because if so, your idiot driver just made a wrong turn."

Quayle was ready. "They haven't taken him to the hospital?" he said gravely, "it would be far too dangerous."

"Dangerous?" She was almost snarling, but his story was ready, and it was good.

"Can't you understand?" he asked. "The work your father is engaged in...no one must know that he's returned until he's

180

had the time to...to set up certain precautions with regard to his safety. The assassination attempt failed, so there'll almost certainly be another, and until he gets everything organized here, he's terribly vulnerable. It's as simple as that."

"You mean he's in hiding?"

"Precisely."

"From whom?"

"The group that's trying to kill him. Your father's not sure yet who they are, he has his man working on it already. Meanwhile, no one must know where he is."

The moment had come, and he took from his pocket the white cloth bag Aida had prepared for him. "And that means you too," he said, holding it out to her. "So if you'd put this on, please?"

She stared at him, aghast. "You really are lacking in natural intelligence, aren't you?" she said angrily. "That kind of order doesn't include me..."

"Oh but it does," Ian Quayle said. He went on earnestly: "*No one*, your father said. And you must know as well as I do that the colonel doesn't allow his assistants to use their own discretion, ever. He expects his orders to be followed to a T. And if it turns out that I was wrong...then I'll apologize when the time comes. But for the moment, I'm going to follow his orders implicitly."

"You are not just stupid...you're mad!"

"No, I'm not. I'm not even overly stubborn, just cautious, I have no way of knowing what was in your father's mind when he said '*no one*' so strongly, but I know what's in mine."

She was snarling now. "Which is...?"

"That if someone were to see you entering the building, one of *them*...they'd know at once where he was hiding, and we'd have another murder attempt on our hands. I can't allow that risk, Mad'moiselle. With a bag over your head, you're not going to be recognized. Believe me, it's for the best."

She just glowered for a moment or two, and then said sullenly, "I hate it!"

But she made no effort to resist as he gently drew the bag over her head. She snuggled deeper down into the seat as though to hide herself more securely, and he knew that the battle had been won.

And somewhat to his surprise, she said after a little silence, "Well, perhaps you're right after all. I may have misjudged your intelligence. But not by much, I'm sure."

He had the impression that under the cloth she might actually have lost that awful scowl, might even be smiling secretly to herself. No, that was too much to expect.

"Don't worry about it too much," he said cheerfully. "People do that to me all the time. Everyone does..."

The warehouse was a low, squat building on the far side of the suburb, its painted walls peeling, its windows shuttered on the inside for the most part, all of them heavily barred.

They drove round to the back and along a fetid alleyway where the monstrous Cairo cats were snarling at each other, three of them ganging up on a husky pi-dog they'd cornered, a huge, emaciated and ulcerous beast that had been foolish enough to challenge the cats for a share of the rotting garbage that was strewn around everywhere; one of them was slashing savagely at the dog's eyes while the other two went for his belly.

The car turned slowly in a second alleyway that was narrower still, and there was Suleiman waiting patiently for them where he was supposed to be. There was another man there with him, dressed in rags, a horribly scarred man whose face had been knifed open years before, a thin and wiry sort of man in his forties perhaps; he was armed with the ubiquitous dime-a-dozen Kalashnikov submachine gun, and there was a long curved dagger stuck into the twist of cloth that served as a belt.

Suleiman said quietly, "This way, please as quickly as you can..."

Once they were inside and the door was closed, Quayle moved to take off the girl's head covering, but Suleiman said, "No, not yet..."

They led her carefully down a long corridor through a succession of doors, and at last down a stone stairway and into the first of the cellars, quite small, through an archway into a second, a little larger, then through a heavily padlocked door into yet a third, which was huge.

And everywhere they went, there were armed men, riffraff from the streets for the most part, though now they were all armed—an assortment of Kalashnikovs, Colt ARs, Hungarian AMDs, Berettas, and even Galils, not an old or beat-up piece of scrap iron among them. The days were gone, Quayle was thinking, when ragamuffins like these armed themselves with ancient Turkish rifles and revolvers they'd hidden, buried in sand, ever since World War One; today, the finest weapons in the world were to be had for the asking or the stealing, there was hardly one of the 'civilized' countries that wasn't pumping arms into the Middle East as fast as it could for one lousy idea or another...

There were crates and boxes of varying sizes stored here by the hundred, with automobile and farm equipment motors lying around, many of them in pieces, stacks of carpets, sacks of farm produce, metal and plastic piping, bags of cement, everything in fine disarray.

A young kid there, nine of ten years old and also dressed in rags (but with a Beretta machine pistol slung over his shoulder), pulled aside an old icebox on its well-oiled castors to disclose what looked like a series of air-conditioning vents, one above the other, fastened into a plywood panel, its gray paint peeling, which turned out to be a hidden doorway when it was swung open.

Quayle saw the men watching him, some scowling, some laughing, some just picking their teeth with their daggers, as they went down a long corridor and into a remarkable room...

CHAPTER 15

From the warehouse side, the door had been just a plaster panel, not even a handle on it; you had to push, and push very heavily indeed.

But from inside, it was a heavy walnut door, intricately carved and fitted with very modern deadbolts. And as it was closed and locked behind them, Ian Quayle saw that they were in a large room of satisfying proportions and fitted out as a living-sleeping-dining room for someone who liked, and could afford, only the best of everything.

And at a nod from Suleiman, he finally took the bag from Lilian Mifari's head.

She blinked her eyes briefly at the bright lights, let out an impatient sigh, and said brusquely, "Good. Now you will take me to my father. At once."

Quayle stared around him, surprised and mightily impressed after all the squalor out there...

The room was some twenty-four feet long by sixteen or so wide, high-ceilinged with good light fixtures everywhere (no windows here at all,) and the floor was entirely covered like an Arabian Prince's desert tent, with excellent carpets, including a priceless and very beautiful tapestry-woven Kerman that must have been, he was sure, at least two hundred years old. There was a large divan against one wall, upholstered in dark blue shot-silk covered with cushions in a lighter shade of the same material, with rosewood tables on either side of it. There was an excellent gate-leg table of turned oak, 17th Century English, there were half a dozen high-backed armchairs in carved walnut and red velour, much the same date but probably from France, and an immense court cupboard of carved and inlaid oak, and a wonderful Hispano-Moresque wood-and-gilt screen in one corner, considerably older than the rest of the furnishings, perhaps 14th or 15th Century, and damask covered ottomans all over the place. And several old cupboards had been converted to bookshelves, with some very fine leather-bound volumes on them.

A bit of a mishmash in styles, he thought, Oriental hedonism mixed with the best of ancient Europe, but a hell of a fine room anyway.

And there were four women waiting there for him. There was Wendy, of course, dressed now in her favorite buff colored safari suit and watching him expectantly; there was a middle-aged, robust, and tough looking dolichocephalic from the Upper Nile, black skinned and with thin lips and a high-bridged nose, a Shilluk tribeswoman he thought, from the Upper Nile region, whom he recognized as Suleiman's seldom seen wife; there was a much younger and very attractive girl, in her late twenties, perhaps, dressed in very mod jeans and tank-top, slim but muscular, tall and wiry, with dark eyes almost as large as Aida's, tight, upstanding breasts under the loose cotton knit, high cheekbones, and an olive complexion. Her lips were very sensual, but she wore a scowl that almost equaled that of his captive.

And then, there was the fourth woman...

Seated on one of the high-backed chairs, she was dressed from head to bare foot in an all concealing peasant's black *abbayah*, with only her eyes showing above her black veil; and she was pregnant enough to burst at any minute now. Or so he thought...

He looked at those eyes, he saw with a start that it was Aida, with a large cushion strapped around her middle under the gown, obviously, but he wondered about that for only the briefest moment before he guessed the reason.

But his captive was raising Cain and her voice again, saying shrilly, "My father! Where's my father? I demand to see him at once, at once, you hear me...?"

"Well..." Ian Quayle began ruefully, but before he could continue, Aida leaped from her seat with surprising speed for such a pregnancy, strode to the girl and said harshly, "Your purse, give me your purse!"

Lilian stared, and Aida snatched it from her in a lightning fast and very strong movement, to upend it on the beautiful gate-leg table. And when the gun fell with a *thunk* she picked it up, flicked it expertly open, and extracted the shells. "A Bayard .32," she said, "a very nice little gun."

She took one of the shells and looked at it. "Hollow-nosed bullets. One of those could make a hole in your belly big enough to step through."

She was speaking French, and she said the girl, mocking her, "Don't look at me like that, you horrible child, or I'll knock all your teeth out. One by one, you understand? You're a prisoner now, so you don't demand anything, you just keep quiet and behave yourself. Or else—you'll find yourself in very grave trouble."

"A p-p—prisoner?" She was speechless with disbelief and fury, and Ian Quayle said calmly, addressing her for the first time like a child or an old friend, "Well, as I was about to say..."

He was gentle with her now, not liking himself a bit for what he had been forced to do.

"It's like this," he said apologetically. "First of all, everything I've told you so far is a lie. Your father is *not* here, you'll be glad to know that he's *not* been hurt, he's still in

Jordan, and he's returning tomorrow as planned. And I am not his friend, I'm his enemy, as he is mine. As for your position...you will stay here under guard for just a very short while till we see what happens next. You have my promise that you will not be hurt in any way at all...."

"Provided you don't try to make trouble," Aida said, and Quayle went on, "Yes, of course. Behave yourself...and we should be able to release you, unharmed, in a day or two."

"Meanwhile," Wendy said, feeling a little out of it, "these two ladies will stay with you all the time. Outside this room, there are twenty or thirty very rough men wandering around, you're only safe from them in here."

"Why?" Lilian Mifari whispered, terribly subdued now. "I must know why..."

"No," Wendy said patiently, "all you have to know is that apart from the great danger to you if you were to try and leave this room—and the doors are locked and barred and guarded on the outside—is that if you make the slightest wrong move, anything that even *looks* suspicious; then your guards have been instructed to tie you up, truss you, hogtie you and gag you as well, a discomfort you can easily avoid. You'll have the divan to sleep on, three good meals a day brought to you, and you can pass the time with your studies."

She went to one of the bookcases and looked the volumes over. "I understand that you're studying political philosophy, a heavy subject for a girl your age. But there's Jean-Jacques Rousseau here, Thoreau, Adam Smith, Thomas Hobbes, Karl Marx, all in French. And a lot of books in Arabic for you to choose from if your studies bore you. Just remember one thing: There is absolutely no possibility of escape, and all you have to lose is your privacy."

She turned to Quayle. "Only one thing left to do now."

She went to a cupboard and took out the Polaroid camera she had put there, one of the nice new Spectras, and handed it to him. "Where do you want her?"

It was hard to find, in this beautifully decorated room, a piece of wall that was absolutely bare, but by moving away the heavy court-cupboard, he was able to disclose bare plaster without a mark on it.

"Here," he said.

Wendy stood the girl there, and as she stared at him, Ian took the first of the shots. He examined it carefully and handed it to Wendy. "She looks...*defiant*, I think. I wonder if that's bad."

Wendy nodded. "Yes, it could be..."

The lithe young woman in the tank top had not uttered a word, just sitting there on her high-backed chair like a feline in repose; and listening. But she got languidly to her feet now and said: "*Moi, je m'occuperai de ca*, I'll take care of it..."

She reached down into her boot and pulled out an eight-inch knife, its thin blade shining, and drew back her arm for the throw, and as Wendy screamed. "No, in God's name no...!"

But Quayle knew what was happening, and he was ready; he pushed the button as the knife hurtled only an inch or so past Lilian's ear and buried itself deep into the plaster and the heavy timber behind it. With a short laugh, the young woman recovered her knife and said to Lilian. "*C'est amusant, hein*...?" then went back to her seat and sat down again as though nothing had happened.

Ian Quayle looked at his picture in silence, and handed it to Wendy for study. "Oh my God," Wendy whispered...

It was a good shot, only the thrown knife blurred and barely recognized for what it was. But on Lilian Mifari's young face there was a look of the most abject terror imaginable; it was even in perfect focus in spite of the speed of his reaction, automatic focusing at its best. The eyes were wide with horror, the head turned a little to one side as though in an effort to avoid certain death or mutilation.

"Perfect," Ian said calmly. "But I want one of her bound

and gagged too, let's get our money's worth while we're being unpleasant."

He tried not to look at Lilian, but caught a glimpse of the tears streaming down her face, and he felt awful. But he forced himself to think only of his daughter Pia now, something that for two long days he had forced himself not to do in order to hang onto the sanity he needed so desperately if he was ever to find her.

One step at a time, I'll think of Pia when I find out just who this monster Abu Jildi is, not before. It's hard. I must do it. You don't win a fight through panic or hysteria, you win it by cold and callous reasoning. But now... Now I've got him over the barrel, where I want him...

Hard?

It was the hardest part of the whole operation, the hardest thing he'd ever had to force upon himself in his whole life.

And now, he was almost ready to explode, to let the violent hatred take over and erupt; almost, but not quite.

He said to the girl in the tank top. "*Comment tu t'appelle, mon petit?*"

She said clearly: "My name is Higran, I am from Turkey."

"You have rope? A gag?"

"*Bien* sure, I have been instructed to tie her if she gives trouble."

"Then tie and gag her."

"*A votre service, M'sieur...*"

There was that ultra-feline movement again, lithe enough to make even the svelte Aida look like a hippo in comparison. She found rope and rag in the cupboard, and in a very few moments Lilian Mifari stood there, still in tears and trembling now, and nicely belayed.

"Not too tightly," he said, but it didn't make him feel any better.

Higran stood back at last, and Ian Quayle got his shot. He signaled Higran to release her, and he said to Aida, "Jesus Christ, do you have any cognac here?"

"Of course."

She went to the cupboard and poured. No snifters now, but fine six-ounce beakers of enameled glass from Vienna, Ian Quayle thought, probably by Anton Kothgasser or one of his pupils.

"One for Lilian too," he said, and Aida laughed. "You are very soft-hearted, aren't you?"

He took the glass to his captive, and he said to her gently, "Drink, it will make you feel better."

She shook her head. She was no longer trembling, no longer quite so pestilential either. "No. My...my father does not allow me to drink."

"Drink it," he said sternly, "all of it. And if you want more, you shall have it."

She hesitated, then drank it down at a gulp and handed him back the glass with a shudder, and Aida said drily. "Fifty years old, and ninety-five American dollars a bottle. But we are finished here now, so shall we depart?"

"Okay," Quayle nodded. "Everything under control here?"

"Naturally."

"Okay, so let's go."

When they were outside at last in the dry heat of the early Cairo evening, Quayle said: "So, will someone tell me who the hell tank-top is? The girl with those tight little boobs?"

"Yes, I saw you studying them," Wendy said caustically. "Me, I thought they looked like doorknobs."

Aida laughed. "Higran? I'm glad you had a chance to meet her. And who is she? She's an acrobatic dancer who works twice a week at the Club..."

Higran's specialty, it seemed, was not only as a dancer,

she incorporated the martial arts into her act, finishing off with a dazzling display of knife-throwing. She'd stopped here three years ago on the so-called Middle Eastern nightclub circuit—Damascus, Istanbul, Athens, the long hard haul to Marrakesh, then Tangier, Tunis, Alexandria, Cairo, and back to Damascus. But she'd found that nightclubs everywhere on the circuit were getting duller and duller with the passing years: and the rise of a certain fundamentalism, and Egypt, even today—though far stuffier than it once had been—was somewhat more liberal than the other capitals. Public entertainment here was the pits, but the very rich loved nothing more than to display their wealth in lavish parties, with top-rated bands, singers, acrobats, dancers, magicians—the best talent the circuit could supply.

And somehow, Aida and Higran had become friends and lovers. And then, step by step, the young Turkish girl had been initiated into the secrets of clandestine intelligence work.

"She's bright," Aida said, "very bright. She doesn't know that she's working for MI6, all she knows is that I'm interested in Intelligence, probably for the Americans."

"Are you sure," Wendy asked, frowning; "that she can be counted on if something goes wrong back there? I have this awful feeling that one of us ought to have stayed there with them."

"No," Aida said emphatically. "First of all, nothing can go wrong. Secondly, if it should—then Higran's capable, believe me. And thirdly, what we have to worry about now is not Lilian Mifari anymore, she's locked up tight. What we have to worry about now, you and I—is *Ian.* Colonel Hassan Mifari, otherwise known as Abu Jildi, returns from Jordon tomorrow by government jet at eight fifteen in the morning."

She looked troubled. "And at midday exactly, Ian has to meet with him. Alone. It's not something I like the thought of, Wendy."

The silence lasted all the way to the apartment.

* * *

Ian Quayle felt a strange emptiness creeping over him, and he couldn't account for it at all.

He wondered how much of it was relief that so far the operation had gone without a hitch, silky smooth with no danger to anyone; yet, wasn't kidnapping the daughter to Egypt's Chief of Security Police, on the face of it, one of the most dangerous tasks even a highly qualified man could attempt?

And he *wasn't* qualified, and he knew it. This was Field work, and the Department's Field Officers went through an immense amount of training at a lovely old country house in Purley, Surrey, England, which had been taken over by a Ministry of the Government that didn't even exist except on paper, and was innocuously called '*The Academy of Advanced Technology.*' It was filled with very gentlemanly gentlemen and erratic ladies who tended to argue at high table over the most unlikely matters, from the effect of the Bolshevik revolution on yogurt made from yaks' milk, to the documentation concerning the length of Casanova's penis.

The men always seemed to wear green sports jackets with the crepe-soled suede shoes that were known as brother-creepers, and the ladies always seemed to make a point of looking like hell while still managing to get laid almost nightly by someone or other, it didn't really matter too much who it was.

And yet, in the space of thirty months (with sometimes the extra six as well), AAT managed to turn out some of the most formidable spies in Western Europe, men and women who sooner or later took up permanent residence in the leading capitals of the world, and sooner or later somehow managed to get themselves killed off.

Field Officer work. Ian Quayle tended to shudder when he thought about how close he had come on occasion to being suckered into it.

He knew now that at least part of that strange feeling in

him was fear, nothing more complicated than that.

With Wendy and Aida, he ate a splendid dinner, a salad called *michoteta* first—crumbled cream cheese with oil and lemon juice, onion and cucumber, and then *kofta*, the Egyptian *shish kebab* made with ground lamb and heavily spiced with cinnamon, cummin, and: coriander, with two bottles of a good St. Estephe, Turkish coffee, and the inevitable cognac.

Quayle liked his food, and he knew that Aida had laid all this on mostly for him, but his heart wasn't in it tonight. He was a little withdrawn, trying now to insinuate himself into the mind of a young girl he had sorely mistreated, trying to imagine her first conversation with her father the terrorist. He thought about Aida's 'pregnancy,' and the efficiency of her simple disguise to protect her cover.

He could imagine the furious young girl saying: "...a Frenchman named Alain Rogers, at least he spoke French but he looked more like an Englishman, and an Englishwoman as well..." (Here would follow a description of Wendy,) "and most important of all, an Egyptian woman dressed like a peasant, which she wasn't, her French was far too good for anything but an educated, woman, and she was pregnant, in her ninth month, I'd say, so that should make finding her very much easier..."

"Penny for your thoughts," Wendy said, and Ian sighed. "I was just thinking," he said, "I'm not going to sleep very well tonight."

Wendy murmured to him: "You will. I'll see to it myself."

When they went at last to the spare bedroom, Aida stood in the doorway and said quietly: "If you'd like me to join you? It might be very amusing..."

Quayle, already stripped down to his shorts, went into the bathroom for a shower. "That's for you to answer, Wendy," he said, his spirits rising a little.

"You bastard," he heard her say as he closed the door. And when he went back she was alone, lying naked on top of the sheet. The air conditioning wasn't working at all, this was Cairo, and it was hot as hell. They spent a sweaty hour or so playing with each other, and he loved her long and ardently and quite furiously, trying, it seemed; to pour his emotions into her as well.

"You think you can sleep now?" Wendy asked politely. "Or would you like another round?"

"For Christ's sake," he answered, "we honestly have to find more logical reasons to make love. You want to give that some thought?"

But he fell asleep at last, lying on his back with a long, soft, and very wet thigh thrown over his, while the mingled perspiration, salty to the taste, trickled in little rivulets down from their bodies and soaked the sheet.

He didn't awake till six-thirty in the morning, when, after a discreet knock and a long wait, Suleiman brought them their morning coffee; strong, no sugar, and a cardamom seed floating on top, ready to be broken open with the teeth.

"Take my cyanide gun with you at least," Wendy said, pleading, but he shook his head.

"They'd find it at once. I'm not worried that he'll blow my head off the moment I open the door. Even the Chief of Security, a Minister practically, can't murder an innocent tourist in the Semiramis Hotel. And once I'm inside that room—that's when *I* take over."

He thought for a moment about Murphy's Law, and surely it applied to the work he was engaged in now more formidably than anything else in the world.

"If something can go wrong, it will..." he said aloud. "But I've got a gut feeling...it's going to be okay."

That's what he thought.

CHAPTER 16

It was two minutes to twelve precisely when Ian Quayle hesitated at the door to Suite 709 in the Semiramis Hotel, situated on the bank of the River Nile, still lovely in spite of the City's continuing and frantic deterioration, in spite of the noise, the pollution, the smell, the flies, and the general chaos.

He looked at the second hand on his watch, waited (forcing an unnatural calm on himself even though his heart was pounding dreadfully) and then pushed the button.

The door was opened at once, just as if someone on the other side had been looking at his watch too, watches synchronized for H-Hour in the trenches...

And there was a Police Sergeant there, a tall and very swarthy man with a fierce black moustache and a livid boil on the side of his cheek, just ahead of the left earlobe. He was in uniform, dusty and un-pressed, the leather work dull, his black boots duller still, and he seemed to be unarmed save for a revolver in his belt; he didn't look very prepossessing at all.

But close behind him and to one side, a uniformed constable was standing with his feet well-spread, and he was holding an Uzi submachine gun leveled, its barrel aimed at Ian Quayle's gut.

Murphy's Law, it was a moment of panic, and Quayle was, thinking *Oh God, perhaps they can kill a man in the*

Semiramis Hotel... He had a morbid fear of Uzis, he'd researched them long ago when the Israelis first produced them and every damn terrorist in the Middle East got their bloodied hands on them; he knew that with a single left-to-right-and-back burst it could cut through a man's belly and drop him to the ground in two pieces before he could even say *oi vei*.

But the Sergeant was saying something in Arabic, quite politely, it seemed. Quayle shook his head, and said in English. "I'm sorry, I don't speak Arabic."

"I am saying," the Sergeant said, "what you are wanting?"

"Ah. Well. My name is Ian Quayle, and I am here to keep an appointment."

"Appointment? What is appointment?"

"I meet someone here."

"Who?"

"Someone, I hope, who is waiting for me..."

There was a soft but sharp word in Arabic from inside the room, and the Sergeant stepped back and gestured him in, then patted him down carefully head to foot.

"I don't carry a gun," Ian Quayle said mildly. "I have this crazy feeling that an intelligent man ought to rely more on his brains than on his arms."

There were three other men there, two other constables armed with submachine guns, and a tall, thin man in civilian clothes seated comfortably in one of the armchairs, with a newspaper on his lap. *A gun under it*, Quayle was thinking.

But no. The man put the paper aside and got to his feet.

He was well-dressed in a light grey suit, white shirt, and dark blue tie, with well shined wingtip shoes. He was in his late thirties perhaps, fairly tall, dark haired, olive-skinned, quite good looking with very expressive Egyptian eyes, a thin, slightly beaked nose, thin and rather cruel lips, and a small black moustache, neatly trimmed. He didn't really look too much of a menace.

"I think you must be Mr. Quayle," he said. His English on was fair, quite heavily accented, and his voice was soft, very soft indeed.

"Yes," Ian Quayle answered, for want of something more intelligent to say. "I am Ian Quayle. And you...?"

The man took a wallet from his inside breast pocket and flipped it open, just like the cops on TV, showing a rather crummy photograph.

"Since you cannot read Arabic," he said quietly, "I will tell you I am Inspector Ismail Kabbaj of the Security Police. Will you please tell me why you are here? You spoke of an appointment. With whom?"

"I am quite sure you know the answer to that, Inspector."

"You will tell me, nonetheless. I must be certain." He gestured. "Surely you must understand that?"

Quayle was looking at the hands; short, stubby, and strong-looking fingers, the nails not in the least well-manicured as his friend Paul Diderot in Paris had said. But then... Would the head of Security come here himself to do his own dirty work? Or would he send one of his minions?

"I have come here," Ian Quayle said, "to meet with Abu Jildi. In answer to a summons he sent to me in London. Last Saturday."

"I see."

The Inspector snapped those peasant fingers, and the Sergeant went to the table, took up a pad and a ballpoint pen and offered them to Quayle, using both hands in the polite fashion.

"What's that for?" Ian Quayle asked.

"You will please write down," Inspector Kabbaj said: "'My name is Ian Quayle, and I have come here from London to meet with Abu Jildi.' Just write it for me, please."

Why? Did they want a specimen of his handwriting?

No, it would make no sense at all. Why then?

He shook his head and said: "No, I don't see why I should do that. It's quite unnecessary."

"You will write," the Inspector said: "*'My name is Ian Quayle, and I have come here from London to meet with Abu Jildi.'*"

"I will not," Ian Quayle said stubbornly, not in the least knowing why he should refuse, just trying to make a point of some sort.

There was that snap of the fingers again, and one of the cops reversed his Uzi and drove the butt of it hard, very hard, at Quayle's solar plexus, and as he doubled up in sudden, gasping pain, swung the butt up again to smash into his face with such force that he was sent sprawling across the room.

He lay there for a moment, searching for breath, and it only came after he had vomited all over the carpet, more threadbare, he noticed, than it ought to have been. And it was a long time before he could stagger to his feet, and he stood there swaying for a moment.

"The bath...bathroom," he mumbled, and stumbled through the open door to stare at his bloodied face in the mirror; and at the cop right behind him.

The cop was not grinning, nor scowling, nor anything else; he just looked like a stolid and not very bright robot.

Quayle turned on the tap and waited for the water to come trickling through, and splashed it over his face. His lip was split open and very painful, and there was a nasty bruise under his right eye, but at least his nose or his jaw was not broken.

He dried himself on the only towel there—it had been used before already—and walked with a bogus dignity back into the room. He took the pad and pen from the Sergeant, went to the desk, and wrote as he had been ordered to write.

He said stuffily. "That was really quite unnecessary, Inspector."

"It was you yourself Mr. Quayle, who made it necessary.

And now...you are under arrest. You will come with me, please."

"Arrest?" Quayle was startled. "What for, for Christ's sake?"

"Under Egyptian law," the Inspector said quietly, "as in any other civilized country, it is an offense to associate with a known terrorist."

He waved the pad. "The evidence against you is clear. In your own handwriting."

"Oh God. That's the dumbest thing I ever heard of!"

So where were they going to take him? Just a short drive away to the bustling slums of Bab-el-Luk, where a body could be dumped in the market garbage there and no questions ever asked about it? A few miles down the Nile where a couple of concrete blocks around his neck would take him down to a never discovered and very unpleasant death in the river's rich muddy bottom? Was all he could expect now a slash across the throat with a sharp dagger? He knew there'd never been any question of Abu Jildi's calmly handing Pia back to him, just a play to get him, Ian unhappy Quayle, where he could more easily be knocked off...

But wouldn't they want to question him first? He couldn't be sure, and he had to be absolutely certain of every move now, there was just no other way to play it.

He said tightly. "Where are you taking me?"

"To Police Headquarters, of course. Where else did you expect to be taken?"

"Good." He took the plunge. "Because I also have some information for Colonel Mifari."

The Inspector was taken aback. "You know him, Mr. Quayle? I don't think you've ever met him."

"No, I haven't. But I know him by repute, it's enough."

"I see..."

There was a certain hesitancy there now, and Quayle had won a pawn, at the very least. He pushed for a knight or a bishop.

"And if by chance anything were to happen to me before I see him... He won't just reprimand you, Inspector, won't reduce you to a constable, won't even imprison you. Believe me when I say with all the certainty in the world: He'll kill you. That's how important it is. To him, not to me."

Taken aback was hardly the phrase: Quayle could almost see the wheels turning in a mind he was sure was very, very devious, he knew that he'd made a very important point now.

Indeed, why should Abu Jildi want to see him? What had he to gain by questioning under even the most severe persuasion? Very little, hardly worth the bother.

The Inspector said at last, very softly: "Perhaps you should give me that information, Mr. Quayle. I'll see that the Colonel gets it immediately."

"Like hell you will," Ian Quayle said. "And you should know that my threshold of pain is at a very low level. If you try breaking my fingers or carving me up—I'm liable to die of shock almost instantly, and then where will you be?"

There was a long, long silence, and then the Inspector spoke briefly to the two cops, something that must have meant '*watch him*' or some such, and went into the other room; the telephone, no doubt. And it seemed an interminable time before he came back.

Quayle looked at his watch, nearly twenty minutes to get through, the Cairo telephone system at its worse, even for high ranking Government officials and the cops; the telephone is no respecter of persons, he thought.

When Inspector Kabbaj did at last return, he merely nodded briefly to the Sergeant and said to Ian Quayle: "We will go now."

And Quayle knew that it was no good asking where.

They shepherded him down the stairs and onto the street, where a blue police van was waiting, and he was pushed unceremoniously into the back, the two cops and the Sergeant with him. Through the bars, Quayle could see that the Inspector was going to follow in his own car, a nice new Mercedes.

The van wouldn't start, the battery was low, but the Sergeant bullied a dozen passersby into pushing, and soon, they were on their way.

And fifteen minutes later, through the great stone and iron entrance to the Kasr-el-Nil barracks, across the parade ground, round to the back of the cut-stone building, through interminable corridors and past countless guards... Ian Quayle was ushered into the office of one Colonel Hassan Mifari, Head of the Security Police, quasi-Minister-Plenipotentiary, and perhaps the third or fourth most powerful man in Egypt.

CHAPTER 17

There was no nonsense at all about Colonel Hassan Mifari's office; it was spartan in the extreme, just an oversized desk, quite modern and surprisingly well-polished, with a large black leather chair behind it and three wooden chairs in front of it, a row of metal filing cabinets along one wall, two big cupboards, not matching, an old and quite dilapidated gun cabinet containing three hunting rifles and a shotgun, and—the only touch of luxury—an expensive looking stereo, complete with receiver, dual cassette, turntable, and CD player.

And somewhat to his surprise, the stereo was playing some very good music, quite quietly; a descant recorder, with a continuo too to add counterpoint to the strings. Sammartini, he thought, that crazy Italian hautboy player and composer who had taken London by storm in the seventeen-hundreds; what was it, the Concerto in F Major?

Or was it Tartini?

Did it matter?

No. And he came back to the earth of his surroundings.

There were no carpets on the stone flagged floor, and the only pictures on the whitewashed walls were a stylized portrait of President Mubarak and an excellent painting of a fine Arab stallion.

The desk was almost empty, just two filing trays on it and

a cheap carafe of water with a tumbler upended over it The single window was barred, and gave onto the big open garage building just across the way.

The man behind the desk was surprisingly young for his position, not more than forty at the most. He was quite ordinary looking except for rather small and very penetrating eyes, with a rather sharp nose and full lips half-covered by a drooping black moustache. His cheekbones were high, his forehead wide, his hair black and very short cropped. Sitting there behind the desk, he seemed to be fairly short, but powerfully built, with very broad shoulders and an unusually thick neck. His arms were folded, and Quayle saw that the fingers were long and surprisingly delicate for so strongly-built a man; and the nails were perfectly manicured and polished.

He was staring into Quayle's eyes with that appraising look that so many cops seem to have, as the Inspector laid a paper down on the desk. The eyes shifted only briefly as the Colonel picked it up, then resumed that probing stare.

"Ah," he said in English. "A confession. It is almost all we are needing. There will be more, of course. My Inspector is telling me you have information for me. I am Colonel Hassan Mifari. He is saying it is important to me. Well?"

"It is information you would not wish anyone else to learn." The Inspector, the Sergeant, and the two cops were still there, a menace...

The Colonel shook his head. "No. First, you are telling me why you come to Cairo to meet with this Abu Jildi? You know who Abu Jildi is, I think? Is terrorist. Number One, wanted everywhere."

"Yes, I know that."

"You are also knowing what is penalty under Egyptian law you are associating with known terrorist?"

"I have no idea at all. I'm sure it's most unpleasant."

The colonel laughed shortly, quite humorlessly: "It is

thirty years in prison. You can understanding, I think, what Egyptian prison is like. Not like American prison, Mr. Quayle." The laugh again. "No television."

He leaned forward and placed those delicate hands on the desk. "So you tell me now what is this important information. If not...then we are finding out in your cell."

Was it the time now? Quayle thought not. Was the Inspector privy to his Colonel's secrets? Maybe, maybe not. If not; then disclosure was undoubtedly premature. And what about the Sergeant and the two moronic cops with their Uzis? The same argument applied, it would open up a whole new can of peas if even one of them was relatively honest and merely being used.

So Ian Quayle stood his ground. He shook his head and said earnestly. "Believe me, Colonel Mifari, it is in your interest as much as mine. I will say no more till you dismiss your men."

The Colonel spoke very mildly in Arabic, and there was that snap of the fingers again from the Inspector. The same cop was there at once with his gun reversed like a battering ram. But this time, Quayle was ready, and somewhat to his own surprise, he found the sudden panic forcing him into something he knew was not wise.

There was just no time to think, no time at all...

He swept the weapon to one side with his left forearm, doubled up his right fist with the second finger bent for a protruding knuckle, and drove it with all his force at the man's throat. The cop went down hard, and the second one ran in with his weapon swinging.

Quayle kicked hard, and the gun fired, sending a half-magazine of bullets splattering into the ceiling. The Sergeant shouted and pulled the man away, then wrestled the gun from him as the Inspector screamed out his orders.

For a moment, everything held, like freeze-frame on a motion picture screen; One cop lying on the ground groaning and clutching at his broken Adam's apple, one standing there unarmed with the Sergeant holding his own gun on him, the Inspector looking to his Colonel for orders; and the Colonel sitting there immobile, even faintly smiling to himself.

'*Calm and not given to hysterics, an unflappable Arab,*' he had said to Mrs. Bloody French after his long talk in Paris with Paul Diderot. '*How many unflappable Arabs do you personally know?*'

Well, here was one, at least; the Colonel had hardly moved a muscle.

Panting from the effort and the fright, Ian Quayle said as quietly as he could, "It is personal matter, Colonel, a matter that concerns only you, and not your department, at the most personal level imaginable. Send your men away. I'm not armed, I can do you no harm. You'll have men outside..."

Outside...?

The door burst open suddenly, and a dozen men rushed in, Keystone Cops; their guns levelled, a young Sub-Inspector in charge, just a kid. They pulled up short, just staring as though they had expected to find a corpse strewn floor.

"You see what I mean?" Quayle asked, a small advantage. "Next time, I'm sure, they won't be so long getting here if they hear a commotion. All you have to do is raise your voice."

"And you're not armed, you say? I'm sure that's true, my Inspector would have found any gun you may be carrying. Nonetheless..."

He gave an order in Arabic, and the Inspector moved forward, a trifle too carefully, Quayle thought, and patted him down once again, far more thoroughly than the Sergeant had done before.

"Empty your pockets onto the desk," he said, and Quayle produced his wallet, the little notebook with the Cross ballpoint in it, the little pocketknife he always carried, the handful of change—still in English currency—the slim silver cigarette lighter that Wendy had given him long ago, and even slipped off his Omega, because watches these days, in his field of endeavor, were not always what they seemed to be and he thought the Colonel would surely know that.

The Inspector went through the wallet very carefully, scrutinizing everything he found in it, and Quayle thought that it was very bright of him, because plastic C-4 explosive these days could be fashioned to look like almost anything; a half-ounce of it could be rolled into a strip of leather so as to be virtually undetectable. He even sniffed it, and Quayle said, not even trying to hide his admiration: "No, it's just ostrich leather..."

The Cross was next, a most careful examination to make sure it contained nothing but an ink refill, no cyanide at all.

He stood back at last and shook his head. "Nothing."

"Very well," the Colonel said: "Is only one more thing."

He bent down and pulled a gun from under the desk and laid it down, and Quayle stared at it. It was the cute little Socimi submachine gun, not much more than sixteen inches long and with a rate of fire of 550 rpm from a 32-round magazine, an almost pocket-sized arsenal and a very fancy piece of hardware indeed.

He gave an order in Arabic, and in no time at all they all trickled out and the door closed behind them.

"Now," the Colonel said, "you are telling me."

"Good. Would you be happier if we spoke French? It is essential that you understand what I am about to tell you."

The Colonel shrugged. "My English very good, excellent," he said. "But if making you happy, *bien, nous parlerons Francais.*"

He went on in French, quite amicably under the circumstances. "I have always regarded English as a rather inferior language. I was at the Sorbonne, you know."

"Yes, I do know. And at Teheran University too, I

believe."

There was a moment of silence, and the very slightest change in the Colonel's expression, a sort of wariness. "That," he said at last, "Isn't that a strange piece of knowledge for you to acquire?"

"Research," Quayle said clearly. "I know who you are, Colonel. I know you to be Abu Jildi. And I want my daughter back." It was hard for him to control his emotions, and he said: "I have the means to get her back."

But the Colonel was staring at him in the most acute astonishment; his mouth had even dropped open and his eyes were wide. "What's that?" he said. "*What...?*"

"I know that you are Abu Jildi."

The Colonel was shaking his head in bewilderment. "Are you quite mad?"

"No. I'm quite sane, I'm quite bright, and I'm quite sure. No. *Very* sure."

"A madman...! And what's this about your daughter?"

"I want her back. And I have the means to force you."

Colonel Mifari was angry now. He rose to his feet and began striding around the room, not quite as unflappable now; not too volatile either, but no longer quite so calm. And Ian Quayle said steadily. "It's no good denying it. I've researched Colonel Mifari, I've researched Abu Jildi, and the profiles match exactly. You know about profiles? Yes, you must. Then you know how reliable they are. Moreover, Abu Jildi called me to the Semiramis Hotel, and where did I finish up? Face to face with Colonel Hassan Mifari. I don't jump to conclusions, but that's enough for me."

"Mad," the Colonel said again.

He stopped his pacing and looked Ian Quayle straight in the face.

"Let me destroy your foolish illusion," he said tightly, "I learned, never mind how, that you had come to Cairo to meet with this infamous terrorist, at the Semiramis as you say. And since I myself have been searching for Abu Jildi for some weeks now, I decided to wait and see if you would keep this highly dangerous *tete-a-tete*. You did. And you walked straight into the arms of the Police. Profiles? Yes, I know about them, I know how dangerously they can lead you astray. Profile two, three, or even four or five men of much the same character and upbringing—and what have you got? One man if you're not careful! Who might well be none of them! I say again, Quayle, you're a fool! An arrogant, reckless, and impetuous fool!"

Oh God. Either the man was a consummate actor, or Murphy's bloody Law was at work.

Quayle shuddered inwardly at the thought of so frightening a mistake, and he felt that he was losing control, even beginning to tremble. Suppose, for Christ's sake, that he really had screwed up? It wouldn't be the first time, but where, in God's name had he gone wrong? And what would happen now? Poor Lilian Mifari, she could be released if he could ever get out of the mess he was in, and if he couldn't—which was likely now—then surely the whole of the city would be turned upside down and inside out in the savage search for her...

What would happen then to Wendy? To Aida? To the faithful old Suleiman and all the others? And most of all...

Most of all—*Pia.*

The wheels in his mind were turning above Mach One in his search for some indication, some slight clue as to where he had gone wrong; where he had put two and two together and made twenty-two instead of four? The profiles? Mifari was right, you had to watch what you were doing like a hawk, if you made just one small mistake they really could throw you for a loop. To hell and gone.

He saw that there were wheels turning in the Colonel's mind too; Mifari was looking at him with a very strange expression on his face, the eyes narrowed a trifle, as though something he didn't quite understand were troubling him.

The Colonel said, puzzled. "But there's something else, isn't there? I can smell a *something else* a kilometer away, and I'm faced with one now. What is it, Quayle? I want to know, and I want to know *now*."

Quayle shook his head. "No," he said, unsure now and mumbling. "I need...I need time to think."

It was a feeble effort at nothing, and he knew it.

Profiles, fucking profiles had thrown him into a pit he couldn't escape from now. Okay, so Mifari wasn't Abu Jildi, but he was still Head of Security, a ruthless and dangerous man you didn't fool around with, not likely to take this kind of indignity lying down...

Ian Quayle was thinking furiously, but the only images he could conjure up were of Marie-France Pages who had been found hanged in her cell, maybe even the same cell where they'd take him for further 'questioning,' the strangling-cord ready.

And what would happen to his Pia then; with no one else to come to her rescue? What would happen to Wendy and the others?

Because he'd talk, for sure.

It wasn't only the cords and the razorblades, it was their injections too.

He knew all about the injections. They weren't truth drugs, there was no such thing. They just gave you a cheap drunk in which nothing at all mattered, who cares, you want to know this or that? Well, why not? Go to hell, Charlie...

Another needle in the butt and you were screaming '*No, leave my fingernails alone...!*' and you didn't care what you said, nothing mattered anymore, and after a few more needles you became a talking vegetable, not capable of any thought at all, just yak-yak-yak, tell the nice man anything he wants to know, stupid. You'd pass out for a while, and when you came round you'd pluck at your lip and mumble: "Hey, did I tell...tell...tell you about that Aida...? She's terrific, all she wants is to get laid..."

"You came here," Colonel Mifari was saying, "with what you called personal information. What? That I am really Abu Jildi? Yes, that could be regarded as personal I suppose. But it's not that, is it? Abu Jildi concerns me, yes, as Head of the Security Police, but it also concerns the whole of Egypt, my Government, my President, every right-thinking man in the country..."

Oh God.

He went on. "So I'm forced to believe that there really is something else. And I want to know what it is, Quayle! I *demand* to know! And I assure you, I will find out! After a few hours in one of our cells, you will talk, believe me! *Je te couperai les doigts, l'un per l'un...*"

Quayle froze.

I will cut off your fingers one by one... It was the phraseology, almost exactly, of that Special Delivery letter that had brought him here; and now, he knew the time had come. All the doubts disappeared at once and he couldn't believe he'd ever entertained them.

He lifted his head and said clearly. "Yes, there is something else, and you shall have it now."

He raised his left foot slowly and placed it on the chair, and as he bent for his shoe the Colonel snatched up the Socimi and levelled it at him; he even pulled back the bolt.

Quayle stopped his movement and held out his hands. "No," he said, "not a knife, not a cyanide gun. Something you must see."

"Slowly, then," the Colonel said.

Infinitely slowly, Ian Quayle eased off his slip-on. He took out the slim package, wrapped in a plastic sandwich bag, and held it up. He put the shoe back on and stood back a trifle; there was still something else to be done.

Unflappable, perhaps. But the colonel was still an Egyptian, and who could tell what violent volatility lay underneath the veneer? It could all end now in a moment of uncontrollable, quite uncontrollable fury.

He said steadily. "Put down the gun, Colonel, and stand away from it. I don't like a loaded gun aimed at my gut, especially when it's cocked and there's a finger on the trigger."

"If you don't give me that package immediately," Abu Jildi said, "I will carve a two inch pattern in your stomach with my gun. It will take your several minutes to die, and I am prepared to believe, idiot that you are, that you can accept that. But can you accept what will then happen to your daughter? I think not."

Ian Quayle said clearly. "If I do not report back to my associates when I am supposed to—then they will commit, automatically and without hesitation, an act of murder. They will kill this person."

"Give it to me!" the Colonel said furiously.

"Put down the gun."

"No!"

"A reflex action on the trigger," Quayle said, "and you will have lost the one person in the world, perhaps, who is dear to you."

The blood was draining from the Colonel's face, it was ashen now. Slowly, he secured the gun and laid it on the desk.

"Give it to me," he whispered.

"Then stand away from the desk."

The Colonel moved back to the wall behind him, and Quayle reached slowly for the gun and re-cocked it. "A precaution, I feel," he said, "that might be absolutely necessary. There."

He tossed the package on the desk and moved away, thinking in a moment of incoherence how easy it was to disarm a dangerous man if you had the right equipment.

Almost hesitantly, as though he were afraid to look, Colonel Mifari stepped back to his desk and picked it up; his hands were trembling as he pulled out the two photographs and stared at them for a very long time.

In a moment, he sat down, completely under control as no man could ever be; and Quayle admired him for it, and took warning from it too—another man who, like Quayle himself, could force emotion out of the way when dispassion and cold calculation were required.

He looked up at last and said very quietly. "Your daughter Pia has not been harmed, Mr. Quayle. You may perhaps find it hard to believe, but for reasons that do not concern you, I have ordered that no one lay a hand on her."

"I know your reasons," Quayle said. "I know how much more valuable virgins are on the slave market. That was part of my research, part of your profile too."

"And Lilian?"

"Unharmed, you have my word."

"And you have made plans for the exchange?"

"I have."

"Where, and when?"

"How long will it take you to produce my daughter?"

"Four hours, a little longer perhaps. And you, mine?"

"Less than that. In the Dead city, then, six hours from now, to give you a little leeway." He looked at his Omega. "Let's say midnight, there will be no one in the Tombs at that hour."

"Midnight it is. Where exactly?"

"You know the tomb of Mohammed Halawi bin Susa?"

"Of course."

"In the little square, then, in front of the big door on the north. You and Pia and no one else."

"You and Lilian and no one else too. We shall settle this matter like gentlemen. Agreed?"

"Agreed."

Quayle was thinking: *Good, the darkness is good, it will be hard for rooftop snipers ready to extract their revenge.*

And for his part, Colonel Mifari was thinking: *Good, six hours is good, it will give me time for what has to be done now.*

Ian Quayle laid the weapon down on the desk and said politely. "Your gun, Colonel. We meet again at midnight. Good-day."

"Good-day, Mr. Quayle."

And that was the end of that.

CHAPTER 18

The extensive necropolis known as the City of the Dead was an astonishing place of great antiquity, embracing the tombs of many of Egypt's more famous leaders; that of the great Imam esh-Shaei, the founder of one of the four orthodox sects of Islam was nearly eight hundred years old, and many of the others were architectural wonders of almost unbelievable beauty.

There was a remarkable ornamented minaret there, slender as a pencil, it seemed, and yet more than a hundred and thirty feet high, that had been built, Quayle was thinking, around the time of da Vinci in Europe. When was it? He wracked his researcher's brain and thought it was 1469; so who was the genius who had engineered this awesome feat? He couldn't remember, though he knew just where to look it up.

Some of the mausoleums here were enormous, one of them encompassing well over fifty thousand square feet, with a central fountain, colonnaded passages, and beautifully intrinsic pulpits on mosaic marble floors. There were friezes of remarkable richness inscribed with Koranic inscriptions and also flagstones bearing the impressions of footsteps said to have been made by the Prophet himself and brought here from Mecca.

All was not so rich, however, as the tombs of the Sultans, and Khalifs, and the Mamelukes; there were humbler buildings here, and even parts of a fairly modern cemetery. And almost all these buildings, rich and poor, were deserted at nighttime, because, in the dark of the moon, the City of the Dead became a place of ghostly, macabre, even nightmarish atmosphere which any honest citizen would prefer to avoid.

And now, it was about to erupt in a nightmare that was all its own.

The dark was good.

"No one else," Abu damned Jildi had said, and who could trust a terrorist to keep his word?

And for that matter, who could trust an honest man when the life of his daughter was at stake? There were no rules now, the hell with Hoyle and the Marquis of Queensbury.

Quayle had a gun now, found for him by Aida. It was the Beretta M93R, which he had researched when Mrs. Bloody French had insisted that all her Field Officers have access to them.

It was one hell of a gun, with a twenty-round staggered magazine of 9mm parabellum bullets that spewed out at a fantastic rate of eleven hundred rounds a minute—but still cut out automatically after every third round to avoid muzzle climb.

James Bond stuff, it was terrific. It was thrust into his belt at the back, under his jacket, and ready-cocked, and his pockets were filled with spare magazines.

They made their way through the deserted cemetery, with only the ghosts of the long-since dead to keep them company, keeping to the shadows the moon cast, a crescent moon that was still far too bright for comfort. The silence was eerie; it seemed that even the night time traffic of the city, only a block or two away, could not penetrate and pass the low mud walls, that phantoms were arrayed there holding up their dead arms to prohibit any sounds of a world they had left long ago.

They came to some heavy timbers, three uprights and two

horizontals. (one of them fallen to a sharp angle), that Quayle figured was part of an old hitching rail, decayed now and serving as nothing more than a landmark; the square was just the other side of the mausoleum that flanked it.

The first step now...

He knelt down beside Lilian Mifari with a length of rope, and tied it to her ankles with two clove-hitches, an eighteen inch length between them so that she could still walk but not run.

(To achieve the same purpose for slaves, he knew, they simply cut a tendon at the back of one foot, so that the poor bastard could only hobble when he was called.)

He whispered. "I'm sorry, Lilian. It has to be done. I don't want you running off before it's time."

He made a little joke to ease the tension on her; "I'm getting too old to chase after young girls. Especially when there's a sniper or two up on the rooftops, as there will be."

"If my father said '*alone*,'" she answered quietly, "then he will be alone. You are the one without honor, not he."

"Uh-huh."

He made her walk a few steps to make sure that the restraint was short enough, and nodded his satisfaction.

A second rope now, a thief knot, quite loose, around her ample waist, three feet of slack, and a slipknot around his own; they were ready.

"Give me a flare," he said.

It was handed to him and he struck the fuse and tossed it over the low building and into the little square beyond it. He hated it, hated it like hell, but the question of identification was very important now.

Was he being too careful and inviting danger by it? He knew Abu Jildi to be a man of some deviousness, a man who liked to *think*; would he perhaps try to foist someone else on him in the darkness? Perhaps not. But there'd be a moment when the two girls crossed each other, and he fancied himself staring at a strange face once he could see it clearly in the light of the flare...

A slight, athletic figure came running to them, and Higran, the Turkish girl, whispered. "*Ready.*"

"Okay, here we go. Keep your fingers crossed."

He took the tethered Lilian Mifari firmly by the arm and walked with her round the comer of the Mausoleum.

Now was the time for the first of the dangers, and he held her very close to his body. Even though he was sure that Abu Jildi would *know*; know for sure that there just had to be someone else covering him.

He stepped into the circle of light and called out, "*Nous sommes arrivés*...we're here! Show yourselves!" and dragged his captive quickly back into the shadows.

The wait seemed interminable, but at last he saw a shadow move on the other side of the square. It was Abu Jildi/Colonel Mifari, moving into the light, too. Alone.

"Show me my daughter again," Abu Jildi said, "I could not see her clearly."

"Like hell. Show me mine."

"No. Not till I see her again."

"If you cannot produce her," Quayle said, "I can only believe one reason. That she is dead, as I sometimes half suspected. If you cannot show her to me..."

He felt that his voice was breaking, maybe she really was dead, he was even sure of it now, and he shouted. "I have backup! A sharpshooter has a sniper's rifle trained on Lilian at this moment! Damn your fucking eyes, show me my daughter!"

There was that long wait again, and then Abu Jildi looked back over his shoulder and called out: "*Viens*, Pia, come!"

And there she was.

Quayle felt himself trembling uncontrollably at the sight of her, felt the tears welling into her eyes.

She was struggling, hobbling and *hopping* toward the light, and Quayle saw that his adversary had had much the same idea; Pia's legs were in a potato sack, a sack race from childhood days, but her wrists were bound together in front of her body.

She called out. "*Papa! Je suis bien, Papa...*"

The tears were almost uncontrollable now. How long had she been a prisoner? How scared to death had she been? How had she been mistreated? And her first words were. "*I'm alright, Daddy...*" he first thoughts, as always, for anyone but herself.

"So show yourself again," Abu Jildi said, "and I will send her to you. As soon as you send Lilian to me."

Enough was always enough, and always would be.

Ian Quayle held Lilian close and moved with her into the light, and he stood there for a moment, wondering what the hell ought to happen now. And then, out of the corner of his eye, he saw a figure rising up on a rooftop only fifty or sixty feet away, above Abu Jildi's head, and he was lifting a sniper's rifle to his shoulder.

He screamed: "*Wendy! Hit him...!*" and threw himself and the young girl too to one side, rolling over and over with her on the pavement as the shot rang out. He felt the dull thud of the bullet as it went through his left side just below the ribcage, and he rolled over and over, dragging a struggling Lilian with him, into a culvert, no more than a foot or so deep.

He flattened himself over her to protect her as he heard Wendy's shot too... And he whipped out his Beretta and readied it...

Wendy Hayworth, champion marksman ('*marksperson*' they called them now, he thought inconsequentially,) at that bucolic Academy down in Purley, Surrey, England. She was damn good with a rifle, better still with a handgun, and was using, he knew, her favorite Walter P38, the best handgun ever made. He saw the man on the roof drop his gun, heard it clatter to the ground, saw him stagger for a moment and then fall to the pavement below, a small round hole in the middle of his forehead.

And all hell broke loose.

He heard Wendy scream: "*Back, Ian, get back here...!*" and he thought that was a very useless comment; the rooftops all around them were alive now with armed men rising up like ghouls against the skyline. He saw Wendy out in the open but running for cover as the men began firing, and then there was answering fire, volley after volley of it, from Suleiman and a score of the riffraff he had rounded up from the warehouse.

He saw Aida, crouched low and running fast, stopping to hurl a hand-grenade before ducking fast back under cover again.

He yelled at the top of his voice: "*Pia, get down...!*"

But in the awful din of the shooting, more hand-grenades going off everywhere, his voice was lost like a fart in a thunderstorm.

The bullets were chipping away at the stonework of his culvert, and then he saw Abu Jildi himself, out in the open and firing his cute little Socimi on rapid, like a maniac, not unflappable anymore, five hundred and fifty rounds a minute, one magazine replacing another with commendable speed. He was firing at where Wendy had been, and Ian Quayle yelled. "Get down, God dammit, you stupid bloody woman...!" and he saw for the briefest instant that wiry, slender body of the girl Higran, standing out in the open as though. she hadn't a care in the world...

He saw her arm drawn back, saw the flick of the wrist as the knife left it at tremendous speed, saw the blade bury itself in Abu Jildi's stomach.

But this man was made of carbon steel. He fell to the ground, dropping his weapon, and with both hands he pulled out the knife and hurled it away. He was on wide-spaced feet again in seconds, firing once more, seemingly unharmed.

And then, to his horror, a sack-wrapped bundle was rolling toward him through all the gunfire, and it was Pia, yelling her head off for no reason at all and doing quite the wrong thing.

He rolled away from Lilian to make room for his daughter in the narrow confines of the culvert, and grabbed at her and yelled: "Are you hurt...?"

She shook her head and gasped. "No, Papa, I don't think so..." He dug into his pocket for his penknife and sawed at the ropes that bound her wrists, and held the sack up at her waist, and then he cut Lilian free too and said to her. "Keep down, don't run yet, it's murder out there"

Once her hands were free, Lilian Mifari, daughter of a monster, raised herself up and slapped him hard, very hard across the face. He fought off the return blow and held her wrists as she screamed. "Wait till my father gets hold of you, you pig...! I'll have him nail your hands to the wall while I slice your balls off, you'll see just how; how, how..."

She broke off; Pia had seized her by the hair and was tugging her head back and saying quietly. "Don't talk to my father like that, you tub of lard, or I'll beat up on you myself. So shut up, you hear?"

The Mifari girl fell silent. Quayle released her and peered over the rim of the culvert, the noise still fearsome out there.

He saw three or four of the riffraff had been killed, rather more of Abu Jildi's Swords of God lying there too. He spotted Wendy and Aida, under sensible cover now, firing repeatedly but carefully, taking their time to make every shell count. He saw Aida place down her gun and hurl another of her grenades, and instinctively ducked back down to wait for the explosion. When it went off, he raised up his head again and saw to his astonishment that Abu Jildi was still on his feet, still firing short bursts from his deadly little Socimi; his face was heavily bloodied, there was blood pouring from the knife wound in his stomach, one hand seemed to be half-shattered; but he was still standing—and deadly.

And then, the flare went out, and there was only the moonlight left.

The firing was more desultory now, and when it ceased altogether. Ian Quayle climbed carefully and painfully to his feet, his own wound giving him a very bad time. He half-saw, half-felt that the girls were rising up with him, and he said urgently. "No, not yet..."

He saw that Abu Jildi had fallen at last and was crawling toward him, dragging a broken and bloodied leg. He was only thirty feet or so away, and in the semi-darkness their eyes met for a moment. And then, Abu Jildi swung his good arm round, the submachine gun in his hand; and pulled the trigger...

Reflex action and a certain amount of panic as well; Ian hurled himself at Pia and bulldozed her to the ground, and felt Lilian fall hard on top of them, all of her maybe hundred and forty pounds, and he wriggled himself out from under. He held on tightly to Pia and whispered. "All right?"

"Yes..."

"Jesus Christ, there's no killing that man..."

But he had heard Wendy's shot, and he knew that there was no way she could miss now. He raised his head cautiously, and there was his enemy lying still at last, on his back, not a movement of any sort. He said to Pia: "Wait here, my love..."

And as he moved up out of the culvert, he heard her hushed voice: "*Papa...!*"

He turned back, and to his horror he saw that Lilian was lying on her stomach with a gaping hole in the back of her head. He wanted to vomit, and couldn't.

There was only silence now, and in a moment he said: "Let me make sure."

Slowly, cautiously, he clambered out, his gun ready.

He walked very slowly and painfully towards the still body there, wondering how much blood he'd lost, and stood over it for a moment, looking down onto a man he had grown to hate so much on paper, and yet, lately, had somehow come to *know*.

He was astonished to see those hard eyes open, but he

made no move, and Abu Jildi said, his voice harsh and wheezing from a damaged throat—there was so much blood everywhere!—"My...My daughter. Send her...send her to me, Quayle."

Ian Quayle shook his head, a sadness on him. He said quietly. "I wish I could, Colonel."

He was conscious that Wendy and Aida were moving towards him now, very cautiously, with Higran a little way behind them; Pia was coming out of the culvert too.

Abu Jildi's eyes were veiled. "You wish...you wish...?"

"She's dead, Colonel," Quayle said: "Your own bullets. That last senseless burst of fire. I'm sorry, truly sorry."

The breathing was rasping, the breath of a man with not much longer to live unless the Egyptian surgeons were damned good and he could be taken to them in time.

Then Abu Jildi moved at last, in slow-motion, a painful roll to his side. He reached out for the fallen Socimi and dragged it to him with infinite slowness, inch by inch, scraping along the ground.

Ian Quayle thumbed back the hammer of his Baretta. "It's no good, Colonel," he said. "It's all over now. It's finished."

Abu Jildi was on the very edge of absolute stupor, lying on the hard ground on his side, the submachine gun flat beside him. His eyes had lost their fire, the veiled eyes of a man already dead. The lips were moving through the bubbling blood, but it seemed that the words could not be articulated.

And then—then there was a sudden coherence, as though a strong man's mind had taken control of a bodily weakness; the sputtered words were clear and quite strong:

"She...She is dead? My Lilian, *dead*?"

Ian Quayle said, hating every syllable of it: "She was in your line of fire. What can I say...?"

He was searching now for the words, and the image of that foolish young girl would not leave him. The words came tumbling out now in very high emotion, and he found that he was almost screaming:

"This could have been settled so easily, but *no*! You had to fuck it up, *didn't you*? So yes; your daughter is dead!"

He found his senses again and said quietly: "You yourself killed her, Colonel."

Abu Jildi's voice was almost inaudible now: "Is it the truth? You swear...swear it by all...all that you hold most sacred?"

"On the life of my daughter, Pia," Ian Quayle said, "I swear it. Your Lilian is dead. You killed her."

There was only a prolonged moment of silence; and then Abu Jildi placed the end of his Socimi's barrel in his mouth and pulled the trigger, and the last ten or twelve rounds in the box magazine blew the top of his head off, splattering blood and brains and pieces of shattered skull across the tiny square where, once, nearly four hundred years ago, the great Sheik Mohammed Halawi bin Mustafa, soldier, statesman, philosopher and poet, had been killed by the thrust of an assassin's spear; he was a man who might, had he lived, have changed the whole course of Islam.

But this was the Middle East, where men of good will were not always allowed the privilege of living.

Pia had buried her head in her father's shoulders, clutching at him desperately to hide the awful sight, and he held her tightly, not knowing what to say now. And in a moment Wendy touched him on the arm and said gently: "Come. We must go now. We made enough noise to wake even the Egyptian Army. A discreet and rapid retreat might be desirable now."

Indeed, the sirens were already sounding, breaking at last even the macabre silence of the city of the Dead.

"The count will not be accurate yet," Aida said, "but at

the moment it seems that four of the street people have been killed, seven more delighting in their wounds. And of the enemy—it looks like nine dead, including Abu Jildi, with another nine too badly wounded to escape the net the Army has thrown around the place. How many got away, we'll never know. But it was a good battle, they must have had twenty-five or thirty men there, almost certainly all from the Swords of God."

She was bandaging Ian's wounds; a bullet in and out of his left side, a long searing wound along his back where another had creased it without his knowing it, a nasty wound in his upper right arm...

"How come you always get shot up when you go into the field?" Wendy asked curiously. "I never do, as a matter of principle. But you're always fart-arsing around out of your depth, aren't you? And getting hurt. Are you going to make a habit of it?"

A cable had come from Robin Harris during the fight, a reply to Wendy's hopeful quest for promotion, addressed to Aida since the original was in her code. It said simply:

YOUR LAST INCORRECTLY ENCYPHERED
PLEASE CHECK AND RE-SUBMIT,

and Aida said blandly. "How stupid of me. I swear it's the first time in my life I ever made a mistake like that. But it's hardly worth correcting, is it? I mean to say—it's all past history now."

"Nice work, Aida," Ian Quayle said cheerfully. "That was really a brilliant move. Good for you."

Wendy said nothing, just looked, and Aida went on. "There's an eight o'clock flight to Paris in the morning, and you, Wendy, and Pia have to be on it, before word gets around. This is a city where secrets don't last for very long."

"Great," Ian Quayle said. "Just one problem. Pia doesn't have her passport with her, she was smuggled here in a wooden crate, remember?"

"Oh. *Merde*!"

"But all problems have an answer, don't they?" Wendy said. "The British Ambassador here is Sir Michael Farrar, you remember him? From Rome? He was transferred here six months ago." She said to Aida. "He's an old family friend, used to bounce me up and down on his knee when I was six years old."

"Ah yes," Quayle said, "child molestation, we call it. And the Embassy will be open for business just one hour after the plane has left. When's the next one?"

But Wendy was already getting to her feet. "Could your car take me to the Embassy?" she asked Aida, and Quayle said: "What, at four o'clock in the morning? He'll be in bed."

Wendy sighed. "Yes. But he's a lecherous old sonofabitch, I'm afraid, so that won't discombobulate him in the least. Back in an hour or so."

And back in an hour or so she was; a little disheveled.

"He's such a nice old man," she said. "Seventy years old, and he still thinks that god made sweet young innocents like me especially for him, I had to *wrestle*, physically, to protect what is laughingly known as 'my honor.' All over his goddam waterbed, and he sleeps in tops only, too. It was a fight like you won't believe, 15 rounds of Spinks and Holmes all over."

"And are we permitted to know," Ian Quayle asked politely, "who won?"

"Shut up, you shitty sonofabitch," Wendy said without any rancor at all.

She fell silent for a moment, reflecting, and she said at last, as though it were a matter for the greatest curiosity. "You know? When a lady's pantyhose are all tangled up in her ankles, isn't it axiomatic that further resistance becomes...well, bad taste? If not downright *crass*? Forget it. All you have to know is that I've got what I set out to get. I have a *laisser-passer* in Pia's name in lieu of a passport. It'll get her on that plane—and that

226

was the objective. Mission accomplished."

Pia was sleeping in the other room, at Aida's quiet insistence. "I know how much you want to be with her, constantly," she said to Quayle. "But a few more hours of the restraint you've shown so much of? After all she's been through—sleep cures everything, I think you know that."

She was great, Aida, a very understanding woman; just *great.*

At six in the morning, old dependable Suleiman—limping from a bullet wound in his leg—produced Turkish coffee for them, with hot croissants, oodles of butter, and wild strawberry jam imported from England, and at seven Ian Quayle took his hand and embraced him.

"You're a good kid, Suleiman," he said to the ancient servant, "and it's my fervent hope we'll meet again." He hesitated, "Is there perhaps some way in which I can express my thanks?"

The old man smiled. "Yes, there is, Mr. Quayle, sir." There was just a little beat, and then: *"Remember me."*

Ian Quayle took Aida in his arms and embraced her, and even placed a hand on her breast to mold it, wondering if Wendy would notice. "How can I think you?" he asked, "there are honestly no words..."

"Just come back soon."

She looked at Wendy, watching them, and she turned back to Ian and said. "I adore your Wendy, she is almost perfection. But next time you come to Cairo... Come alone, okay?"

"Bitch," Wendy said amiably, and Aida moved to her and hugged her. "Or you come alone, *l'une ou l'autre,* the one or the other. I love you both and it's hard to choose. Go now, or you'll miss your plane. Abu Jildi is dead, and the Swords of God are dead with him. Cut off the head—and the arms have lost their power. It's what you came here for. Isn't it?"

* * *

The Air France 747 was Paradise.

It was scrupulously clean after the dirt of Cairo, whisper quiet after Cairo's god-awful noise, and wonderfully efficient after the city's hugger-mugger imbroglio.

They sat together in credit card First Class, and why not? Mrs. Bloody French would object, Ian Quayle was sure, but they could at least put Coach on the expense account, and the rest was a gesture for his beloved daughter Pia; and yes, for his paramour Wendy too...

He would not ask questions of his daughter, he was far too wise for that; and when she said, just once: "*I have not been hurt, Papa, not seriously,*" he made a vow to say no more on the subject. (He'd find out all he so desperately wanted to know from his mother Claudine, Pia's grandmother, when the time came. But not now.)

Now...?

Now was a time to relax in the comforting idea of safety, secure in the knowledge that the next stop on their journey was Paris, far from the dangers of the Middle East in the luxury of the St. Cloud apartment where his mother would lose at once all her dreadful fears; it mattered a great deal.

St. Cloud, Paris, and then for Ian Quayle and Wendy, the safety of the London flats and the little thatched cottage in Austel-in-the-Woods where, at this time of the year, the herbs in their own special corner of the garden would be ready for drying and finishing up in the little jars on the kitchen rack—tarragon, oregano, thyme, marjoram, rosemary, chervil, parsley, the verbenas, horehound, the stinking weed coriander, chives, sage, skirret and sorrel, germander and even mugwort... He was very proud of his herb garden.

Wendy could not so easily put her work on the back bummer.

She said gravely, interrupting his herbal reverie. "You do know, don't you, that Abu Jildi was one step ahead of you all the way down the line? A goddam double agent in our own office, it makes me sick to think of it! *Bahram*! God damn his bloody eyes! You know what it means, don't you?'

"I know," Ian said calmly. "Do you?"

"Yes! It means that when you sit down at your typewriter and peck out your report—as your Case Officer I don't want to see one mention of the name *Aida*! When I've finished with it, it goes automatically to Mrs. Bloody French, who passes it onto Ops. G for general distribution. You pulled this thing off by *yourself*, you understand? If Bahram doesn't know about Aida, which may well be—that's the way it has to stay. Is that understood?"

"Let me buy you another Bloody Mary," Ian said caustically, "they're free in First Class. I know what has to be done...and I'm going to do it. I'm not entirely a fool, you know. My report is going to be a masterpiece of duplicity."

He grinned, "just remember that nobody ever believes absolute truth, you have to fart-arse around with it a mite, anyway, to make it believable. It's going to be so easy for me..."

He laughed shortly. "Mention Aida? No! I may go back to Cairo one day, and if I do—I don't want to discover that the libidinous Aida has hanged herself in a cell of the Security Police, who'll probably be after her guts if Bahram ever gets to learn about her. So just leave it to me, Luv, and have another Bloody Mary."

Wendy fell silent, and Ian Quayle took his daughter's hand, and he whispered: "Soon now, Paris and your grandmother Claudine for you, London and the Surrey cottage for Wendy and me. We're all going to be *safe* now. No more danger, no more fear, and no more trauma, my love."

Pia, only half-awake, nodded. She looked marvelous now, in designer jeans and a navy blue cashmere sweater that

Aida had procured for her, with high-sided black boots of camel leather and a silver-coin belt around a very slender waist.

Yes, she nodded...

But she knew that 'safety' for her father and his sometimes lover Wendy was a very relative kind of word.

It always meant, in their dreadful business, until the next time.

THE END

ABOUT THE AUTHOR

Alan Lyle-Smythe was born in Surrey, England. Prior to World War II, he served with the Palestine Police from 1936 to 1939 and learned the Arabic language. He was awarded an MBE in June 1938. He married Aliza Sverdova in 1939, then studied acting from 1939 to 1941.

In January 1940, Lyle-Smythe was commissioned in the Royal Army Service Corps. Due to his linguistic skills, he transferred to the Intelligence Corps and served in the Western Desert, in which he used the surname "Caillou" (the French word for 'pebble') as an alias.

He was captured in North Africa, imprisoned and threatened with execution in Italy, then escaped to join the British forces at Salerno. He was then posted to serve with the partisans in Yugoslavia. He wrote about his experiences in the book *The World is Six Feet Square* (1954). He was promoted to captain and awarded the Military Cross in 1944.

Following the war, he returned to the Palestine Police from 1946 to 1947, then served as a Police Commissioner in British-occupied Italian Somaliland from 1947 to 1952, where he was recommissioned a captain.

After work as a District Officer in Somalia and professional hunter, Lyle-Smythe travelled to Canada, where he worked as a hunter and then became an actor on Canadian television.

He wrote his first novel, *Rogue's Gambit*, in 1955, first using the name Caillou, one of his aliases from the war. Moving from Vancouver to Hollywood, he made an appearance as a contestant on the January 23 1958 edition of *You Bet Your Life*.

He appeared as an actor and/or worked as a screenwriter in such shows as *Daktari*, *The Man From U.N.C.L.E.* (including the screenwriting for *"The Bow-Wow Affair"* from 1965), *Thriller*, *Daniel Boone*, *Quark*, *Centennial*, and *How the West Was Won*. In 1966-67, he had a recurring role (as Jason Flood) in NBC's *"Tarzan"* TV series starring Ron Ely. Caillou appeared in such television movies as *Sole Survivor* (1970), *The Hound of the Baskervilles* (1972, as Inspector Lestrade), and *Goliath Awaits* (1981). His cinema film credits included roles in *Five Weeks in a Balloon* (1962), *Clarence, the Cross-Eyed Lion* (1965), *The Rare Breed* (1966), *The Devil's Brigade* (1968), *Hellfighters* (1968), *Everything You Always Wanted to Know About Sex* (*But Were Afraid to Ask)* (1972), *Herbie Goes to Monte Carlo* (1977), *Beyond Evil* (1980), *The Sword and the Sorcerer* (1982) and *The Ice Pirates* (1984).

Caillou wrote 52 paperback thrillers under his own name and the nom de plume of Alex Webb, with such heroes as Cabot Cain, Colonel Matthew Tobin, Mike Benasque, Ian Quayle and Josh Dekker, as well as writing many magazine stories.

Several of Caillou's novels were made into films, such as *Rampage* with Robert Mitchum in 1963, based on his big game hunting knowledge; *Assault on Agathon*, for which Caillou did the screenplay as well; and *The Cheetahs*, filmed in 1989.

He was married to Aliza Sverdova from 1939 until his death. Their daughter Nadia Caillou was the screenwriter for the film *Skeleton Coast*.

Alan Caillou died in Sedona, Arizona in 2006.

DON'T MISS ANY OF MICHAEL KASNER'S HARD HITTING MILITARY NOVEL SERIES

BLACK OPS

Formed by an elite cadre of government officials, the Black OPS team goes where the law can't - to seek retribution for acts of terror directed against Americans anywhere in the world.

3 BOOK SERIES

Armed with all the tactical advantages of modern technology, battle hard and ready when the free world is threatened - the Peacekeepers are the baddest grunts on the planet.

4 BOOK SERIES

CHOPPER COPS

America is being torn apart as criminal cartels terrorize our cities, dealing drugs and death wholesale. Local police are outgunned, so the President unleashes the U.S. TACTICAL POLICE FORCE. An elite army of super cops with ammo to burn, they swoop down on the hot spots in sleek high-tech attack choppers to win the dirty war and take back America!

4 BOOK SERIES

FROM CALIBER BOOKS

www.calibercomics.com

DON'T MISS ANY OF NEIL HUNTER'S
NOVELS FROM CALIBER BOOKS

Reporter Les Mason is completing an expose on the Long Point Nuclear Plant. But before he can finish he dies an agonizing death. The doctors are baffled—and there are similar cases to follow...Chris Lane, his girlfriend, and organizer of the Long Point Protestors, discovers Mason's notes, and decides to find out for herself what the plant has to hide.

2 BOOK SERIES

In middle of the 21st century America – over-populated decaying cities are ruled by hi-tech gangs pushing every vice and wastelands are controlled by bands of mutants. Ordinary citizens are oppressed and face a hopeless future. But Marshal T.J. Cade is a new breed of law enforcer. Teamed with his cyborg partner, Janek, Cade takes on these criminals and works in the gray areas of the law to get the job done.

3 BOOK SERIES

The village of Shepthorne England wasn't being gripped, but strangled by a winter's blanket of heavy snow and Arctic temperatures. The trouble began innocently enough with a massive pile-up of autos on frozen roads leading to and from the village. Then, from the sky, a military transport plane with its top secret cargo of devastation crashed down towards the center of the village. Hell was just beginning to touch Shepthorne and its unsuspecting citizens...

FROM CALIBER BOOKS

CALIBER
B O O K S

www.calibercomics.com

CALIBER COMICS GOES TO WAR!
HISTORICAL AND MILITARY THEMED GRAPHIC NOVELS

**WORLD WAR ONE:
MO MAN'S LAND**

ISBN: 9781635298123

*A look at World War 1 from
the French trenches as they
faced the Imperial German
Army.*

**CORTEZ AND THE FALL
OF THE AZTECS**

ISBN: 9781635299779

*Cortez battles the Aztecs
while in search of Inca
gold.*

**TROY:
AN EMPIRE UNDER SIEGE**

ISBN: 9781635298635

*Homer's famous The Iliad and
the Trojan War is given a
unique human perspective
rather than from the God's.*

WITNESS TO WAR

ISBN: 9781635299700

*WW2's Battle of the Bulge
is seen up close by an
embedded female war
reporter.*

THE LINCOLN BRIGADE

ISBN: 9781635298222

*American volunteers head
to Spain in the 1930s to
fight in their civil war
against the fascist regime.*

**EL CID:
THE CONQUEROR**

ISBN: 9780982654996

*Europe's greatest warrior
attempts to unify Spain
against invading foreign
and domestic armies.*

WINTER WAR

ISBN: 9780985749392

*At the outbreak of WW2
Finland fights against an
invading Soviet army.*

**ZULUNATION:
END OF EMPIRE**

ISBN: 9780941613415

*The global British Empire
and far-reaching influence
is threatened by a Zulu
uprising in southern Africa.*

AIR WARRIORS: WORLD WAR ONE #V1 - V4   *Take to the skies of WW1 as various fighter aces tell their harrowing stories.*
ISBN: 9781635297973 (V1), 9781635297980 (V2), 9781635297997 (V3), 9781635298000 (V4)

  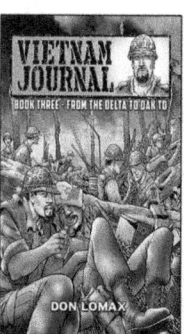 

FROM AWARD-WINNING COMIC WRITER AND ARTIST
WAYNE VANSANT

COMES TALES FROM WORLD WAR II

An action/adventure tale of the French Legionnaire soldier, Battron, who is involved with the liberation of a freebooting French ship, the Martel, from a heavily guarded Vichy French port during WWII. The Allies want the ship destroyed; the Germans have sent serious resources and firepower to save it. But a critical security leak in British intelligence could jeopardize not only the mission but Battron's life. The key is the beautiful former mistress of the Martel's captain, enlisted in the hope she can convince him to join the Free French movement with his ship. But has she told the Allies all she knows? And can Battron and his skillful commandos complete their dangerous mission in time under the luming shadow of the pending Allied invasion of North Africa?

Collection of tales involving the German Waffen SS from acclaimed creator and comic artist Wayne Vansant. These stories deal with the German Panzer troops during World War II and collects the highly acclaimed Battle Group Peiper story, Witches' Cauldon saga, along with three short tales. Knights of the Skull covers the war experiences of young German troops on the Eastern Front to the massacre of American troops near Malmedy Belgium to the harsh conditions of a crushing winter and engagements against an unrelenting Soviet troop onslaught.

The epic and incredible telling of the early days of the United States during the Second World War. Days of Darkness covers the darkest days of WWII for the US, when the country went from the tragedy of Pearl Harbor to the triumph at Midway. Covering in detail is the attack of the US Naval base and the devastation of the fleet in Hawaii, then the action moves to the evacuation and fall of the Philippines to the horror of the Death March of Bataan, and finally to the dramatic Battle of Midway which stopped the Japanese juggernaut in the Pacific.

"Heavy on authenticity, compellingly written and beautifully drawn." - Comics Buyers Guide.

WWW.CALIBERCOMICS.COM

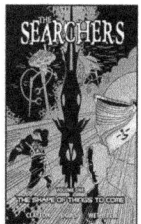

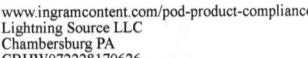